NICAEA

NICAEA

a book of correspondences

MARTIN ROWE

Lindisfarne Books
Great Barrington, MA

2003
Lindisfarne Books
P.O. Box 799
Great Barrington, MA 01230
Copyright 2003 by Martin Rowe

Printed in Canada.

Library of Congress Cataloging-in-Publication Data

Rowe, Martin.
Nicaea : a book of correspondences / Martin Rowe.
p. cm.
ISBN 1–58420–020–0
1. Council of Nicaea (1st : 325)—Fiction. 2. Council of Nicaea
(2nd: 787)—Fiction. 3. Iznik (Turkey)—Fiction. I. Title.
PS3618.O873N53 2003
813'.6—dc21

2003012897

printed on 100% post-consumer waste paper, chlorine-free

Acknowledgments

This book has marinated for nearly fifteen years and, but for the good graces of Christopher Bamford at Lindisfarne Press, it might have been another fifteen more before this particular book was cooked. I would like to thank Antonia Gorman for her thoughtful reading of an early draft, my colleague Sarah Gallogly at Lantern Books for her commitment to and care with the manuscript, and Dianna Dowling for her enthusiasm and sharpness of mind. Thank you, too, to Tzyh Ng for her inspired cover design.

Among the books and articles that helped me with *Nicaea* I would like to recognize particularly Metin And's *Karagöz: Turkish Shadow Theatre* (Dost Yavinlari, 1975). For the stories in, and style of, "Karagöz and the Sultan," I am indebted to *Arab Folktales* translated by Inea Bushnaq (Penguin, 1987), particularly "The Girl Who Spoke Jasmines and Lilies." For thoughts on the epic and Helen of Troy I was helped by Mihoko Suzuki's *Metamorphoses of Helen: Authority, Difference, and the Epic* (Cornell University

Acknowledgments

Press, 1989). *Cassandra* by Christa Wolf (Noonday Press, 1988) was the impetus for "Courtly Love," and I turned to *Women in Purple: Rulers of Medieval Byzantium* by Judith Herrin (Princeton University Press, 2002) for the life of the Empress Eirene. *Grazie* to my good friend Christopher Abbott for his invaluable insights on courtly love.

My love and appreciation to Mia MacDonald, who was before The Beginning and will be after The End: Our life together continues to offer me a richer story than any book could tell. I would like to acknowledge all those who made my time at the Çagdil Language School in Bursa, Turkey, in 1989 such a formative one. I wish to extend my gratitude to the Turkish people and the citizens of Bursa for their hospitality and generosity of spirit—as well as the expert medical attention of their doctors, with whom I lost an appendix and regained my spirits.

It was while I was in Turkey that I heard of the death of the individual who was the reason this book was written and who was, in every way, a better person than I will ever be. It is to his memory that *Nicaea* is dedicated.

Contents

In Memory of
R. W. H.

Chronology of Nicaea/Iznik

BCE

323   Death of Alexander the Great.

316   Antigonus the One-Eyed, a general under Alexander, founds Antigonia.

301   Death of Antigonus, defeated by Lysimachus, another of Alexander's generals, at the Battle of Ipsus. Lysimachus renames Antigonia after his wife Nikaia.

281   Lysimachus killed in battle at Corupedium by Seleucus, also a general of Alexander.

CE

113   Death of Pliny the Younger, Governor of Bithynia, Nicaea's province in the Roman Empire.

250   Birth of Arius of Alexandria.

260   Birth of Eusebius of Caesarea.

273   Birth of Alexander of Alexandria.

297   Birth of Athanasius.

309   Martyrdom of Pamphilus, Eusebius's mentor.

324 Constantine the Great becomes sole emperor of Rome.

325 First Council of Nicaea.

326 Death of Alexander of Alexandria.

336 Death of Arius of Alexandria.

339 Death of Constantine the Great.

341 Death of Eusebius of Caesarea.

373 Death of Athanasius.

755 Eirene becomes Empress of Byzantine Empire.

787 Second Council of Nicaea meets and permits the creation of icons.

798 Blinding of Constantine VI, son of Eirene.

803 Death of Eirene.

1078 Nicaea falls to the Seljuk Turks.

1096 Kilij Arslan I surrenders Nicaea to Godfrey de Bouillon. Recaptured.

1106 Nicaea recaptured from Muslims by Byzantines under Alexius I Comnenus.

1204 Byzantine Emperor Theodore I Lascaris flees Constantinople, which has been overrun by Latin crusaders (in fourth crusade), and sets up court at Nicaea.

1258 Death of Theodore II Lascaris.

1261 Nicaean Byzantines successfully reclaim Constantinople for the Byzantines.

1280 Death of Ertogrul, father of Osman I, founder of the Ottoman Empire.

1324 Death of Osman I.

1331 Orhan I, son of Osman I, conquers Nicaea and renames it Iznik.

1330s Orhan marries Theodora, daughter of Byzantine emperor, John VI.

1362 Death of Orhan I.

1390s First performance of Karagöz puppet theater.

1453 Fall of Constantinople to Ottomans.

1500s Iznik tiles and ceramics used throughout the Islamic world.

1920 Iznik invaded by the Greeks.

1924 End of the Ottoman Empire. Mustapha Kemal, known as Atatürk, declared sole ruler of Turkey.

Historical Note

Although Eusebius, Arius, Athanasius, and Eirene are heavily fictionalized, I have tried to capture something of Eusebius's long-windedness and the matter of the debate between Arius and others. Eirene is generally held responsible for the blinding of her own son. Pliny's handling of the deaconesses and the story of the nun recounted in "Synapsis" and "The Iteration of the 'I' " are historical events. I had the pleasure of an afternoon with a man named Soner, who was a cook and who did indeed make great pizzas, although he has not to my knowledge suffered the indignities of his fictional counterpart. I should note in fairness to my family that one of my ancestors, the poetaster and dissolute publisher Edward Moxon, was the inspiration for "The Belletrist," although, unlike me, he did not to my knowledge visit Iznik.

Topos

 Out from the shadow of the old city walls, their sorrow and their ruin, where the sun bucked among the cypress trees and flung itself onto the cobbles; along the back of School Street, where children swooped and stormed, where old men mumbled over their sweet-lipped tea and old women hung out their sullen washing—the sun fighting its way into alleys, harrying mud streams down the roadside, ducking into shops while their keepers slept, catching cats as they skulked through iron and stone, accosting the guard in front of the fearful synagogue; where lovers floated in their own recklessness, the sun licking brown eyes and olive skin, stroking silk and muslin and cotton, hearing a blandishment or a prayer, feeling between its fingers a stray thread of hair, or a glance, or tears: at last, having mounted our chargers, bid goodbye to our loved ones, departed to the waves of aged warriors, wailing women, second sons, and unmarriageable daughters; having traveled across waving plains of virgin corn and bars of infinite sand and run alongside the soft edges of lakes

1

and over the poppy fields, crossing the hills and the val-
leys, past crag and scree, vale and riverbed; having dined
in hovels and palaces, advanced by cities and sages,
accosted armies and farmers, confronted solitaries and
packs of hunters; having answered riddles and anointed
kings, scaled cliffs and swum torrents, braved great heat
and desperate cold; having followed the stars and trusted in our senses, killed dragons, rescued maidens, buried
the dead and baptized the newborn; having watched
cities crumble and new ones rise up; having forfeited all
we had and won more than we could dream; and having
loved deeply and been betrayed, we left the turbid city
of Bursa and arrived where the sun was absolute as it
struck the diamond city of Nicaea.

"That was quite a beginning, wasn't it?"

I turn and you are there, unchanged, still young, a
slight indulgent smile.

"Mock heroic," I add redundantly.

"So I gathered." You sit down on the grass next to
me, gazing along with me out at the lake. "And such a
lot of it as well." You grin. I notice that your face is still
pockmarked with acne scars. The same thick brown
hair, the full lips, clean-shaven. Is this really how I
remember you? "Why, *mock*, Adam?" you continue,
trying to disguise your annoyance. "Why does it always
have to be *mock*?"

"You haven't changed," I reply, unable to ignore
your brown corduroys and tweed jacket, with a white
pressed shirt and a blue tie. A preposterous outfit, utterly unsuitable for this climate.

You seem to sense it as well and cast an eye over

your clothing. "Why would you expect me to have changed?" You smile at me again.

"It's been twenty years."

"And I'm just as dead as I was twenty years ago. You see me as you last saw me—another place, another time. That must be obvious to you, mustn't it?"

I turn back to stare out at the lake. Of course it must.

"You haven't answered my question, Adam. Why *mock?*"

"Because I set out to go to Nicaea and arrived in Iznik, isn't that *obvious*, too?" I am not handling this well, and I don't know why I should be so irritated.

"Well, on one level it is obvious." I remember how pedantic you can be. "Nicaea ceased to be called Nicaea five centuries ago—or thereabouts."

"I wanted to use a lot of literary commonplaces— *topoi*—in order ironically to point out that this is only a common place."

You give a brief snort of laughter. "I am aware of the intent, Adam, and of your labored effort not to split the infinitive. It was not subtle."

"But all the roadsigns said Nicaea...."

"Well, they would, wouldn't they?" You turn to look at me. "After all, tourists are coming to see the place where the Nicene Creed was instituted. They want to see the Roman city and not the little Turkish town it is now. Isn't that why *you* came?"

I say nothing.

"Of course, there are the Iznik tiles—which might be of interest to some...." I recall those flashes of arrogant dismissal and remember how much I hated them. "So, is it just *disappointment*, then, that makes you want to use the mock heroic?"

Once again, I feel absurd. A little too earnest, not willing to laugh at myself, needing my ego massaged, as you once put it. And yet not taking the moment seriously enough.

"I *am* disappointed, I admit. I had wanted to come to Nicaea for all the reasons you mentioned, and somehow thought it would be more impressive." I am annoyed at how self-aggrandizing and pompous I sound. "But all I found was a dirty, dusty little town with nothing to remind me of the councils of 325 and 787 that took place here. Instead, there are a few Roman and Byzantine ruins, a dilapidated mosque, and a desultory museum showing a few artifacts and displaying some elaborate blue tiles that are apparently the zenith of the town's once-glorious tile-making industry."

"You've been reading the guidebook, I notice."

"Ever the dutiful student," I reply.

"I should probably remind you that you wanted to come here because of me, didn't you? Let's not forget the fact you summoned me up."

Even though your face is turned away I can see you are still smiling with that damned Cheshire Cat equanimity that infuriated me when we were growing up.

"Yes, since you seem to require the flattery, I wanted to come here because of you." I lean forward to disguise how awkward I feel. "Because I wanted somehow to come to grips with your death."

You turn to me and raise your eyebrows exaggeratedly. "I'm impressed. It's been a long time." You pause.

"I'd have thought you'd have moved on."

"That's what Marianne keeps telling me."

We glance across at her and see her throwing stones irresolutely into the lake. You turn again to face me. "She's probably right."

I do not respond.

"After all, Adam. I am dead and there is nothing you can do about it. I know that I died in a particularly horrible way, and perhaps my funeral service was a little too triumphalist for some people's liking...."

"Your parents, perhaps?" I do not hide my bitterness.

"Yes, my parents perhaps. But I don't see the point in dwelling on it."

All your "friends" celebrating and applauding your death because you had finally thrown off this decaying, mortal body in favor of the holy raiment of purity in heaven. Your parents in the front row, stoic and unmoving, their faces set in some kind of holy terror. What must they have been feeling? The child whose conception and birth was attended to with bodily pleasure and pain, whose talents were so large and generous, whose prospects were so wide and pregnant with possibility, declaimed as a mere prelude, an unimportant hiatus between blissful states in heaven. Were they meant to be consoled by that? Were they meant to go home that night and say to themselves that it was just as well that you died when you did, so young, because it meant you got to sit with the cherubim and seraphim that much sooner than the rest of us?

"Why not?" I ask. My voice is raised loud enough

that Marianne looks at me and asks me what I'm talking about. "Nothing," I say, and she returns to whatever she is doing. I self-consciously continue in a whisper. "That seems like a pretty good thing to dwell on to me."

"Well, I'm not going to be able to change your mind if you don't want it changed. But you must know that it's no use, Adam, because there's no way you can prove whether I am a 'soul in bliss' or not. I am a figment of your imagination, not some angelic spirit come to provide you with a glimpse of heaven. In addition, I'm not here to convince you of the reality of God or the fact of an afterlife—or to persuade you of the unreality of both. That's your affair."

You take a deep breath and lean back on the grass.

"It's good to see you again."

"Oh yes? I always thought you were angry with me."

"I was some of the time; but, in spite of what seems to be disgust for who I was and what I represented, Adam, I liked you then and I still do. You take things seriously—perhaps a little too seriously. But you're a little directionless, and not knowing where you are going and how you're going to get there encourages slowness and staying in one place. And that in turn can foster humility—always a good thing in my book. Then there is the fact that you've decided to run off to Turkey with another woman who happens to be married to someone else. Not—to use an unfortunate metaphor—my particular road to heaven, I will admit, but something of a bold gesture nonetheless. It makes you interesting. A son of a bitch, maybe. Something of a cliché of a midlife crisis, definitely. But nevertheless interesting." You pause and glance across at me. "Well, isn't it?"

I nod briefly and you continue. "You need to trust yourself more. Your instincts in coming here were correct. I appreciate your concern for my life. I am glad that you cared—care—about the manner of my passing. These are good, generous things. But you can't expect an obvious, reciprocal 'something' to happen or be given— especially if that something is only some sort of salve for your infidelity. It, whatever that 'it' you're looking for is, doesn't work like that."

There is silence. I feel once more the heat of the noon sun on my head and the cool breeze that comes off the lake. My ears open to the sound of the frogs in the sedge to my right. I can see tiny fish swimming among the rocks near the water's edge, bordered as it is with some yellowish pollution that I presume has come from the factory I can see shimmering on the other side of the lake.

"Why not?" I ask.

"Because God only makes himself manifest with a lot of trumpets and a host of angels in stories, Adam. You took the road to Nicaea, not Damascus, remember. Revelation is not going to happen because you want it to happen, or—and this is the position I think you believe you are in—because you *deserve* it. Plus, I'm not convinced you really *do* want it to happen. Thus, the mock heroic, right?"

You lean over toward me. "You have to stop fighting so hard—beating up against these big things called God and Faith. If you see them as great monoliths needing to be chiseled into shape, then you're going to expend an awful lot of energy for very little reward."

You stand up and walk to the edge of the lake, throwing your voice over its placid surface. "When we were young I asked you to come to Bible classes because I thought you might like to explore what I was exploring. I didn't have the answers; I just thought these ideas were worth getting to know more about. They seemed to have exercised a lot of intelligent and passionate people over the years and that seemed to me to count for something. And that was about it."

"Why didn't you tell me that at the time?"

You turn and face me. "You'd have never believed me or listened, Adam. You shrank away as soon as I mentioned God or the Bible or *anything*, as a matter of fact. Didn't want to commit. Thought it was uncool, effeminate, something as stupid as that, I imagine. And I, perhaps, was a little aggressive. We were *very* young."

"I envied the confidence of your faith. Was that real?"

You bend down and begin to pull up strands of grass with your fingers. "It was, yes. I know they're words and sentiments you loathe, and I will admit that they can seem a bit trite, but I did indeed discover a personal relationship with Jesus Christ. Or rather Jesus offered me a personal relationship with him, and I said yes, which is not quite the same thing. And it was a gift of grace and none of my choosing. There was no sounding trump or tinkling cymbal, no sudden rushing in of pentecostal-wind or fire, although I was filled with *something*. Does that help?"

"How do you mean 'help'?"

"I mean, does that make it clearer?"

I nod a doubtful yes.

"But when I was caught in the car-wreck, I felt as much pain as anyone would, and I prayed to God to be with me, and I didn't feel relief from my pain. And, before you become too critical, it didn't diminish my belief in his saving presence. My death did not invalidate the joy I got from having him in my life."

There is a large splash and we both turn toward Marianne, who smiles back sheepishly at me.

"Tell me about her."

"You know everything already," I reply. "You're part of my imagination."

"I'd like to hear you say it, though. It might help, don't you think?"

"What do you mean, 'help'?"

"You have a lot of problems with that word, don't you, Adam? It doesn't seem to be a word you're familiar with."

"All right." I feel the anger reddening my cheeks. "We've come back to Turkey to recapture the energy of our first meeting."

"The *energy*? You can do better than that, surely Adam! She's not a power station! Do you love her?" I look across at her: strawberry-blond hair, still slender; open-faced, quizzical eyes; older now, but still something generous and youthful about her. "Or perhaps that is too difficult a question at the moment."

You get to your feet and walk to the edge of the lake. "That's what I always liked about you, Adam. You were ready to make the grand romantic gesture—commit yourself to God, leave your wife, and steal your first love away from her husband and take her back to where you first met. These things take courage, some sort of restless self-belief."

"I thought you'd be angry."

"Remember, Adam. I am not the admonishing angel. I am your creation, although not as self-serving and palliative as you might want me to be. Unfortunately for you, your conscience, sense of guilt, superego, or perhaps—may I suggest?—your guardian angel is particularly fractious and makes me seem harsher than I was in real life."

"You were pretty harsh."

"If that's what you want to believe, then perhaps I was. I was also unforgiving of myself, as well as you and others. I was an ambitious young man, wanted to get ahead, had lots to do. But a wayward car put paid to that. Anyway, given that my role in this discussion is to be the gadfly, I should probably remind you that Sarah is devastated, as are the children. They are at a loss, sleepless at night, wondering what you are doing. You know how organized Sarah is, how competent she is— well, how shall I put this delicately? She isn't anymore."

"Now she knows what it feels like."

You throw your head back and laugh. "Adam, your petulance is wonderfully refreshing, if appalling. I don't believe you're the sort of person to be pettily vindictive just because your wife chooses to spend time with other men. And you don't really care, do you? I very much doubt she is sleeping with them; sex doesn't interest her particularly, as you have lamented often enough. In any event, her behavior is convenient for you, an excuse because you're too scared to ask her why she likes to spend time with others more than she does with you. Allows you to be the martyr and feel self-righteous, all at the same time.

"But your absence. Well, of course, *that* matters. And I'd be lying if I said things were easy. Far be it for me to be the recording angel with the broken record, but, as I'm sure you have read in the self-help manuals and popular magazines, what has happened is tough on children. They don't understand grand romantic gestures at that age. It merely seems like abandonment to them. I think Sarah has rationalized it by telling herself that you are on some sort of Odyssean quest to find yourself, and that if she just acts like Penelope then you'll come sailing back, having got whatever wanderlust you have out of your system." You look around. "Kind of appropriate thinking, I should say, given where you and Marianne met."

You turn back to look at me. "And Sarah isn't entirely wrong, is she, Adam? You don't follow through, do you, with the great romantic gesture? It always ends up being a half-measure—in the end, *only* a gesture. A self-regarding wave of the hand at the heroic."

You glance at Marianne. "Why don't you talk to her? Find out why she's unhappy."

"Why should I? Why doesn't she tell me? I ask her often enough."

"That's not asking, that's *telling* her not to be unhappy. Can't you tell she's locked in somehow?"

11

"Then I don't see why I have to unlock her. That's her job."

"Of course it's her job. But you don't need to bolt the door on the other side, do you? You might consider giving her a chance to voice her concerns. After all, you brought her here."

"She said it was all right."

"Of course she would say it's all right, Adam! She's in love with you. The stakes for leaving a spouse are so much higher for her. The stakes always are for women, you know that—given what society expects of them."

"*She* doesn't have any children."

"I'll ignore that, Adam. Don't judge her. Just listen to her. Pay attention. If she feels she is being listened to, then things can change." You pause and look toward the town shimmering in the heat to the right of the lake. "At the risk of being as pedantic and arrogant as you always accused me of being, I might point out that listening has never been your strong suit. That and asking for help. You never seem to have countenanced the possibility that there are wonderful mysteries that require only a little humility and a little attention, and things that seem intractable and impossible to believe in become supremely...well, *present*, for want of a better word."

I look at you. "You're saying I should shut up a bit?"

You stop and give me one of your sobering looks, the kind you used to give me when you felt I wasn't matching up to your good impression of me. I feel myself bristling.

"Nicaea," you continue, dwelling on the word. "I admit—there is a ring to it. A lot went on here—a council of faith, the permitting of icons, seat of the Byzantine Empire for a while. A definite resonance. Perhaps it may offer secrets, if you listen to it." You raise your eyebrows conspiratorially. "Unfortunately, you seem to be stuck on Iznik. Why are you so scared of Iznik, or even the possibility that there may indeed be traces of Nicaea in Iznik, that you've decided in advance to be disappointed by raising your expectations so ridiculously high? True, this place is no paradisal location or enclosed garden of delights, and, flattered though I am, I am no sage old man disguised as a boy to provide you with great spiritual wisdom. Yet, truth and beauty and ugly reality don't have to be so ruthlessly separated through your disappointment. Simply not getting what you expected hardly seems reason enough for you to encompass both the possibility of success and the certainty of failure in a verbal trick like *topos*?"

You sit down once more beside me. Your voice is coaxing, soothing. "Listen. Twenty years is a long time. You've had other friends—less taxing than I was and a good deal more rewarding. You've had love affairs, got married, had children. You've seen both your parents die. These are all differences, all gifts in their way. And now you're older and I'm not. I can see how you've aged, how everything is less open in you and more defeated. And that's all right as well. But you can't lie to me and be too sanctimonious, because I am well aware, Adam, that for long stretches of that time I never entered your head. So isn't it time to move on and accept that what is, is? I am not, was not, will never be, a particularly special person—although I'm flattered you are so concerned. You made me that way. My death was one among many, and my life, as short as it was, was rich, and how my Christian friends chose to express that is their concern. It was you who has lifted all of it into this huge crisis of conscience between faith and unbelief, between God-fearing and God-rebellion, as if you're trying to wage Lucifer's battles all over again."

"I thought you might be pleased."

You laugh again. "Why does it matter whether I'm pleased or not? I'm a dead man! This isn't about me. It's about you and Marianne and God."

"Of course it's about you!" I stand up and walk away along the shore out of the range of Marianne's hearing. "It's about how that Orphic cult you belong to that calls itself Christianity ripped your body apart. It's a lamentation, a jeremiad, a yell from the lion's den, a rivers-of-Babylon ululation. It's about saying, 'I object. I accuse. I do not submit.' Somebody had to say 'No. This is not acceptable. This is not as it should be,' and that someone was me. Is me. Somebody had to make a little noise to offset the great hypocritical silence of God in the face of the suffering he allows." I close my eyes. Shouting is merely confirming your disdain for me. I bring my voice down to a lower level. "I am merely trying to establish a balance."

"You're trying to be heard, Adam," you say gently. "I understand. You want God to pay attention to you, and you think the best way to do it is to make as much noise as possible, and be as bitter as you can be. But cries from the heart only work when you don't hold anything back, and you're holding so much back. Change means letting go of it all."

"Really? I thought Christianity was a little less therapeutic and more doctrinal than that."

You shrug your shoulders to tell me that the remark is beneath me and that you're going to ignore it.

"You can think anything you like, Adam. The living have that prerogative. Given your hostility to all things Christian I thought it best to couch my advice in the language of spirituality. Make it more acceptable." You pause. "Apparently I failed to convince you."

"You've failed for twenty years," I mutter.

You smile. "I'm not sure I'd use the word 'failed,' Adam. And even if you accept that there has been a failure, I don't think the failure's mine. But we'll let that pass." You pause. "All I'll say to you is that you should give Iznik a chance. Who knows? It might be that God is willing to speak to you even here. And it might not be some triumphal expression of imperial will, some strong-arming by those muscular evangelical Christians you liked to lump me with—the kind of display you seemed to look forward to resenting. It might be completely different. I don't know."

"And you're sure it won't come through you?"

You give a little laugh. "That's right, Adam. Just keep protecting yourself with your irony and you'll be fine. Irony's a wonderful thing—keeps you safe when you're feeling vulnerable and makes sure you don't take any steps outside of that big palace of misery and self-disgust you've built for yourself."

"You're telling me that you think a teetotaler being run into by a drunk driver is not ironic?"

"No, I do not think it is ironic. Stuff happens, life is short; this is all I can say on that point. Was I ready to die? No. Did I want to die? No. Did it hurt? Like hell. But that doesn't invalidate my faith, and it doesn't invalidate my belief that you would have been, and would be, a whole lot happier if you had attended the Bible classes as I suggested. God forbid, you might have learned something or even, heaven forfend, found happiness."

"I read the Bible after you died. Twice. Didn't do me any good." I hear the smugness in my voice.

"I know you read the Bible, Adam. I'll be sure to tell teacher to give you a gold star. But you read it with so much resistance, as if you were reading it as evidence for the prosecution. You never actually bothered to listen to it, to let it speak to you, did you?"

You notice we have reached an impasse and take a deep breath. "Listen, take some time in this town. There are things to see. There's a shadow puppet theater you might enjoy. There's even a group of dervishes conducting a *zhikr*. God is all around you here, even in the kids on motorbikes who are annoying you so much by whizzing up and down the road. Take some time to open up to the history of this place, hear the voices of the people, think about what went on. Who knows what will happen?"

"What happens if nothing happens? It hasn't in twenty years."

You raise your hands in exasperation. "Then nothing happens! And you've gone around thinking that nothing is going to happen for all those twenty years. You've allowed all this rejectionist noise in your head and you can't hear 'the still small voice of calm,' as a rather saccharine hymn likes to say."

You pause. "But you came here today and there is the option for something else to happen. Isn't it worth trying to let that something else speak to you?"

I look out at the lake and see the little yellow dots of pollution and the tiny fish speckled by the sunlight swimming between the reeds. Signs of Christ, perhaps.

"There you have it," you interrupt. "Signs of Christ is a start."

I look up at you. You are smiling. I am incredulous. "It's as straightforward as that?" I ask.

"It's a beginning a lot more convincing than yours."

I glance across at Marianne, who is now sitting on a rock, her hair lifted by the hot wind. Her feet are dangling in the water. I can see the shape of her body through the T-shirt and skirt she is wearing. I feel a brief surge of lust.

"What are you going to do about Marianne?"

I am surprised you are still there. "What do you mean 'do'?"

"Your relationship, such as it is. You haven't been very nice to her, have you?"

"Nice?"

"Respectful, decent. Why do you have to be so unpleasant?"

"I would have thought you would know the answer to that question."

You smile. "You can't blame me for every flaw in

your character, you know. I'm certainly not responsible for your tendency to feel sorry for yourself. Think again."

I am tired of your interference. You, too, could use some discretionary silence, I think. "I didn't know you were interested in human relationships as well?"

"I am interested in you, and you are preoccupied with your relationship with her. What's wrong with that?"

"Shouldn't your mind be on more heavenly matters?"

You laugh. "Don't you think God cares about relationships? You forget that Christianity is an incarnate faith."

"I don't want to discuss it with you. After all, you were a virgin as far as I know."

"As far as you know, yes." There is a grin all over your face. "Really, Adam. You do say the stupidest things sometimes, don't you?" My teeth clench and I hold my peace. "I was not talking about sex. I was talking about other forms of intercourse. I repeat: You can do a lot by listening."

"So you say."

"What I don't understand is what you hope for in this relationship."

"Do I have to 'hope' for anything?"

"I think she hopes for something."

"Such as what?"

You look at me severely. "Why don't you ask her, Adam? You might be amazed to find that she too has a spiritual life—or rather a life that she wants to shape to attain a larger goal than sex, or family, or whatever great goals we set out on our lives to achieve."

"Goals that your Christian friends apparently thought inconsequential."

You let out a brief laugh. "Yes, death came a little too soon for me to achieve them. But that doesn't mean they're meaningless. To my mind Marianne seems as restless and dissatisfied as you—and it's got precious little to do with you or Michael."

"And you think she's going to tell me, do you?"

"I don't know, Adam. That's a risk, isn't it? It's a risk you're going to have to take."

And, suddenly, you're gone. I look at the fish swimming in the lake. Images of Christ—an image that is acceptable to you—icons of faith. Signs to the true way.

Yet I cannot avoid the memory that all morning as we drove through the dust it was Nicaea where we were headed. From sign to sign we moved in this town, past ruined mosques, on Roman roads, by unroofed houses, all signifying through the word "Nicaea" the great sign of faith once made here. Light of Light, true God from true God, begotten not made. And I feel the flesh of my hands, the cool touch of water on my feet, dust thou art and to dust shalt thou return. Body and blood, sun lighting the blood in my hands. Nicaea, begotten not made, an image born from the mind.

So, all morning across eternity, through groves and avenues, along the sides of the dam and the edges of cliffs, by rivers and streams, across passes and flats, the sun slipping through the sky, trees, and high grasses; with the pulse of all existence leading towards the resolution of place at that time, at that hour, your image within and without leading me on; with all this I came to Nicaea and found it broken into the infinitesimal fragments of light on the lake, the flecks of dust, and the fish around my feet. I came to expiate, forgive and be forgiven: and all three states have been thrust joyfully at my unbaptized feet, where the only images of Christ are the fish beneath the mortal, decaying dust warmed by an uncaring sun.

Yet I cling to the past, the Nicaea that is pointed to but never arrived at. The Nicaea of long vowels and days, lying opposed to the squat consonants of Iznik. Nicaea: city of follies and sepulchers, porticoes and bays, arcades and cloisters, of dialogue and design. Nicaea: where what is spoken is automatically done, and what is achieved is instantly understood. Nicaea: kaleidoscope of meaning, coruscation of light and language, where qualification and contradiction dissolve in the certainty of a singular sun.

I ask that Nicaea be found in a sudden unspoken revelation, where it was neither looked for nor expected. I ask that Nicaea be known and not experienced, an equilibrium at the back of the mind, an understood configuration of sense and statement. I ask that Nicaea let me reach beyond word and difference, and apprehend the body as it comprehends the soul; that it lead me through the city and its splendors as a brother, away from the common and the commonplace. Away from here.

Logos

To my most blessed brothers and sisters in Christ of Caesarea in Judea, greetings and peace from your loving bishop Eusebius, given honor through and for your piety at this the most major of ecumenical councils yet convened by our noble Emperor Victor Constantinus, Maximus Augustus, it being near the twentieth year of his reign as liberator of our faith from the dungeon of its oppression, for which we must thank God, and less than one year after his great victory over the traitor Licinius; at Nicaea in Bithynia in Asia Minor, a place said to be founded by the pagan god Dionysos yet denoting true Christian victory and renowned for its felicitous climate and convenient location; to refute utterly the dangerous and misleading heresies of those who follow Arius, a presbyter of Alexandria, and his disciples (notably Theonas, Secundus and, most heinously, Eusebius of Nicomedia, the last whose name if not ideas I share, and whose apostasy most keenly wounds the Emperor); and to establish a creed at once binding and true whereby the Church might continue its mission to bring light into a

21

world where all is at its darkest; to you all, greetings, and may God and Christ Jesus bestow upon you blessing.

You will, of course, be acutely aware of the excitement with which I greeted the news of the Council. It was indeed an honor for us all that the Emperor allowed in his goodness so humble a bishop as myself, not only to present him to the assembled throng, but also to be the recorder of events at once momentous and decisive as have taken place at Nicaea. You above all are aware how keenly and with what anticipation I hoped for a swift resolution to this most damaging and divisive action of Arius and his followers, so terribly misled, and who have been punished fairly and through due course of law; and you can therefore imagine consequently how great is my joy that a creed has been decided upon that is both to the satisfaction of every party present and the final word on the nature of Christ and the Logos.

Poor though my words are, it is incumbent upon me and my earnest duty to attempt to describe the occasion and the number and importance of the representatives of our Church gathered at Nicaea. From Phoenicia, Cilicia, Libya, and Thebes; from Egypt, Syria, and Arabia; from Mesopotamia and Palestine, Thrace and Macedonia; from Pamphilia and Cappadocia, Asia and Phrygia; from Epirus, Achaia, and Persia, Scythia, Pontus, and Spain—in short, from the whole world—prelates and representatives arrived, a passage made easy through the largesse of this most considerate of emperors, who laid his transportation at the disposal of us all. This company was not one of casually gathered men, with a passing interest in religious affairs and an idleness in their modes of thought, as may have been the case before our enlightenment; but it was the most choice and most revered of all the nations under the Emperor's benign command who gathered in front of his delighted eyes. This Council will long be remembered for the brilliance of the assembly and the grace of its moving spirit, the Emperor himself. Nor was there anything wanting to men young and old, both known for the fire of their conviction and force of their debate. Sumptuous banquets were prepared, and the very finest provisions garnered from the wide world. I say, in truth, it was as if Heaven had come to Earth and bathed us in its bounty.

At the opening ceremony I delivered an oration which reflected the due magnificence of the occasion. It does not befit a mere cleric such as myself to fill these pages with my poor words, especially since those of the Emperor overwhelmed even the most studied and schooled of rhetoricians there assembled; nor does it suit that I should attempt to place in the forefront of this letter the creed I suggested might be adopted by the congregation. It is in any event one well known to you as fellow celebrants of our congregation. Both were mere introductions to truths more pressing and, because addressed so fully and with such wisdom, greater than my paltry efforts. Nevertheless, a brief outline must suffice, if only to show how dedicated was the gathering to solving this most contentious of issues.

I welcomed on behalf of the Emperor those who had traveled from far and wide. There may be those who would see my adopting such a stance as a presumption of the highest order; yet I felt that, since the Emperor himself was too modest a man to venture his own views before all had stated their own, how much more would he be unwilling to be seen to dominate the proceedings from the very beginning, when it was to be understood that he was to act as a first among equals, with due consideration to those more fully schooled in the scriptures and of higher benefice than he within the Church. Furthermore, I here record for posterity a letter written to me personally, in his own handwriting, by our most gracious Emperor, giving me authority to speak on his behalf.

"Constantinus Augustus to his friend Eusebius Pamphili of Caesarea. I am not an eloquent man; that you know. I am neither as well versed in the scriptures nor in the schools of rhetoric as you. I speak Latin, the language of soldiery, and not Greek, the language of thought. Because I am a soldier I cannot use such language. Be my spokesman and prepare all men's hearts for the truth, which I am sure you know as well as me. See to it."

As you can well imagine, I was deeply impressed by the commission from the Emperor, as well as flattered by his attention towards such a lowly bishop as myself. Thus was I authorized, and thus did I speak.

I wondered at the great diversity of peoples present, the representation of all ranks and points of view, and expressed thanks to the Emperor for providing so great a number of people with the transportation necessary for the journey. I then sternly impressed upon the assembly the importance of their mission. "The whole world has turned its eyes upon us," I said. "Those eyes, dimmed through suffering and torture, are now bright with expectation; those hearts that had become faint as promise after promise was broken, church after church destroyed, family after family parted—those hearts are driven with a stronger beat as they await our decision. Across the whole world, men, women, and children are bending their goodwill toward us. Indeed, as I prayed to the Lord this morning, I felt him gather me up and lift me to the very heights of Heaven and bid me look upon the millions as they themselves prayed for a solution to these problems.

"My brothers, we are at the crossroads of our faith. In one direction lies the path of Anarchy, a route which leads to Hell. It is paved with the bodies of lost souls, who through mistrust and blindness slew each other in their jealous efforts to speed more quickly than the other to their eternal doom. It is a wide and tempting road, for it is the road of decisions which at first sight seem easy but lie in wait like robbers to entrap those foolhardy enough to look no further than their own nose. In the other direction, however, lies the path toward Heaven. This road is always hard, because it has to be trod by the traveler whose sights are always set upon the target and never on the path immediately in front. This road is paved with the bodies of those who died for our cause, slain by evil times. Should we stumble upon these bodies, they are not a source of terror for us, but a source of joy, for they speak to us of sacrifice and true faith and urge us onward to receive the gift they have been given. At times the road is almost impassable, at times moving further from and not nearer to the goal; but at other times, when the end is most clearly seen and the signs (so obvious and yet so easily misconstrued) the brightest, it is a road which is blissful to walk upon.

"The whole world, as I have said, awaits our decision. Are we to take the easy route and bring upon the world dissension and strife; are we in a few days of false debate and facile argument going to place upon the shoulders of every trusting Christian the burden of horrors which do not bear contemplation; are we going to fail them now at the hour of greatest need? Or shall we be recorded in history as the great justiciars of the Church, the benefactors of the Christian world, the heirs to the Kingdom of God who understood the most serious crisis yet to face it and acted decisively and magnanimously to resolve it?

"The answer, my friends, is clear. But the solution will not be easy. At times it will seem almost impossible. But I beg you to have faith and trust in the superior judgment given to you by God, so you may be guided by the light within you to come to a conclusion that is of benefit to us all. Finally, give thanks to God that we have an emperor in whose soul the Holy Spirit has made its home. We likewise shall find a home in his wisdom as he has housed us so near his home and in a place so pleasant and comfortable. As I look around me, I am struck by the contrast with former years. Who would have thought we would be debating openly here when so recently we were looking over our shoulders expecting the advent of the persecutors? Who would have thought the image of greatest fear would become our most trusted friend and counselor? And yet, it is not surprising at

all if all is duly considered. For God was clearly prepar-
ing for our release even as he punished us most severely
for our sins. For God is always just, and his mercy
knows no bounds.

"I have spoken too long, for our business is pressing
and the figure to whom we owe our thanks and reverence is most anxious for the business to commence
without delay. I shall end, therefore, and wish you well.
May God be with you."

At this, trumpets sounded and the Emperor
appeared. Although I had made an attempt to prepare
the assembly for the arrival of the Emperor, words
proved inadequate in this instance; for the Emperor out-
shone so markedly any description, no matter how effu-
sive or precise, that all were dazzled.

How can I hope to convey the impression the
Emperor made upon us? It is my duty and yet I fear I
will fail in my task. Nevertheless, I shall try, so you may
understand the sweet grace and majesty of our lord. It
was as if a messenger from God had arrived, his face
illuminated from within by the divine light of Heaven;
and to look upon his visage was to behold a part of
God's bounty, so piercing was the Emperor's beauty. He
himself looked upon the company with eyes so benign
that at once all felt both at ease and yet subordinate to
this celestial manifestation walking among them.

I addressed the Emperor as follows:

"Lord of us all, whose eminence almost seems to
deny that we are fallen, your presence here gives us a
glimpse of a world from which we departed many centuries ago, and a world to which we hope to return

when we have breathed our last. With you here among us, we ourselves feel raised to unknown heights of grace and can observe our soiled, daily lives beneath us. We are your humble servants, ready to do your will; and we know your will is that of the world's, for in your palm you hold the world and its future. In you are brought together the two great institutions of the Empire and the Church—which are images themselves of the Kingdom of Heaven—and you bring down upon us the Logos of the Father in your rule as the vicegerent of the Lord over the Kingdom of Earth. Surely this day will be recalled by future generations as the day God and Man were briefly reunited through your presence. Before you, my lord, are gathered the wisest men under your aegis; with you as our chief and guide we are ready to follow through the mire of debate and storm clouds of dissension born from the scoundrels that sit, like vipers in our midst, to spread discomfiture and defamation where there should be reason."

There is not room in this letter to report all of the Emperor's speech. Moreover, these words I offer you, my brethren, are mere dross in comparison with those offered to the assembly by the Emperor, and I am an idle chatterer when I think of the simplicity of his tongue and the force of his argument. Not for him were the obfuscations of rhetoric, the masking of speciousness and falsehood in the cloak of fine-sounding but empty words; not for him the elaborate extensions of ideas through exemplar and simile in order to provide with beauty what is hideous and deformed. No, Constantine's words, formed from the source of all language, which are the Lord's words, are as open as his face. Again, a brief extract will suffice to give you an idea of the brilliance of his speech.

"My friends, it is indeed good we should have such commendable weather today, for the tough task ahead will be more easily completed with the blessing of God's sun upon us. I am a soldier and use the Roman tongue; the way you think doesn't suit a mouth accustomed to giving and an ear to taking orders. Nevertheless, I hope you will both give ear and listen to these words, rough and ready as they may be.

"I have not been happy at the idle speculations made by both parties concerning the nature of Christ and his relationship with the Father. I am not happy because I consider it imperative that we present a united front both for those who still do not believe and for those who waver in their faith when they are pressed about with such difficulties. I therefore commanded this Council to meet, and I am grateful to you for coming to Nicaea in such numbers.

"We are on the verge of a great decision, for the day will soon come when we will either perish or gain life eternal. I hope and trust we will take our opportunity to achieve reconciliation, for the consequences for life on Earth are undoubtedly dire should we fail. Riot and disorder stand on our heels; the world waits for a conclusion. Shall we be defeated? No. We must not be defeated, because failure would exact too high a ransom. Shall we not win, rather? With our talent, combined to good effect, and our goodwill also added, we shall triumph over the enemy and destroy them utterly."

Be assured, my brothers and sisters in Christ, that this was not the only time the Emperor spoke; for when all was at its most divisive—with both factions unreasonably arguing over the issues and addressing each other as "heretics" and such like accusations—the Emperor, who until then had been an image of silent authority, delegating to his trusted envoy Ossius of Cordoba the menial task of overseeing the debate, intervened, indicating that he was here to bring goodwill and consensus, and to punish not one Christian who argued reasonably and for the common good. He then brought to bear his great intelligence and offered, by way of compromise, the word *homoousios*—"of the same substance"—as a description of the Son's relation to the Father.

The silence that greeted his suggestion was profound—it being undoubtedly a silence of astonishment that the Emperor could cut so boldly through the thickets of over-clever and indulgent sophistry with the sword-stroke of illumination. After a moment's pause, I asked, on behalf of all of those gathered, for a clarification of what the Emperor meant—since such a word was not present in any form in the scriptures, which were, and will remain, our guiding light through the dark, storm-tossed nights of our confinement. The Emperor then asked whether this phrase was so important as to cause such division among us, and he offered by way of explication the phrase "being of one substance with the Father." Even to me in person did he speak, for taking me aside he laid the conditions of his idea clearly and exactly—as a kindly father to an uncomprehending

child—which can but confirm, as if confirmation were
lacking, the generosity and intelligence of this emperor
our redeemer. All the assembly, except those fools and
madmen unwilling to accept any compromise or reasoning, then agreed upon this.

O my friends, would you had been there to see this
gracious man dispense justice! It is impossible for me, as
a mere mortal, to describe the radiance emanating from
our beloved Emperor, Solomon himself, whose majesty
and wisdom were clear to see, and to contrast this vision
with the subtle and devious counselors who had so cruelly deserted the offices entrusted to them. The former
was the image of clear and reasonable authority, with
sentences duly weighed and considered in the balance of
his perfect understanding; the latter spoke the confused
and excited nonsense of those who vainly constructed the
tower of Babel. Even as our lord the Emperor revealed
the light of God in his compassion, so did these serpents
whisper their subtle falsehoods from the fog of their own
error. And yet, these victims of sophistry were their own
worst enemies: for the more they attempted to persuade
the assembly of their point of view with false syllogisms
and distortions of piety, the more did they make manifest
the contortions of their evil minds. Thus the opposition
were utterly defeated and downcast, while the Emperor,
bringing upon them the full weight of his imperial
majesty, a majesty invested with the authority of God,
needed only to voice the opinion of the whole company,
that these offenders be excommunicated forthwith, for
the deed to be done. Immediately the judgment was
sounded, and the recusants who had failed to sign the

Creed agreed upon by all departed the town, the somber mood accompanying the authoritative command of our lord seemed to lift, and the sun shone once more.

Before I relate to you more precisely the details of the Creed, it is incumbent upon me to inform you that this was not the only business of the Council. For many years, the day of our Lord's resurrection has been a matter of debate. It has dismayed all true Christians, and especially our Emperor, that we could not celebrate such a day together. Now, through the benefices of our Emperor and the collective will of the body gathered here, it has been decided that Easter shall fall upon one day, and shall be celebrated across the imperial world. Also it was decided that the Church, for it to become the mighty force in the world which the Emperor clearly so wished it to become, required a restructuring along the lines of the Roman government. Therefore, the Church has itself been split into provinces, and each province is to be administered by a synod of bishops which will in turn be headed by a bishop of the capital of the province, known as the metropolitan. These decisions are yet more examples, if any further were needed, of the goodness and far-sightedness of our Emperor; for he has foreseen our faith will spread most effectively if it is unified in all its parts and ceremonies.

With regard to the Creed, it has been decided upon and confirmed that the Son is consubstantial with the Father. There never was a time when the Logos was not, for God the Father is only so because he has the Son. The Logos remains perpetual through Time, created from the Father but indivisible from him. To those who deny that the Logos is infinite, to those who would divide the Son from his Father and talk of the Son in terms of a lesser being, I say this: observe the first words of the holy Gospel of John. Here is it most clearly stated that the Logos was at the beginning with God and remained within him, acting as the silent language of thought within us at all times, even though we do not utter a word. In such a way, brethren, was the Logos both a part of God and yet God himself.

Likewise, and in similar fashion, note also how the Gospel says the Logos took upon himself the flesh of which we are made, and became man. The Logos dwelt within Jesus, that is the Christ, until he had fulfilled his mission and the Logos returned to his Father. In this act, God revealed to us the true mystery of eternal life, and sought to show us, in forms and words we might understand, what we ourselves must undergo in order to attain that end—namely life everlasting. This stands written in the opening lines of the Gospel, and you can read it there. These, then, are the words you must say.

"We believe in one God, the Father Almighty, maker of Heaven and of the Earth, and all things both visible and invisible; and in one Lord, Jesus Christ, the Son of God, begotten of the Father, God of God, Light of Light, and true God of true God, begotten not made, being of one substance with the Father, by whom all things in Heaven and on Earth were made; who for us men and for our salvation came down, and was incarnate, and was made man. He suffered, and he rose again upon the third day, ascended into Heaven, and is coming to judge the living and the dead. And we believe in the Holy Spirit.

"But those who say there was a time when he was not, or he was not before he was made, and he was made out of nothing, or say that the Son of God is created from a different substance, or is a creature, or is alterable or changeable, they are anathema to the Catholic Church."

You will see that the Creed is not so very different from the creed we use, my brothers and sisters in Christ. All of importance that has been inserted is the phrase "of one substance with the Father"—which, as has been reported, has the authority of the Emperor himself and is, thus, to our eternal blessing, of both temporal and spiritual authority.

Surely, therefore, it is incomprehensible such clarity should be so misinterpreted by all these sons of Simon Magus. It is imperative that you are not dissuaded from your current course. Do not seek, you mortals, to understand what God has not revealed to us. Do not question what has been decided upon by men more godly and learned than yourselves. Do not believe that any version of the Creed but this will suffice.

And to those who still labor in the mire of their own ignorant superstitions and barbaric rites, I say: how can you hope to find truth when you propagate so many lies, at once blatant and absurd, for your own ends? You are fools, all of you. Say nothing, then, but listen to those who have experienced the grace of our Savior and through him have known the glory of God's love; say nothing but the Creed laid out by this Council in its wisdom, and rejoice at the unification of its earthly and heavenly power through the presence of our lord and emperor Constantine Augustus; and above all, say nothing but praise for him who has most bountifully brought about the release of our faith and who convened this most successful of councils. For we live in times that are historic in every way.

Remember how but twenty years ago we were under the yoke of the collective madness of the misled Roman State. Let us therefore rejoice at our liberty with the restraint borne of our suffering; let us acknowledge the generosity of our enlightened Emperor who has blessed us with the authority of the leader of the whole world; let us bask in the rays which shine from his eminence only so that we may illumine the shadows of those who prepared the way for the Emperor's revelation through their suffering.

Be vigilant in the Lord's work, my brothers and sisters. Understand that it is upon our backs that the burden of responsibility lies, a responsibility made more acute by our newly established role in this society, a role confirmed and strengthened by this Council at Nicaea. And love each other, trusting always in our Lord Jesus Christ, believing in this creed for the good of all mankind.

Eusebius Pamphili, Bishop of Caesarea

The Absence of the "I"

My dear friends at Baucalis, greetings from your servant, Arius of Alexandria, and blessing to you all. May God shine his light on us all.

I believe some explanation may be needed after my recent outburst during the service conducted by Alexander, bishop of our great city. I have heard that some of you have commented that this was conduct unbecoming two men not in the first flush of youth, and I would be the first to agree with you, were it not for the fact that the distortions put out by the bishop, and the prevalence of misconceptions concerning our beliefs, made it necessary for me to speak out there and then.

To get to the heart of it, the sermon the bishop was preaching shamelessly argued that the Father and the Son were both of equal eternality (his words, not mine— you know I've never been one for all that scholarly talk). In any event, the phrase was so flagrantly contradictory that yours truly felt it necessary to interject. I stood up (deep breaths all round and a bit of throat-clearing from the assembled congregation) and quite calmly said that to state the Father and the Son were co-eternal was to deny the absolute transcendence of God who was, of course, indivisible and singular. I continued, "God willed the Son to be born, but that birth was neither inevitable nor was it incipient at any moment."

As you can imagine, Alexander was shocked that anyone would dare to interrupt him, especially, as it were, on his home turf. When he's rattled, he becomes even more pompous than normal, and his chins wobble as if they have minds of their own. "Are you saying..." he began. "Are you saying that it was an act of random creation?"

I told the bishop that there was no need to shout, but that I merely wanted to correct some doctrinally speculative elements in his homily.

This did not go down well.

"But surely the Son of God cannot be the Son unless he is part of the Father. The Father begets the Son and does not create him."

"I disagree. The title of the Son of God was given to Christ by God because of the former's perfect goodness. But the Son does not possess either by nature or right any specific qualities of God, such as perfect knowledge, immortality, absolute goodness and kingliness. These attributes belong to God alone since they are indivisibly contained within his oneness."

"But this is nonsense," Alexander blustered, and looked around for support from some of his cronies, who appeared startled by the whole exchange and remained glued to their seats. Actually, I think Alexander was more embarrassed than angry—and, my friends, he was *very* angry—but he carried on regardless of the scene he was making.

"Surely God was made man through Christ and through him came to save us from sin."

"But this is not the point," I replied. I tried a different tack—trying to sound reasonable at least. "Look, I am not saying that Christ was just one of us. He is the firstborn of all creatures; by his actions he achieves the status of godhead, although he is not absolute God. It is simply impossible to say that the Son existed before the Father or existed within the Father always. Otherwise the Son would have no relation to the Father that could be conceived of as separable from him. Instead, let us think of the Son as uniquely privileged in his access to the Father so as to provide us with a model of wisdom and brilliance given him by the Father. He is a pathway for us to reach the Father, but, because he is not the Father but only from the Father," (at this point, I should add, friends tell me I began to wave my arms about a lot) "he cannot know God perfectly. As with all of us, the Father extended his grace towards his Son, who is sinless and without change through the practice of his virtue, but we cannot say he is sinless and unchangeable by nature."

This seemed to exhaust Alexander, along with a great deal of the congregation, who began to stand up and stretch and give longing looks at the back door.

"Have you finished, Arius?" he said.

I hadn't.

"I am merely warming to my theme. The Son is one of the very first creations of God—he indeed existed apart from God before all things came to be."

"Well, I can accept that," says Alexander. "You must not believe that when I say that the Son is co-eternal with the Father I am speaking in terms of chronological time. That too makes no sense, since God is outside time. Therefore, the Son and God are co-eternal with respect to their being."

"But how can you have two beings, both eternal and both ungenerated? One of them must have produced the other, or both been produced by a higher one."

"The Son was not begotten in the way we understand as begotten."

"That still doesn't answer my point. How was the Son born if he wasn't born? Or rather, from what was he born if he wasn't born?"

"Your mockery does you little credit, Arius."

"Your answer does you even less, Alexander."

Then he plays his trump card. "If all this is simply because you were passed over for the archbishopric of Alexandria...."

He strikes a nerve. I will admit, he strikes a nerve.

"That has nothing to do with it. I was unjustly treated, yes. But I would still like an answer to my question."

"The Son and the Father are co-eternal and of the same substance."

"You've said that already."

"And I will say it again until you and your mad ideas are driven into the wilderness where they belong."

At that point, he got down from his perch, stopped his speech, walked out of the church, giving me a very hostile look, and the service was abandoned. Naturally, I would have continued, had I had the opportunity, to tell him that it neither made sense nor fully valued the nature of Jesus to say there was no distinction between the Son and the Father in any way at all. I would have reminded Alexander that we must always be aware that the Son entered into the soul of Jesus—as he enters into all of our souls—and became it. But he did not assume the whole of Jesus' nature, or the Son would have died on the cross with Jesus, and, as we all believe, this is not the case. I would have referred him to John 17:3, Proverbs 8:22, and the letter of Paul to the Colossians 1:15 for evidence as to the fact that Christ is viewed there as a distinct and lesser entity than God.

But I didn't get a chance, and was hustled out of the church by some of my loyal supporters—I've told you about them in previous letters—and narrowly avoided being stoned to death by some of Alexander's more robust (so to speak) parishioners. Still, that's the cut and thrust of doctrinal debate, I'm afraid.

Now, if all this seems a little dry and academic, I am composing some verses that I believe will more easily carry our ideas to those who would believe them more readily without the kind of intellectual ramblings we Alexandrians are so known for.

Yours in faith,

Arius of Alexandria

* * *

Friends,

As I promised you, at your request your intemperate leader has written to Alexander again trying to clarify some of the misunderstandings he seems to possess in reference to the Son. Alexander seems to believe that my denying the absolute godhead of the Son would not only make it impossible for us to be redeemed but also mean that the Son was also lacking in perfection and therefore in need of redemption.

These are telling points only if you believe, as Alexander does, in the fundamental illogic of God being anything more or less than God. God created his Word as an instrument for the creation and the redemption of the world; in such a case Jesus Christ is the bridge we can use to move from this world to the next. But, as befits a bridge, this says nothing that is at all verifiable about the Son's character. Moreover, any attempt to do so is needlessly complicating the issue by making up personalities that needn't be made.

I won't bore you by enclosing my copy of the letter, but will sum it up. I began, rather suitably I thought, at the beginning. I argued that there are three individual realities—the Father, Son, and the Holy Spirit. Each is dependent on the other, but the Son is subordinate to the Father and the Holy Spirit is subordinate to the Son. The Father is the reference to the Son, who is Christ Jesus, and the Holy Spirit is that which descended upon the disciples after Jesus was taken up into heaven. They all, however, stem from one God—who is indivisible. All three persons belong to God but none are either equivalent or of the same substance as God.

So, there you have it. I have tried to be polite and not insult Alexander's intelligence too much. Believe me, I am not interested in schism.

I have as yet received no response.
Yours in faith,
Arius of Alexandria

* * *

From Arius of Alexandria, Friends, etc., etc.

My best efforts over three years at placating the portly prelate in my letters seem to have come to nothing. I have to report that a council of Egyptian bishops was convened by none other than the bishop himself to discuss this and other incidents pertaining to my beliefs, and henceforth I am no longer a member of the Christian Church. Alexander also, however, devoted much of the precious time at this council—time he could have spent either saving souls or more likely lining his pockets—accusing us of such impieties as would make the worst excesses of the Roman Empire seem tame. We are thieves, despots, licentious, and, what is more, idolatrous, although we have, as far as I know, never had a graven image in our churches and are not likely to have one in the future.

Apparently, so run the accusations that were both publicly posted and publicly handed to me by one of Alexander's self-described amanuenses, we also commit sins against nature and against our fellow men. Given these accusations, it's amazing we have any time at all, between running from orgy to orgy, to engage in the theological speculation that seems to have upset the good Bishop of Alexandria and his merry band of men. But it seems as if we have. For good measure, we are also all followers of Sabellius, whoever he is. And that, my friends, is that.

You may, of course, rest assured that I will not change my beliefs or compromise them in any way. They are too important to be toyed with in the way that Alexander does with his. Yours in faith,

Arius of Alexandria

* * *

My friends, blessings upon you and so forth.

I have already written to some of you informing you of the letter the Emperor Constantine himself wrote to our mutual friend Alexander and myself, urging us to set aside our differences—"differences"!?—over what he considers to be a theological trifle and unworthy of such schism in a Church so newly gathered together. He even had the gall to suggest that such deliberations were the result of too much leisure bestowed upon us through the rulership of Rome! Given what many of us can remember about the Roman Empire before Constantine, that came as a surprise, I can tell you! I've had copies of this letter made and ask those of you who possess the letter to circulate it among our supporters with the utmost speed.

After reading what I believe—at my most charitable—to be ill-considered ruminations from an emperor not supremely gifted in either philosophical or theological speculation, you will be able to determine more clearly the principled stance I have adopted, and the shameless cowardice of my earnest disputant and fellow

troublemaker Alexander. You will also be aware of how
the Emperor asked that, if we were unable to reconcile
ourselves with the heretics, we should agree to differ—
like, he said, the ancient philosophers, no less—in the
cause of the unity of the Church. While we were, as we
have always been, willing to consider the Emperor's
requests seriously, we were not about to surrender to the
hopeless, indeed blasphemous, illogicalities of others. I
must thank you with my whole heart for the strength
your prayers gave us in deciding to reject the Emperor's
plea (as well as the curses I presume you bestowed upon
the bishop).

You will also, perhaps, have been informed of my
most recent meeting with the Emperor's envoy, Ossius—
a man, I believe, from Cordoba in the westernmost
reaches of the Empire and, I further believe, one who,
although he means well, is too inclined toward the quick
and simplistic compromises of the West rather than the
lengthy disputations and absolute schisms so favored in
the East! Needless to say, we were unable to reach an
agreement as to a course of action except for a desire on
both our parts to bring forward the proposed meeting
about this issue from next year at Ancyra to this year at
Nicaea. I will write again when the Council has given its
decision.

In the meantime, please send your prayers to
Eusebius of Nicomedia and Asterios the Sophist—both
of whom have labored tirelessly to persuade the
Emperor and those who will be convened at the Council
at Nicaea to further our cause. I also have to report that
Eusebius of Caesarea—who is well known to you as a

historian of the highest rank—has indicated most strongly to me that he will help put forward our case at the forthcoming council. As you know from other letters, he has also been hard at work both before and since Antioch—where he too joined the ranks of the excommunicated—to impress upon the Emperor the truth of our ideas. As a consequence of these good Christians' work on our behalf, my heart is high and my trust in God absolute; it shall not be long before the ridiculous fallacies of Alexander and his like will be shown up as precisely those.

On a separate matter, I am grateful indeed you have responded so warmly to my *Banquet*. I must say I very much enjoyed writing it, especially those parts in verse, which, as I am not used to composition, taxed me greatly. Encouraged by your support, I have begun putting together a number of songs for some of our followers who travel on the sea or land. I would welcome any ideas for topics. Are clerics allowed to enjoy the act of creation so much?

Yours in faith,
Arius of Alexandria

* * *

Friends, etc.

Well, here we are at Nicaea and things, it seems, are not going well. Eusebius of Nicomedia gave a reasonably spirited defense of our claims, although he proved a little muddled over some of the key issues, which I won't go into here. Alexander, meanwhile, had brought along his young deacon, who goes by the name of Athanasius and who is something of an ecclesiastical prodigy (if that is not a contradiction in terms), having written a work on no less a subject than the Incarnation itself when barely in his twenties. Oh, to be young! Athanasius has already called my *Banquet* the work of an effeminate and degenerate old rogue (his words, not mine—you know how much I have fasted and practiced certain asceticisms for the glory of God) and questioned my theology because of it. So much for youth's respect for the elderly. As to his arguments, it is the standard stuff: the Logos joined in union with man and, by so doing, restored to the fallen Adam the image of God in which he had been made, and by his death and resurrection from it conquered sin and its consequence, death. Blah, blah, blah. He also said that God became man in order to deify us.

Eusebius of Nicomedia commended him for the felicity of his ideas but said that he (and I) were unwilling to entertain quite so metaphysical a concept as that we were all gods incarnate. I enjoyed that one, but it seems his tone must have annoyed them—Alexander and Athanasius, that is—for they accused me—me, Arius!—once more of degeneracy. (What is it about me that encourages all these insane fantasies about my immorality?) Then they went too far. They accused me of not believing in God. This, needless to say, was not what I wanted to hear, and I could not remain silent any longer.

"How dare you question my belief in God? My belief in God has never been in doubt—either by myself or from others—until you grotesquely brought it up. That man," and I helpfully pointed to Alexander, "has constantly impugned my honor, suggesting that myself and my supporters engage in the kinds of actions you wouldn't conceive of from your worst enemy. We are here to discuss the nature of the relation between Christ and God, not to deny that either or both exist."

I had just begun to gain my stride when Ossius, who had taken over from Constantine in governing the assembly—presumably because the latter's head had begun to hurt—said that such argument was unworthy, etc., etc. and told all of us to sit down. "My honorable friend Eusebius of Caesarea wishes to make a statement."

I have mentioned before, I believe, the hope we all shared over Eusebius of Caesarea persuading both the Emperor—with whom he claims he is friends—and the assembly of our cause. He also, as I think I told you, was excommunicated last year at Antioch, and so was eager to find a compromise. As you know, therefore, I hoped he would act as our intermediate.

Well, unfortunately, he has proved not only open to persuasion but absolutely spineless. My heart had fallen slightly when he had risen magisterially to his feet at the outset of the Council and given a turgid and mostly incoherent address to the assembly, exhorting us (as far as I could make out) to come to a decision and thank the Emperor very much for getting us all together. This address—full of extremely long and preposterously over-elaborate sentences—lasted a good hour and probably contributed substantially to the bad mood in which myself and Alexander began to debate our little topic of dissension. So I was hardly looking forward to his defense of our case, and I am afraid my fears were well founded.

Instead of offering a sturdy defense of our doctrine, based on his studies of the history of the Church—on which he is willing to bore you until you are pleading for mercy—he weakly put forward the judgment that the Father, Son, and Holy Spirit were separate individual personalities (or hypostases, as he insisted on calling them). At that point, there were murmurs and some shouts from the hall that this was "false doctrine," and Eusebius backed down rapidly. Instead, he suggested that the creed his congregation uses in Caesarea might be a basis for creating a creed acceptable to all. It later transpired that the first plan had been suggested by Constantine—"to test the waters," as the Emperor put it—and that Eusebius hadn't believed a word of it was clear from his pathetic justification.

For whatever reason—probably because they were so bored that they hadn't been listening—the assembly accepted it as something to work with and began to run through word by word those elements that would be acceptable to myself and Alexander. And we arrived at the old sticking points and the old insults began flying.

Then came the bombshell. It was announced by Ossius that the Emperor had thought of a compromise. I saw a number of prelates cover their mouths with their hands—presumably to stop themselves from laughing—and I raised my eyebrows at this and looked at Alexander, who also seemed a little shocked. But everybody else seemed eager to hear what this compromise solution was. It turned out that Constantine had decided he could solve all our problems by inserting into the creed the word *homoousios*—"of the same being"—a word, I might add, that appears absolutely nowhere in the scriptures, as far as I can recall. The Emperor read out, in his best military manner, that he didn't want anyone to think that this was an attempt to make solely physical the divine essence, and glanced at me. I looked instead at Alexander, and—rather sheepishly, I thought—he looked back at me as if to say, "Well, he is the Emperor, after all."

When the Emperor had left, to his credit Eusebius protested, standing up in front of the assembly and saying, with the kind of strength and emphasis I hadn't thought he possessed, that this would not do. And Ossius looks at him in disbelief and mumbles something about adjourning for a few moments and consulting the Emperor. Eventually, the Emperor emerges, takes Eusebius aside and, in full hearing of quite a number of the assembly (including yours truly), tells him that obviously he doesn't know *quite* what he is saying and hasn't *quite* understood what the Emperor means and hasn't thought out *quite* what the implications might be if he refuses to agree with him. Eusebius turns a bright red and resumes his seat and doesn't say a word for or against anything for the rest of the Council; indeed, he does very little more except sign his name with the rest of them to the Creed at the end.

So our assumptions about Eusebius were correct and, therefore, beloved companions, I have to report the

worst possible result from the much hoped-for Council
of Nicaea, where the ridiculous arguments and blatant
inconsistencies of Alexander and Athanasius have—
through the inspiring assistance of Eusebius—become
irreversible statute. As a result, myself, Theognis of
Nicaea, and Secundus of Ptolemais, as well as Eusebius
of Nicomedia and Theonas of Marmarice, have been
fully excommunicated, *again*. In addition, myself,
Secundus, and Theonas are shortly to experience the
delights of the banished in Illyricum.

Friends, we must now choose our words advisedly,
for we are to be hunted down and flushed from our
churches like wild beasts. And yet the matter in full
revolved around just that one blasted word, *homoousios*,
one that will hang about our hearts like a dead weight for
a long time to come—for the rest of the Creed, while inel-
egant, is acceptable. Naturally, being an imperial word—
coming moreover from that thinker among thinkers,
Constantine himself—*homoousios* has a certain practical
permanence that makes it difficult to remove without
removing the Emperor himself—a sentiment which, I am
sure, you like me refuse to countenance. Eusebius of
Caesarea babbled something sycophantic to me about
the Church and State being indivisible in this the great
Constantine's reign, but so tortured was his grammar
and so foul was my mood that I have no idea whether he
was offering consolation or mocking me.

Of course, it is not as if Constantine is an actual
Christian yet—no, that would be too bold a gesture to
make. He's waiting for his deathbed, probably, so that—
as Eusebius at his most glutinous would put it—he

might go sinless into Heaven. The real reason is that he wants to keep his options open for as long as possible. But from his unbaptized head we are now to believe— along with this Creed (which will follow in another dull encyclical, I have no doubt)—that the Empire and Christianity are consubstantial; that there never was a time when Christianity and the Empire were not and that the Empire gave birth to Christianity but did not create it, yet is at the same time indivisible from it. Put like that, however, that's a lot more credible than the rubbish you will be forced to say in your churches by the Council of Nicaea. When you get the letter containing the Creed, please read it, because I want you to see what impieties these heretics want us to swallow. Be especially aware of the phrase *ek tes ousios tou patros*—"from one substance of the father"—and how it sticks in the throat.

Yours in the true faith,
Arius of Alexandria

* * *

Friends,

I should begin by saying that Illyricum is relatively warm in the summer, although extremely cold in winter, but at any time of year is emphatically not home. Thank you for your prayers, which I know have been with me. I have been taking the time of my heavy exile by composing some rather inspired (if I do say so myself) tunes for millworkers. I will send them to you for their proper dissemination.

Now, I must confess I am both confused and not a little angry that one of you has suggested you might compromise with the Creed from the Council of Nicaea by inserting an iota into the word *homoousios* and making it *homoiousios*, or "of similar being." While, as a writer myself, I appreciate the wit and not little elegance with which this was done, I cannot countenance a statement of faith that merely plays around with the words and inserts letters where it suits. Statements of faith are serious issues and cannot be solved by orthographical sleights of hand. Naturally, while *homoiousios* is nearer to a more acceptable definition of the nature of the relationship between God and the Son, it smacks too much of a derivation from *homoousios*—a word I simply cannot abide in any creed I want to recite. I certainly don't want to feel I've undergone such indignity and now suffer expulsion for the mere reason that an "I" was missing.

Yours with some indignation,
Arius of Alexandria

* * *

Friends, brothers and sisters of Baucalis,

I fear after my last letter I was overly harsh in not offering you more sympathy. Truly, I know how much you wish to be accepted back into the Church and how deeply distressed you are by my exile. I wish I could be of more comfort to you, offer you a little broadsheet of sayings or one of my songs with which you could fluster or flatter our right-speaking betters in the unexcommunicated Church. But I cannot—not will not, but cannot. If we are down to the components of language themselves as the ultimate arbiters of what it means to believe, then we have nothing upon which we can rest.

This issue is not insignificant, and nothing more than the removal of the word *homoousios* itself will suffice. So do not use the "I"; consider that we have been rendered dumb in our faith and pray.

My heart is with you in these difficult days,
Arius of Alexandria

* * *

Friends,

I have received missives from you asking for advice on those whom we once considered friends and who now have renounced the true way for the impieties of the false doctrines decreed at Nicaea. I must ask you to let them go, forget them, for we are undoubtedly in the right, and, but for the fanatic Athanasius—who insists on keeping us out of the Church in spite of our favorite Emperor's requests for me to be allowed back in—we have no pressing opposition.

I must ask you, however, to keep away from Eusebius of Caesarea, who, while he has the ear of the Emperor, has vacillated too greatly and too contemptibly for us to hold him in high esteem again. He is a talker and would run like a hound to any particular master should you speak to him. He is also, as some of my letters last year made clear, very boring, and I would save you from that. You wouldn't believe, judging from his recent actions, that Eusebius himself suffered excommunication the way he is carrying on condemning this person and that person. It depresses me more to think about him when, at the moment the Emperor let it be known that he thought *homoousios* might solve it all and allow us to go home, Eusebius caved in. But, enough. Just watch out for him.

I am baffled as to who these Arians are who have taken my name. What do they believe?

Hold steadfastly to the right, my friends.

Arius of Alexandria

* * *

Friends,

Good news. I have been summoned by the Emperor to see if I will not reconsider my position and retract my complaints concerning the Creed made doctrine at Nicaea. Those are Athanasius's words, as you can gather. Once more, the vehemence and absolutism of the young! Constantine simply wants to have one of his "talks" in which he tells you, yet again, how he is only a soldier and that to him it all seems very simple...lot of noise about nothing...knock heads together...why, for the sake of the Church, we can't move on he has no idea. Usually, Athanasius completely ignores him and takes off where the late but unlamented Alexander left off, except toning down the invective to suit the sensibilities of an emperor who doesn't think "you people in the Church" (as he calls us) should speak to each other like that. Needless to say, you need not fear that I will in

any way submit to a creed that contains ideas abhor-
rent to us.

I would suggest you avoid these Arians—as you
seem now to be calling them. Their views concerning the
Father and the Son are too mystically oriented for me.
As you know, I have always been concerned with the
practicalities of faith.

Yours in trust,
Arius of Alexandria

* * *

Friends.

I am sorry I have been unable to write to you concerning my meetings with the Emperor, but illness has
prevented me from doing anything at all, let alone writing. But then, at a rough reckoning—only my mother,
God rest her soul, knows when I was born—I am over
seventy years old, an age when the Good Book says
one's lifespan has reached its limit. However, I have
news that can only be good for us. As you know, the
Emperor asked me to come to Constantinople—which is
growing to be a very impressive little town with a
delightful view of the waterway—to discuss the events at
Nicaea, and perhaps arrange something whereby we
might gather together the Church. You are aware with
how much passion I have argued for the Church to
remain together, and how the schism at Nicaea angered
and distressed me because we who had struggled for so
long to be allowed to worship freely and without fear
were now fighting each other again.

It was in this spirit that I met the Emperor and in sum, I, with the others, am to be gathered back into the fold along with you, my fellow believers. This has been done through a statement of faith I have made, detailing what we believe in and why we believe it. I have sent a copy to various of you and ask you to distribute it. I shall remain here for the next few months in order to recuperate.

With joy,
Arius of Alexandria

* * *

Friends,

I am amazed, shocked, and saddened by the hostile reception you have given the news that I signed an act of faith. Please believe me when I say I did not compromise in any way the beliefs we all share concerning the Father and the Son, and I made it very clear to no less a person than the Emperor himself that I spoke for all of you in this.

As it is, your anger is academic, for, after some consideration, Athanasius has rejected once more our reacceptance into the Church—no doubt still poisoned by Alexander's deathbed condemnations of me. But this does not excuse the force of your criticisms, my friends; and, because I have done nothing to deserve them, I will treat them as undeserving of a response.

Yours who yet remains true to his faith,
Arius of Alexandria

* * *

Friends, etc.

Can I still call you that, after what you have written to me? Since you insist on full answers I will give you full answers. You asked me why I was willing to write and sign such a statement of faith when I had so condemned the vacillations of Eusebius and his kind. Don't you see that the conditions were wholly different since I did not deviate in any way from the principles we hold dear? Moreover, the accusation made that I was attempting to gain favor with Athanasius is nonsensical and offensive. If I had sought either his or Alexander's favor I would have agreed to the damnable Creed of Nicaea when it was first offered, and I did not— emphatically did not. Athanasius remains as implacable as ever, even though he will eventually be forced by Constantine to let me in. He is not and never will be a friend of mine.

You ask me to describe my relationship with God, as if I have to prove to anyone my belief in and love of God. But it is not a simple question of throwing in a word or two or even a letter or two, as I've told you. How can I know God? How can I name God? How can I see or hear or talk about or feel or touch God? If I say "God," that is not God; if I think of God, that is not God. If I pray to God, that is not God. God is beyond us and outside us— that is why you and I have been unable to countenance his divisibility in the Son and the latter's co-eternality (the words Alexander shouted at me many years ago). The extraordinariness of God lies in his transcendence and the hugeness of his compassion for all of us. Your blithe assertions that Christ can sometimes be the Son of God and sometimes human is emphatically not the same type of compromise I made with Constantine. It is the compromise of those who have neither intellectual nor spiritual strength—and you know that.

Listen. My reasoning in this whole wretched affair remains simple and I will answer you frankly: I believe I will be more easily able to remove the scourge of *homoousios* from our statements of faith if we are within the Church than if we are languishing in the wilderness. It is in this regard that I urge you to comply with the directives of the Emperor and myself concerning the worship of the Creed agreed upon at Nicaea.

Yours in anger,

Arius of Alexandria

* * *

Fellow Christians,

Now that, under your direction, I am unable to call you friends, I call you by what I expect you believe to be true of yourselves, although given your recent treatment of me I highly doubt whether others would accord you the title. I have been hurt once more by your ignoring of my commands and by the contemptuous letters I have received during my recuperation. Many years ago, you entrusted me with the care of your faith, that it should not go astray or be confused by false doctrines and misleading words. I will admit that there have been times when I have been cavalier in my actions and thoughts, and possibly too confrontational when it comes to what I believe in. But have you so quickly forgotten that responsibility you placed upon my willing shoulders? Have you so ignored your own responsibilities in this matter that you send me invective after invective rather than trusting me in the pursuit of your best interests? Have you been tricked into such anger towards me by some charlatan who disguises his falseness through rhetoric? I need not add that such letters only delay my recovery from what has been a long and disabling illness. I am, I repeat, no longer a young man. I must ask you—for the sake of your presbyter Arius and for all we have worked for—to comply with my request. Unless you do so, then I fear I do not have long on this Earth. This is all I request.

Yours in need,
Arius

* * *

Fellow Christians,

I see. It has come to this. Where once I received insults, I now receive nothing—no news, joyful or otherwise, from those I have always considered nearest my heart. I can only take this as an indication that you wish me to die. Please respond as soon as you are able. Even as you are finally showing your true colors, that pompous fool Eusebius of Caesarea has come to the good—he has brought it about that Athanasius himself now feels the yoke of banishment upon his shoulders. I have to hand it to him—that unprincipled rogue Eusebius will outlast us all.

With the love I still bear you all and the peace I offer

in spite of your hurtful silence,
    Arius

* * *

My people,

This is a last—and, I will confess, desperate—plea from a dying man. My bowels have collapsed and I can no longer walk far from my house in Constantinople. Athanasius paid me a visit yesterday—as he does more and more in these my last days—and sat on the end of my bed and laughed long and loud at my discomfort. He said he wouldn't be surprised if I died in the latrine, which, he added, would be a suitable end for someone who had always been full of shit in the first place. In spite of his having experienced banishment and excommunication, as well as accusations of disorder and confrontation among his soldiers, he is still remarkably brazen. Yet the Athanasius who visits me is the young man who attacked me at Nicaea; and I have no answer for his snide and twisted mind. But then again, these are only nightmares that, when I am lucid, amuse me; but when I am scream-ing in the night—as the wide-eyed children who come to my door in the morning tell me emphatically I do more and more—he seems as real to me as the hand that writes this letter. When Athanasius, just last night, appeared in his usual place at the end of my bed and accused me, for the thousandth time, of betraying my people and my faith, I summoned all my strength, sat up in bed and tried to tell him once and for all to leave me alone and let me die in peace. I vomited instead.

Yours in love,
Arius of Alexandria

*　*　*

My people,

My dear companions and believers in a Christ for all
of us, the Christ of parable and laughter, the Christ of
forgiveness and anger, the Christ of discussion and compassion, last night I sat on the great mountain which lies
outside Nicaea and watched my words fly away on the
breeze towards the place where once our fate was sealed.
I listened to the heavy stillness of its silence and felt
again that what happened at Nicaea was not what was
ordained by God, but that, when the time was propitious, I had no response to those who believed it was. I
have tried and I have failed, though in my failure I have
always tried to do the best by you and what I considered
always to be right.

My friends, perhaps it is because these are my last
breaths that I can say that it no longer matters what you
say. Build in silence your own language to God. A few
years ago I expressed distress that you were inserting
into the Creed's *homoousios* the extra "I." I don't care.
It doesn't matter. Do what you want, pray in any way
you want, inserting your individual "I"s in any way that
will be pleasing to God. Unlike I did all those years ago,
he will accept them. And go in peace, for that is all that
is left to us.

As the light thickens in front of my eyes,
Arius of Alexandria

Gnosis

My beloved friend and mentor, Pamphilus; greetings from your beloved son, Eusebius.

How do you write a letter to the dead? They either know everything already or they are past caring—and with you I fear it is both. Yet I have to write, if only to tell you how much you were in my mind during the Council; how both amused and saddened you would have been at those who were assembled—the dividers, the excommunicants and excommunicated, and the betrayers. It will come as no surprise to you to know that once again I was among the last.

I remember when it was all so clear: you and me working together in the great library at Caesarea or talking about your experiences of God. Then we had a common enemy, a common fear. But since your death, it has been so difficult, so confusing—harder and harder as our lives become easier and easier. And I have still not forgotten the manner of your death—at the hands of that old murderer Diocletian, in the darkness, in pain, your silence your eloquence. You were one of the last martyrs, one of the final ones of a discredited, unregretted dispensation.

After they had taken you, they took me. You had gone by then; at least, I believe you had gone. I hope you had gone. Otherwise, you would have heard my screams. And you would have heard my words. You know how I have always talked, Pamphilus, how I always enjoyed the spirals words could make in the air. Well, I talked then—talked and talked and talked— because I hated the pain you had laughed at, could not bear the suffering you welcomed, was terrified that there was nothing at the end of that agony, whereas you knew, you *knew*, where you were going and what to expect.

That was years ago—a world away now. But the smell of my terror and the stench of the prison cells came to me again at Nicaea, because it was here that I betrayed you once more. I thought of your sacrifice and every time I got up to speak or protest I remembered how you loved Christ so much you were willing to give your life for him. Now it is easy to talk. No one to silence us. No one to stop us from expressing our faith. No one to torture us or kill us. Yet.

It should be a cause for rejoicing, that the day that you and I prayed for has come about and that the Empire has seen the light of Jesus Christ and the one true God. But I have no peace and I have no joy, because all I can think of is your suffering and your death and compare it with the trivialities we have had to contend with. Pamphilus, did it really matter to you in the end whether Christ was "before" or "after," whether he was born from being or non-being, whether he was man or

God? Was the question of whether the Logos was created flesh or dwelt in Jesus as a separate entity running
through your mind as they set about your body and
smacked your ears until you heard nothing but the
blood in your cracked old head? Surely the concerns of
Arius and Alexander and Athanasius would have been
nothing to you—you who denied nothing, admitted
everything you were, laid bare the nakedness of your
soul for them to whip and spit upon. Yet I, who denied
everything, and admitted anything they wanted me to
admit because of the pain, because of the fear, because I
knew how angry and insane Diocletian was, have failed
even the test of courage set for me here.

I had seen the headless corpses in the amphitheaters
and the alleys; I was witness to atrocities of which I cannot even write, so appalling were they. Was it so wrong
of me to want to protect you from being a witness, so
that I could somehow survive the tyranny and record the
martyrdom of those better than I? Pamphilus, I honor
your name: its sonorous sound is so much easier to hear
than your actual words admonishing me for my failure,
sternly teaching me about principles and justice and the
courage of one's convictions.

Because I had betrayed once, was it not obvious I
would do so again? Because I had used words once when
pain was beating in my head, surely it was inevitable I
would use words again, the pain of abandonment and
excommunication no less sharp for being subtle and
unenforced by the cudgel or stick. So I offered up the
Creed we use in our congregation in church, and it was
rejected. And Constantine—whose voice is all I am but

who holds our only hope, the bishop for external things—offered his blasphemous *homoousios* and all was changed.

Then came the cries of "Heresy! Heresy!" and the debates over jots in words. I should have been in my element, shouldn't I? I should have been able to outspeak them all, outmaneuver all of their sophistry with some well-chosen phrase—except you were there, in my mind, forcing me to listen to myself, to hear my hollowness. Now all differences have merged into one inadequacy, and I have lost the will to care whether the Logos is consubstantial with the Father or merely similar. It all points to the same thing, the same ending, which is the corruption of the same word, proceeding from the Word.

Now we believe in oneness, movements towards the oneness and the essences of what we see, the invisibility of existence. Again, we believe in one Lord, Jesus Christ, who rescued us from the oppression of ourselves; born of God, of his substance, God of God, Light of Light, verifiably God because we verify it, created from God but not of God, the face of God, his mask, but not separate from God, the essence of all, his articulation, his quiddity, God and yet not-God but his manifestation of himself, existing when God uttered his being and things were, and yet ever-present through time; the word within and the word without. And if you do not believe this, you are to prepare yourself for judgment. For this is the case; there is no other way, there is no other possibility, there is no other. For we, the Church, have decreed it thus, for we are the Church and we the Creed. And those who dispute, who suggest that there are alternatives: we banish you as heretics, disown you for your heresy. Who are the torturers now, Pamphilus? Who are those who wield the rod of doctrine over the bleeding body of belief? It is us, we who are alive.

So I said, "Yes. Why not?" I agreed because I had lost the will to disagree. And I agreed because I was frightened of losing you forever, losing the sense you always had that your faith reached beyond the fragile inconsistencies of human thought to an inner knowledge that extended its arms over the books we wrote or the ones we studied together. I was also frightened that I might look back on our life together and dismiss that as heresy, add you to the list of heresiarchs that I have compiled in my history as the abhorred ones among all Christians.

And, my beloved Pamphilus, I was frightened I would forget your body. I wanted to remember how once I felt that the Logos had been within you, putting on your flesh, knowing suffering with you. When we were in prison together, when we were left to work in peace or when you were taken away and I heard the beatings and the lashes, I felt you inside me all the time, giving me the strength and courage to think and to resist. Why, then, did you desert me at the end, as the fires licked, the rope tightened, the blade bit, the beasts breathed on my skin? Father, why did you forsake me, your son, your scribe, your inscription? Am I not, and am I not still, the taker of your name—Pamphilus's son—formulator of your phrases, recorder of your posterity, the panegyrist of your martyrdom? When they brought your body to show me—to do with as I wished, they said—I saw a peace on your face that in my wretchedness and shame made my

ears throb and my eyes fill with tears. I resolved to be
your Word, then; to make you known to all, use the
name you gave me as my own.

But all my resolutions fail.

Pamphilus, I am old. But I am not wise, as you were.
I am a victim of two worlds. The one world is the world
as it was before Constantine, when faith was a matter of
life and death, requiring complete trust in yourself and
your fellow Christians or all was lost. It was a time of
innocence and absolutes: there was evil and there was
good, but the evil was the entire evil of the State and its
instruments and institutions of torture, and good was
the total good of God and Christ, our communities and
the love that supported us. We seemed to be more tolerant of our faults then, more able to break bread together, to accept that we are all fallen, all fallible, all simply
trying to point our way to God.

But this world is one of a different certainty, a certainty born from conformity and regularity—one that at
this council has become rigid and resistant. To be sure,
there were heresies before, heresies of as complex and
academic a nature as the one rejected here at Nicaea; but
somehow they seemed to be part of the organic struggle
of the great tree of our faith. Those branches died, off-
shoots from the trunk but not fundamental to its roots.
This world threatens to kill the tree because it is the
trunk that is being divided. What we have done is to hew
and not to heal. We are the wielders of axes now.

A different world. These days one can move about
easily; as you know, the coaches of the Emperor are at
the disposal of the prelates. We are honored by, and

honor in our turn, the figure who was once the very worst of evils. I wish I could believe that the Emperor embraced our beliefs, or even that he understood them. But I fancy this change has come about because there are simply too many of us for the Roman Empire to ignore. So, while everything has changed, nothing has changed. The state has absorbed us and absolved us. Those who had power within our communities before still have power—and a lot more of it. Yet I am too old to fight, too old for sides or factions or divisions. That is why I advised consensus. In return I got an ultimatum. My opponent, in this world where opponents and friends are to be guessed at and argued with, rather than stoned to death, is a young man called Athanasius. He is too young to remember the torture and the covert meetings, secret signs, tacit acknowledgments of where and when—things you and I knew well, Pamphilus. It was like that with the supporters of Arius, I myself among them. Except this time it was our own who hounded us out: not Romans, not Jews, but Christians.

But Athanasius is too young to remember anything like that. He is still a boy, and has all the certainty and conviction of one who has not seen the flyblown corpse of a dear friend thrown at him and left to rot in the sun. I like Arius, robust and amusing as he is with his ridiculous rhymes and his fearless love of intellectual disquisition. But his overly sophisticated efforts to understand the incomprehensible and find subtle ways of marrying his tendency to Greek mysticism with his practical Christology is no match for Athanasius. They are creatures from different eras. Athanasius presents the immutable and the ineffable as though defending a client in court. The case stands thus, therefore it cannot be otherwise. Neither Arius nor I can argue against that. We speak on different levels, from two different worlds, about two different Christs.

* * *

As I was walking by the lake, the afternoon sun on my back, Athanasius approached me, and walked a little while with me, saying nothing. I knew he was there because I sensed his eyes on me, but (perhaps pettily) felt that to look at him and engage him in conversation, no matter how insignificant, would be for him a kind of victory. His eyes, Pamphilus, were as clear, untroubled, and glittering as the lake; yet they were also hard, covered by eyebrows that arched both in concentrated anger and detached amusement, as if waiting for a slip, a glimpse of exposed flesh into which a verbal dagger could slide. Who knows? Perhaps one day it will be a real dagger. As I grow older my lids hang heavily over my eyes, which, in turn, muddy and dim, clouded by the silt of doubt and sense of failure the eddies of my soul stir up. So I kept my head down, watching my aimless feet brush forward the pale grass beneath me. Let him ask me, let him approach. Let the young and unwise ask the old and wise. I was always proud, and always self-deluding.

"I'm puzzled, Eusebius."

"Puzzled?"

I looked up, avoiding the eyes as best I could. His face was so unwritten, Pamphilus, unlined and unarticulated. Nothing to read, no semblance of an obvious personality that could be decoded by crow's feet around the eyes or pinched downturned lines around the mouth or furrows on the forehead. Nothing. When at the Council I had offered him my hoarse, tentative suggestions for compromise, he had laughed almost without guile and had wondered out loud why I could possibly think the situation could be anything other than what he said. He seemed to possess no doubts; he gave no evidence of having any dialogue with himself. God for him was self-evident; Christ's relation with God, with all its confusions, tautologies, paradoxes, ineffabilities—a source of anxiety, at the very least, for myself, Arius, and countless others—were to Athanasius clear and supportable. There is something terrifying about all this, Pamphilus, as though we are entering a new age where doubt, with all its humanity and humility, is as punishable as Christianity was so recently. And yet Athanasius was puzzled. Was that possible?

"Or rather surprised."

"Oh?"

I feel him at my side, searching me with his eyes. What must he think of me, broken and old as I am? Am I not to him a relic to be handled with a degree of baffled devotion but vague contempt at its dubious authenticity? Friend of Constantine, unswerving apologist and hyperbolic rhetorician—am I to him simply one of those too shocked by the change from fear to fortune to be taken seriously? Used to the scurried interchanges of faith hidden in corners of houses in the middle of the night rather than the caustic brilliance of the case for and the case against and the sharp exchange? His faith seems at once simpler and more sophisticated: it can afford to be more sophisticated because it is safer; it can simplify because it has power.

"I am surprised you concurred with the Creed."

"It is a very good creed."

"But it isn't your creed."

"It is the creed decided by this council and therefore it is my creed."

"But it isn't *your* creed. The one your congregation has used under your direction for years. The one you suggested to the Council."

"The creed I put forward was never meant to be final. The creed we used was the one used by our congregations in Jerusalem. My creed was something to work with, something that would suit."

He laughed, showing his perfect teeth. "Perhaps it was always that for you."

"I don't understand."

"Something that would suit."

I look at him. Because Athanasius feels I belong to the past, my creed is not absolute. It is tendentious and malleable, suitable for the hurried communions and the frightened congregations. It is a creed that travels with little baggage, on a mule to Egypt, a miasma of the half-crazed in exile. It is a creed that lives on nothing but what it can take from a worried sleep or a barely decent meal. Very well, let it be...*suitable*...and nothing like the magnificent and ornate palace of this new creed. Athanasius's creed is an imperial creed. But, silence. This is no time for rhetoric. Be conciliatory.

"Maybe."

"They say you sided with Theonas, Secundus, and Eusebius of Nicomedia in the cause of Arius."

"And 'they' would be…?"

"Your erstwhile supporters, Theognis among them."

I briefly taste the bitter relish of treachery. "They are wrong."

"You were, of course, present at the recent synod in Antioch, were you not?"

I nod that I was.

"This was the synod, you may recall, where a creed was agreed upon very like the one to which you have so readily added your signature; and you refused to sign then."

"I did."

"Why didn't you sign?"

"There were others."

"They were excommunicated." He looks at me quizzically, rubbing a hand over his chin. "As were you, I believe. Albeit provisionally."

"Yes, I was excommunicated. I was unclear as to the exact nature of the heresy of Arius, then. He is a very persuasive man."

"And you were a very persuasive advocate for his cause, especially for one so 'unclear' as to its nature, weren't you? A letter has come into my hands from Arius himself, praising you above all others for the zeal you showed before and after Antioch in communicating the message you have just signed away as heresy. So you can stop being so coy."

I do not hide my shock and distaste.

"How did you come by such a letter?"

"It doesn't matter, Eusebius. But it is genuine; you needn't worry."

I stare out at the waters of the lake, my mind filled with images of the transactions of my friends, their fears of losing position, of displacement from the elaborate dance we all join in this, our new imperial age. Athanasius knows that not only would I have no way of disproving his letter, but that I do not have the energy to disprove it—even if it weren't true.

"My position with reference to Arius is a complex one. Yes, I believe the Father exists before the Son, but these things cannot be measured in terms of the conventional meaning of 'before' and 'after.' "

There is a pause. "Eusebius, I am not particularly interested in discussing the nature of God. It has been decided upon by the Council already. Spare yourself the need to try and impress me with your rhetorical sleights of hand."

"So be it, then." Anger and shame join bitterness in my mouth. There now seems no point in holding back. "I confess: I met Eusebius of Nicomedia and the others before the Council began. Is that enough? I confess: I was one of the leading exponents of Arius's ideas. Does that satisfy? I confess: I formulated a creed to please all of us, and had our supporters winking and smirking with pleasure. Is that what you need? But I also confess I was misguided, or wrong, or I have doubt, or something like that." Athanasius pauses, begins to walk away from me, his eyes looking out over the lake.

"Well?" I wanted something from Athanasius—

some sort of corroboration or even outright condemnation, I don't know which. But I wanted something. And I hated myself for it. He, as if knowing that, ignored me, turned back to face me with that look of sly incomprehension unique to him.

"I take back what I just said, Eusebius." There is a slight smile on his lips; his eyes are filled with fierce amusement. "Your theology *does* interest me. Or rather it bemuses me, since it seems to be even further than the ridiculous Arius's from the self-evidence of the eternal and consubstantial existence of God and Christ. For Christ to be anything other—anything less—is to deny the reality of our salvation and eternal life and to offer the unthinkable thought that God created a deliberate imperfection. The Creed we have now makes all these things abundantly clear. Christ is the focal point of our salvation: through him we are saved. This appears far easier a concept to grasp than your rather tortured logic would suggest."

"I would not have called it tortured."

"That Christ is somehow later than God but not in time? That Christ possesses the qualities of the Father by default of his practice but not through his innate nature? That God's substance is not synonymous with his likeness but is only reasonable or within the mind? I call all these ideas decidedly tortured."

"Athanasius, you know nothing about torture. Why speak of it in those terms?"

He pauses; looks back at me. Even his silence—which in my vanity I take as a kind of apology—is a challenge.

"Very well, 'tortured' was an ill-chosen word. What would you have called them, then?"

"Believable."

"Enough to make a creed from?"

"Perhaps."

"Eusebius, Eusebius." The words float into the air and hover above the lake, my name an accusation of failure, of incompleteness, of something at some point gone awry. "Creeds are as easy to form and break as the heretical groups that make and then disavow them. That is why they must be founded on truth. We all recognize that for God to be God he must exist outside as well as within time. He wouldn't be God otherwise, would he?"

"Don't patronize me, Athanasius."

A flash of anger. "Well, don't behave like a child. Be the man, as Paul would have you be, and comprehend the beauty and gravity of God." Athanasius begins to pace up and down the borders of the lake in front of me, his hands cutting the resisting air. "Nicaea is not about the casual discourse of the old days, when there was no need for stricture because there was no power. Now that we have power, it throws upon us a great responsibility for order and clarity. Above all, clarity. It must be absolutely clear what our faith is about if it is to grow and become the driving force in the Empire."

"You think imperially then?"

"We have to. It is our duty by God."

"Well, God be with you then."

I aimed to walk away, as I have always done, Pamphilus, and as I always will. If it is Athanasius's punishment always to feel he is right, then it is mine to recognize the power of his rightness. Him and others like him. But Athanasius follows me, takes me by the arm, leads me to the edge of the lake, bids me sit down on a rock (the reverence due to age). I look at him, and am impressed by the concern in his face.

"This is all meant in love, Eusebius."

My eyes narrow. Whether from the sun or disbelief, I do not know. "Of course."

"Surely it should be taken in love."

"That is for me to decide."

Silence. The lake stares back at me as if waiting for an answer, a justification for my faith and myself.

"You will write about this event, of course." Athanasius's voice is different, more concerned than assured.

"It is all I can do."

"And you will give the Emperor the credit for breaking the deadlock, I presume."

I look up at him, surprised. "Why wouldn't I?"

"Please, Eusebius. There is no need to be so defensive on this issue. I am merely concerned you place everything in the correct perspective so history can judge us properly."

"Judge us or judge you, Athanasius?"

"Can there be a difference, Eusebius?" I sense him beside me, leaning on me. "Hmm?"

"I will do my best to make sure I record the events at the Council properly and with..."

Athanasius claps his hands together. "Oh, for the sake of heaven, Eusebius! I have no patience for your blessed oratory again—covering everything up, glossing everything over, with that ridiculous lapidary prose you insist on using. Just tell the history of how the Council was. I expect you to make clear that Arius and his followers were justly excommunicated for being grossly in error and that the Emperor supported, as he had to—because he belongs to the party in the right—those who argued for the consubstantiality of the Son and the Father."

"Surely it is for the future to decide..."

"No!" Athanasius gets up in frustration, angry and exasperated, his hands clenched in fists in front of him, beating the hot air. "The future must be told the truth; it must be in no doubt as to what was determined here and how we arrived at our decisions. We cannot have any more of these random sects and their irresponsible interpreters throwing us off course." He swings around to face me, suddenly, half threatening, half pleading. "Do you understand that, Eusebius?"

"I will do my best." My head looks down into the water and I see tiny fish swimming between the rocks. I do not know what to think. I hear Athanasius breathe out and say "Good." I sense that this interrogation might be all over, but then I feel Athanasius's hands upon my shoulders.

"What is it, Eusebius?"

"What is what?"

"What is the matter? What has gone wrong?"

He speaks tenderly, with genuine concern. Is it simply because he is so sure that he has such authority? I felt so like a child, Pamphilus, so untutored, as if, in spite of all our talks and all your stories, I was learning about

God and faith for the first time. So I broke down, and once again—as all those years ago—I decided to tell everything. And it came pouring out, like the blood from your head.

"The work I have done, the hours I have studied, the respect in which I am held: these are all known to you, Athanasius. You have read my history; it is a good work. Christ is there in his full majesty, working through history to let the Church grow so that come the End there will be triumph. It is all there. And I have thought long and hard about my faith. For years I believed with Origen that there was always a spiritual union with God that transcended the body and that I too could reach beyond it as a perfect Christian and experience the Word inhabiting the Father. You mentioned it when you scoffed at my beliefs concerning God only being known within the mind. I did believe that. Once. I searched the world, as Origen did, for its symbols and patterns of something unseen to me, looked for the connections that would show me the infinite creativity of the world and God knowing himself within it. By creating—by writing my history—I would attain that mirroring of God filling the world with himself and through Christ descending into it to save us all.

"I thought God understood that—I thought this was, as it were, my *understanding* with him. Even when, as I grew older, there was no revelation, I held on to that belief. I promised to be the witness for the countless who have given and would give their lives for their faith, a faith founded in the knowledge that by believing in the sacrifice of Jesus Christ they would gain everlasting life.

You see, I can be orthodox sometimes."

A gentle smile.

"But nothing happened, Athanasius. Nothing happened. There was no blinding revelation, nor even a gradual dawning, some kind of shifting in the light. I never had a sense that what these martyrs experienced was ever for me or for my life—even though I knew some of them personally. Constantly, *constantly*, I examined myself for the inklings of anything more than pity at the fact of their passing or admiration at the manner of their death. But it was simple conscience or duty, and nothing more. As a result I had to formulate a different creed.

"So I believed only because the beauty of the idea appealed to me. I believed because I saw the suffering of those who truly did give their lives for it, and I was moved by that. I believed because it was once a brave thing to do, and because a scholar whom I admired and loved beyond all others died for that belief. But that creed always went so far and no further. As Pamphilus, the scholar I loved—you may have heard of him..."

Athanasius nods distractedly. He has heard of him.

"...as he lay dying from his wounds, I was confessing everything and lying without reservation, because I felt pain, and the pain was more than I could bear. I don't know how many I betrayed, but it still haunts me."

Athanasius's hand on my shoulder feels like a dead weight. I know how I have fallen in his estimation, even further than I have already. But I also know that it is not important anymore. His voice is uninflected with emotion. "We are not all called upon to be martyrs, Eusebius."

"But none of us should be traitors," I reply, misery spilling out of me. "You see, Athanasius, I had forgotten the body; I had lost the incarnation. I had not realized that Pamphilus's suffering and the magnificence of his faith could not live outside his body. It was all theory until then, all sympathy and pity and feverish scratching on a page. And when the time came, when it came to the practice, when the time of writing it out was over and the time for the inhabitation of the words had come, I failed. I failed utterly, and completely, and unreservedly, and undeniably. There was no resistance, no final threshold crossed, no calling out to God for aid.

"And now I know what I am. A recorder. It is for others to suffer and to die; and it is for others to believe—truly, absolutely. I thought the knowledge of God might be attained without surrender or pain; that it might transfigure me without crucifixion and allow me to join the saints without injunction or request. But I never suffered as the martyrs suffered, and now that even that perverse and vicariously small amount of suffering has vanished, I am left to record the misery of the doubters and the triumph of the believers."

"Do you not believe, then?"

"I believe in the need to believe."

"That is something."

"But it is not Christianity; not the Christianity decided upon here. Don't you see, Athanasius? I have in my imagination Christ's suffering, the bleeding hands, the festering wounds beneath the ribs, the thorns biting the crown of his head. I can feel his faintness, his eyes pressed from behind by blood, his hands and feet still throbbing and stung with agony from the nails. But that is as far as it goes. If I try to imagine the risen, bodily Christ, the wonder and the joy of the apostles as they, like children—astonished, perhaps laughing, aghast, afraid, asking over and over again, 'could it be? could it be? is it really?'—dare to touch the resurrected Lord; if I try to see the ascending cloud, or feel the rush of pentecostal wind and the tongues of fire, the transfigured speech, the words pouring out from overflowing souls; if I try to approach the image of the transfigured Christ: all I see is Christ crucified, his body drained of life-blood, gray in the evening, a wrecked and decomposing body for his disciples to weep over."

"We all of us believe in the body and blood of Jesus, Eusebius. Both of these were his greatest gift to us, and in the Eucharist we celebrate that fact. Jesus is the Christ because of his incarnation; without the incarnation, the physical fact of his existence, then the resurrection is meaningless, and Christ nonexistent. What more do you want than this wonderful truth?"

"I want it to be more than an article of faith. I want it to be real."

"But it is real."

"I want it to be real *to me*. This creed we have just agreed upon asks me to believe in the reality of Christ while emphasizing beyond everything how unreal he is. That seems to me to be a step beyond the many intellectual paradoxes of faith so easy to justify as beautiful and true. Nothing is real to me anymore, in the way you see it as real; but all that suffering and death is more real than I ever conceived of, and it has destroyed all I proclaimed to believe. I have seen too many changes, too much persecution, and too much unnecessary and expedient forgiveness to believe that there will not be change again. There will come a time, no doubt, when the Creed we have both signed will be dead paper, and you arraigned on some heresy or other."

"At your instigation?"

"Athanasius, I am too old to be concerned with plots and insurrections and court intrigues. You can concern yourself with those. This creed is very well, but it solves none of the problems."

"Why not? It is absolutely clear. It defines the position of Christ and God very clearly."

"Of course; to the philosophers and the logicians this creed could not be more philosophically and logically sound. Moreover, I have read and written on Christian truths I only half understand and made them ring with the authority of both knowledge and understanding. In spite of your frustrations, Athanasius, there are uses for my kind of rhetoric. I can write about it and praise it, give it all the intellectual words you want to make it sound respectable enough as a doctrine. I can even say in all conscience and with great seriousness that it is not words that matter, but deeds. I can recognize the magnificence of concepts that define the absoluteness of being in terms of a single, unrepeatable, inimitable act of love. I can realize that cohabitation of knowledge and life, whereby the acquisition of one leads to the other, and that neither can exist in their purest state without the other: Christ gave us knowledge through his life, Christ gave us life through his knowledge; knowledge is life and life is knowledge. I can comprehend the totality of God and the wholeness of Christ, and adopt postures for creation, generation, time and the infinite that explode in the mind like thunderstorms, so brilliant and terrifying are their sounds and so stark is their illumination.

"But it is not enough to be a philosopher, and it is not enough to be a logician, and it is absolutely not enough to be a rhetorician; and one man, who was all of these, showed me how weak are philosophy, logic, and rhetoric when the pain is more than almost anyone can bear. I am, as I have said, simply a recorder of other people's revelations. More to the point, I am an ordinary person, who has woven, as ordinary people do, my hopes, fears, and random associations into a faith where God and Christ, and their relation to each other, are meaningless answers to unimportant questions. Such a faith, perhaps, doesn't solve anything, it lacks rigor and it lacks discipline, it is not for everybody and it will not protect me. But it is all I have.

"And as for Arius—well, it is much the same story. As I suggested to you, I once hoped I would believe, simply and absolutely, by intuition, by an inner knowledge that had nothing to do with others' experience and ideas. I waited, as I have said, and nothing happened. When I began to study, I deduced that this sudden illumination, this emphatic ecstasy that transformed their minds, was not only the gift of the saints. It was also the gift of those we—I—have denounced as heretics, an ecstatic gift for which many paid with their lives.

"I castigated them, of course, because their vision

was different from the vision I had been taught to accept as the true vision. But what right had I, who had never experienced any visions myself, to deny these ordinary men and women the right to their own particular versions of infinity? I denied their visions and eloquently banished them from orthodox history not only because it was wise to do so, but because I was jealous and frightened that people could be so sure. I also denied them because I was studying, as I have said, to believe; and I thought that by believing in heresy I would not receive the proper divine message. That got me no further. The more I learned about other peoples' actions and beliefs the more it made me understand how little were mine in comparison. If I have any knowledge and wisdom now, it is that I see how ignorant and unwise I am.

"Last year I decided I had to make a decision, a valuation of an event of which I was a part. So I opted for Arius's among the latest revelations; and I placed myself in the vanguard of the argument for better or worse. But once more, I suppose, I lacked the courage to see it through. So, you find me here, neither wise nor brave, neither illumined nor damned, a victim without redemption and a conqueror without a victory. I am no longer the champion of heresy or the champion of orthodoxy; I am to be watched, I am under suspicion. I have been found to be uncertain; I, who was never certain of anything. There you have it. I have said it all, and my position is now untenable."

"Why?"

"How can you have a bishop who doesn't believe?"

"Well, I thought I would never come to say this, Eusebius, but it seems to me you do believe, in a way."

"But not in the *true* way." The irony is half-baked. I look at Athanasius and find him staring blankly at me, attempting to bridge a gulf so new to him that it is genuinely curious rather than obviously condemnable.

"Tell me about this meaninglessness, Eusebius." It seems absurd when he says it. What does Athanasius know about meaninglessness?

"Well, it is not meaninglessness as such."

"What is it, then? And please be clear. Remember, I am one of your over-formulaic logicians." Again a smile.

"I said I believed in the need to believe."

"You did."

"Well, I also believe in doubt."

"Rather a contradiction in terms."

"No less so than the paradoxes we must swallow in this creed, Athanasius."

"A questionable point, of course, but I'll let that pass. Continue."

"Doubt for me can be a positive thing; not simply in a skeptical sense: I don't want to be paralyzed in passivity by doubt. I only want to draw attention to the dialogue of existence, how we exist as entities relating to other entities, and how God and Christ, by being removed from us by the Creed decided upon here, lose contact with us."

"I'm surprised to hear all of this coming from such an apologist for Origen."

"Athanasius, I am not going to be labeled. I am already a heretic in some people's eyes. I have also been labeling all my life, and I am tired of its ease and falseness. It is all part of the oversimplification of our existence and beliefs since our faith was sanctioned."

"Very well. What point are you trying to make?"

"The Creed I have signed here at Nicaea is a creed from the Greeks and not the Jews. It deals with the Logos on an intellectual plane, and once I would have accepted that. True, the Creed indicates how Christ came down from heaven, but it leaves him an abstract divinity. The mystery remains, as you have said, in his mortality, in the capacity to doubt allowed him at the end. I think this is what Arius senses: that Jesus as the Christ is more human and thus lesser than God at this moment. Arius has merely attempted, as all so-called heretics have tried to do, to make a dogma from this paradox of divine mortality. Thus Arius's hierarchy; thus his saying the Logos postdates God.

"But I confess, Arius's doctrine most attracted me because in the Arian Christ there is more of the face and body of the martyr than I see in this creed. I see in the Arian Christ more of the charity towards mankind than I see in the abstract Logos—simply because Christ is human, able to understand the pain and the torture and the fact that some stay silent and some speak. I admit: the Christ of Arius may be no more than an angel, or a demiurge, or a poor, deluded, but generous and trusting servant of the Lord; and so this heresy may be no better than the other self-indulgent theologies that have sprung up over three centuries since Jesus' death and resurrection. But it struck a chord in my susceptible old age, and I decided to stand by it, however weakly. It made me revere life even more as a beautiful thing, rendered meaningless when filled with a faith that impels us ever onward toward eternity; but as delicate and fragile as a precious vase when bordered by the finite and glazed by the mortal.

"Beyond all this, Arius's ideas have allowed me to have some hope in myself; because they have made me grasp that Jesus showed just how good and noble man could be. In his goodness, his honor and his bravery, Jesus proved it was possible to apprehend death and still be filled with life. Of course, Jesus knew death as merely a prophetic fulfillment, as the necessary step before the more important act of resurrection. But I like to believe that, on a human level, Jesus understood that his brief time on earth had more purpose than talking about the world to come and waiting to be killed."

"And is all that in Arius?"

"No, of course not. If I were to propose that to Arius, he would, like you, laugh in my face at my lack of rigor and my sentimentality. After all, he believes that the Son is secondary to the Father and, as you have seen, if anything, I believe the reverse. I do agree with you that the Son was begotten by the Father, and not created. But this is all irrelevant—I do not know what it means to agree or disagree anymore. In any event, Arius's creed allows difference, doubt, and humanity, at least for me. This one doesn't."

"Why did you sign it then? We seem to be moving in circles."

"I don't know, Athanasius. It was half fear and half hope. I thought it might change something."

"A sudden revelation?"

"Something like that. I don't know."

"I see."

Looking up, I saw him staring out at the lake again. He picked up a stone and threw it in.

"I can't say I understand you, Eusebius. As you know, it is theology fraught with contradiction and misunderstanding. You don't seem to know whether Christ is Jesus or at what point, as you seem to imagine there was a point, the one became the other. And I am simply confused as to your beliefs about God and Jesus—perhaps, however, not as confused as you appear to be about them. I am not going to argue it over with you either, because you are familiar with the arguments, and I don't think you really care about them enough to discuss them.

"But I sympathize with you. It seems to me your doubt, or your belief in doubt, or whatever it is compelling you to make such a confession, has brought you nothing but misery, which to me hardly seems the positive thing you suggest it might be. On the other hand, my belief has brought me nothing but joy. It is not simply, as you suggest, an intellectual joy, the joy of a finely honed argument or a watertight logical series of steps toward a brilliant conclusion. It is a spiritual, daily joy; one rejoicing as your belief does—when it is happy enough to be extrovert—in the variousness of things and the fact of existence. But then, as you say, I have never seen a dead body."

"I would rather be miserable in doubt than joyful in certainty."

"Really? Given what you have just told me, I find that very hard to believe, Eusebius."

"Yet, in the end, that is probably how I feel. Doubt and misery are part of the human condition; I wish I could believe joy and certainty were the same."

"The human condition is a fall from grace." Athanasius's voice hurries forward. "It is a fall that Jesus' sacrifice on the Cross has made reversible, if only we would be humble enough to accept it as such. There was a choice, there was always a choice, and we chose wrongly. We would be foolish to choose wrongly again. But pardon me; that is dogma. Perhaps you wish to question the truth of the foundation of faith?"

"You're very tolerant, aren't you, Athanasius?"

"Only when it suits me, O friend of Constantine."

"So it's as simple as that, is it?"

'You forget, Eusebius, some of us are blessed, or cursed, with a sense of humor. You should not believe the propaganda of Arius about my fanaticism; one man's fanatic is another man's believer. Well, are you going to question the foundations or not?"

"What? No. That is, not the facts. The foundations of our doctrine seem so far away from the reality of being here at Nicaea that the bonds between them have been stretched to invisibility in my head. What I mean is that, since all we know is what we are, it is futile to pretend we could be otherwise. God, for want of a better word, allowed Adam and Eve to fall because they desired knowledge. Well, if that is the case, and we still want knowledge since it is part of being human and intelligent, then let us remain fallen."

"But God, and there is no better word, Eusebius, let me remind you of that, only condemned knowledge beyond our limited understanding, not all knowledge."

"But what is beyond our understanding? Jesus has shown us that knowledge can reach beyond all our imaginings, many believers have experienced knowledge in ecstasy, and I am sure others will feel the fire of God in their souls. But is it only for the chosen, the few? What about the recorders of this life, whose passion is eternally vicarious, and whose faith only shimmers at a third remove from the source? And why the fire of God? Why not the fire of self? Why not the capacity to value oneself by trusting oneself, admitting we are enough?"

"But Eusebius, you are making no sense. You are disproving your arguments even as you speak them. It is clear we are not enough; and it is not simple delusion that allows us to look beyond ourselves to God. We recognize, as God recognized for us, that we cannot know everything, and to allow the will and the imagination free rein is to be at our most absurd. We are, if you like, in the process of saving time as well as being saved. Christ was made flesh for you, Eusebius; and God loves you for your doubt. It is not a sin to doubt, nor is it unhuman to believe. You must trust in the sacrifice of Jesus. Through Christ you must trust in God."

"Yes. But I must also wrestle with his angel."

"Let the angel win."

"I am still fighting."

Athanasius watches the stones ripple in the water. Does he know?

"They used to kill people with those."

"They still do, in some places. We have a long way to go, Eusebius. That is why we need the Creed."

"The State decrees it?"

"The situation demands it. The Church is not only a rock, it is also a stone. Like those ripples the stone makes in the water, the Church must reach out in wider and wider circles until everybody is touched by it. To change the image again: should the rains come, nobody will get wet, because there'll be room inside the Church."

"And the likes of me?"

"The doors are always open, and there is some fine company inside. There is a choice whether you want to enter or not."

"But none once you're in?"

"Inside there are obligations."

"I see."

Athanasius has the sun on his face, cooler now, moving toward evening. Services to go to, decisions to be made, feasts to be attended. He gets up, helps me up as well.

"I've enjoyed talking to you."

"Likewise."

"And before you ask, I assure you this will go no further."

"I feared, after your performance over the Creed that..."

"I'd expose you?"

"Yes."

"I'm sorry to lead you to suspect that. I have to say,

however, you overestimate your importance. I deal with dangerous subversives, people like Arius who make things up and fool people who know no better, which is why I was surprised when you agreed."

"I should take that as a compliment, Athanasius?"

"You can take it any way you like, Eusebius. Remember, it is up to you. In any event, however, you are neither dangerous nor particularly subversive. You will live through this, believe me. I wish you luck in your unhappiness."

So Athanasius turned and walked toward the town, leaving me with the sense of the placid lake in the evening sun, demanding nothing and giving nothing in return. Constantine was right, Pamphilus, Nicaea is a beautiful place. The silence is so great, so full of sadness, it is the right place for me now, in my old and uncertain age. Pamphilus, I wish I could talk to you now, if only to fill the silence with words demanding response. I have so many questions to ask, questions from my youth, when I could ask questions and still hope to live to hear the answers. But I fear you would not understand even if you were here. You would be as kindly and puzzled, and as distant, as Athanasius.

Being without faith is the most lonely thing in the world. It throws you upon the frailty of your self. What makes it worse is all the evidence of my books and speeches that will survive to record the image of what I hoped I would be: the great orthodox chronicler, the one they will all turn to for truth. Well, let them turn, my conscience is none of their concern. All the events are true; it is only the soul which is not in it. Pamphilus, I wish you were here today. Do you believe that? Do you understand the desperation lying within that question?

The evening deepens, and the distance is becoming gray with night's approach. I must go back, for they will wonder where I am. I would ask if you would allow me to leave you, Pamphilus; but I know the question is futile for both of us. You never will, and I will never let you. But there is a certain sense of peace to be gained by being here, given in a certain manner. And it will do. For now.

Courtly Love

An-ne. Mother. An-ne. An-ne. Children's voices sur-
round me, calling your name. An-ne. An-ne. Mother.
They demand that their mothers look at them, pay them
attention as they play around the edges of the lake. I
cannot tell whether these mothers, swathed in those
heavy black robes, are deliberately ignoring their children or not. Their faces are hidden from me. But their
tented bodies seem collapsed in on themselves or lean
toward each other conspiratorially. But I am looking,
An-ne. I am looking, Mother. I can hear the trick in the
name: An-nie. Annie, my mother.

My pen comes to rest just above the whiteness of
the back of a garish postcard of Iznik—the lake and the
sky an improbable blue, the shadows a little too suggestive of unwelcome secrets. My hand is hesitant,
almost fearful. What is there to say? How can I begin to
explain and tell her that I still care what she thinks of
me, even though she cannot forgive me for what I have
done to Michael, and not remind her of her own wayward husband, called away by the sirens only to return

a few weeks later? I can understand why she called Michael when I left—I would have done the same. I can hear him telling her about what happened: calm, subtly censorious, and self-pitying in a stoical kind of way, wondering how Adam's wife and kids are dealing with it. I want to explain, or say something, or say that it shouldn't change our relationship—or rather that it might bring us closer together, abandoned and abandoner. But I sense this might be a final breach, and I know that to her what I have done matters most because it makes it even less likely that I will give her a grandchild.

And how these children accuse me for her! Towheaded, wide-eyed, with smooth, honey-colored skin, the girls so pretty in their pink dresses and bows. I wonder whether they find it strange that their mothers are covered in black, or, rather, what mysterious change is maturation that what was pure and open suddenly needs to be enclosed to remain pure. But they know nothing of the bathetic rules of adulthood. Instead, they wheel and swirl around their mothers. I look at the white square of the stupid wish-you-were-here postcard that is to be the repository of all that can't be said. Yet I have to do it, have to begin somewhere, if only because these children's voices are demanding that I do it: An-ne. Mommy, mommy. Look at me.

* * *

I first hear Adam's voice again when he steps off the plane from London and rings noisily from the airport saying he's in town and asking if he can see Michael and me.

"It's Adam," I say. "Adam Williams. He wants to come and see us."

Michael blinks at me, pauses slightly. He is bad at hiding pain. He remembers every slight, every fault, every betrayal that has happened to him in his entire life, and this time is no exception. His eyes narrow and his mouth purses, and he nods. "Of course."

I tell Adam that Michael agrees, and ninety minutes later I open the door and am surprised by how comfortable it feels to see him. I invite him in and he kisses me on the cheek and the corner of his mouth touches mine. He has the same warm, soapy smell I remember, and I can sense how robust his body is, how assured he feels in taking up his space.

"Michael, Adam's here," I shout. There is a noise of shuffling and a door shutting. I take Adam's coat. He looks at me and smiles, and in that moment I don't quite know what has happened but know that something has. Michael comes down the stairs, and I am annoyed that he is still wearing his old sweater and battered jeans. His hair is a mess and he hasn't shaved. It is, I feel, some kind of protest. Love me as I am. *I'm* not a fake.

"Adam. Good to see you." Adam moves toward Michael to shake his hand. Michael offers his at a distance. "It's been...."

"Twenty years." They touch.

"Really, that long?"

"Yes." Adam looks at me. "That long."

"Although we appreciated the cards from you and your wife," I say.

"Yes," says Michael. "How is Sarah?"

"She is well, thank you Michael. Unfortunately, I cannot say the same for our marriage. We are separated."

Michael makes some noise that is meant to express sympathy, and wonders aloud why we hadn't known.

"I e-mailed Marianne some time ago with the news," says Adam. "She didn't tell you?" The answer is no. "Marianne's letters and now e-mails have been a solace to me over the years."

I feel the need to explain to Michael. "Adam is a fan of my art. We like to discuss it." It is, I know, no kind of answer to all the questions that cannot be asked.

"I dropped in to see your 'Red Ariadnes' show at the Fifty-Seventh Street gallery," Adam says, ignoring Michael. "I think they're the best you've done."

"You should have looked us up when you were in town," says Michael. How long? he is thinking. How long?

Adam looks at Michael. "I came so rarely to New York, and my schedule was always full. The time was never propitious. Also, it never quite seemed appropriate," he adds quietly. "I'm not sure we parted the best of friends."

There is silence. Naturally, Michael is not going to contradict him.

"You're looking well," Adam continues, "both of you." The compliment dies in the air.

"But why after so long?" continues Michael, and I

hate the tone in his voice. A kind of angry desperation mixed with a cloying fear. It is going to be a long evening.

"Silly, really, of us not to have seen each other more," I say, too emphatically, trying to bridge the silence. "Shall we sit?"

We do. "I should congratulate you on your appointment, Michael," Adam says.

I can sense Michael's pleasure and the annoyance that comes with feeling it. He hates to be surprised by emotion. "I'm amazed you know about it."

"Why should you be? You are one of the best paleontologists in North America and Columbia had a vacancy. Who else could have filled it? It has caused quite a stir within the academic world. Lots of people I know wanted that job." There is silence. "But to clarify the question, since I suspect it might be important..." Adam's voice quiets as he looks at Michael. Adam leans back on the sofa and spreads his arms across the top. I sense again how powerful he is, how enabled he feels in making his presence felt. "It seemed only reasonable to come and visit finally," Adam continues. "After all these years."

It is not an answer, of course. It is not meant to be.

"You haven't changed much," I say, again trying to break the tension. I hate the role of appeaser. It's a part I play too easily.

"Nor you," replies Adam, looking directly into my eyes. "Nor Michael, for that matter."

It is a transparent lie and, as if to confirm it, Michael brushes a reluctant hand across his balding head and pats his stomach. "Except for a great deal of hair loss and a great deal of added stuff around the middle," he laughs, and I feel a surge of affection for the self-effacing, studious, unhappy man whom I married when we were far too young. Adam smiles indulgently.

"What would you like to drink?" I ask. "Beer, soda, scotch, or red wine is all we have at the moment."

"Wine will be fine," says Adam.

I rise and get the drinks, and I know they are fighting each other in silence. I speak from in front of the drinks cabinet. I feel myself observing my actions, the way my hands tremble slightly. The fact of my smile.

"So what are you doing in New York City?"

"Well," and I can hear Adam stretching back, "there is an exhibition on medieval manuscripts I helped curate that is opening in New York in a few days at the Public Library. It's been making the rounds of Europe and finally made it to the Big Apple. So I thought I'd join the exhibition in town and see you at the same time."

"We're delighted to have you," says Michael. "Where are you staying?" Once more there is anxiety in his voice.

"The Yale Club."

"Oh, I remember reading something about that exhibition," I say, too enthusiastically. I sound like a girl. "*You* were involved with that?"

Troy, twenty years ago. His blue eyes remind me only of that. I can tell he is remembering that as well, and the brief silence is filled with it. There is so much to say and none of it can be said.

"For my sins, yes. Myself and a few others gathered

together some manuscripts from around the world—the Gawain manuscript, *Romance of the Rose*, *Confessio Amantis* by Gower, some troubadour transcriptions, Chaucer, that kind of thing. Called it 'Courtly Love' because it sounded sexier than 'Medieval English, Italian, and Romance Manuscripts,' and, lo and behold, we had an exhibition. Of course, it's a controversial term. People even wonder whether there was any such thing as 'courtly love' or a type of writing dedicated to it."

"Forgive me for being a dull paleontologist," says Michael, loading the words too much for the irony not to be leaden and unappealing. "But what *is* courtly love, apart from fancy poetry and troubadours and all that stuff?"

"Oh, good. I never regret a chance to lecture," laughs Adam. "Well, some of it *is* just fancy poetry and troubadours. But it's really quite interesting." He leans forward. "Do you know the stories of Tristan and Isolde and Lancelot and Guinevere, Gawain and the Green Knight's wife?"

"Not really, no. Apart from Wagner's opera, which I've never seen, and a movie about King Arthur's round-table I saw when I was a kid, I've no idea," Michael says impatiently.

"My apologies for assuming too much," replies Adam carelessly. I can see Michael sink a little in his seat. "Well, all these stories and poems carry the usual allegorical overtones of religious quests and spiritual journeys and that kind of thing. They tend to be somewhat formal expressions of devotion to the beloved— apple-red cheeks and white skin, broad forehead, pearl-like teeth, that kind of thing. In fact, so standardized are these descriptions that one might suggest the poet was more interested in his own poetic skill than in the genuine depiction of the object of his love.

"Nevertheless, what's really interesting is that a sizable number of the poems feature adulterous love stories. Gawain is betrothed to another and yet comes dangerously close to making the beast with two backs with the Green Knight's wife. In fact, for the rest of his days he has to carry a mark on him caused by the nick of the Green Knight's sword because of his almost-adulterous liaison. Likewise Lancelot and his affair with Arthur's wife, Guinevere.

"What fascinated me, however, is that the idea of courtly love—or 'fin amour' as it is more accurately called—might be *necessarily* adulterous. Also that the loved woman herself is barely actualized, merely a residue of tropes of beauty—the rose, virtue, and so forth, a kind of crystallization of perfections without any obvious faults, or grain, or texture. Nevertheless, for such an evanescence must the hero turn himself into being the knight of love and the enamored courtier before he returns a sadder and a wiser man to his true path as the Christian knight of faith. And somehow, I fancy, not only does the object of desire know that it all must end but the betrothed knows what must happen as well. They are all engaged in something greater or nobler than themselves. It is, I might go so far as to say, an obligation."

"And what about the husbands?" asks Michael. *Husbands*, not *betrothed*.

"It isn't only husbands. After all, these knights were often affianced to other women who were equally betrayed. This is where the fascination lies. These others, as much as we ever know about them, are nearly always good people, loved and lovable in their own way."

"The betrayal then seems all the greater."

"That's right. But that is essentially our modern, puritanical view of things, isn't it? I think the medieval European court culture had a much more sophisticated view of amatory relations than we do in the emotionally desiccated place that is our Anglo-American heart. Sophisticated and yet somehow purer; erotic without all of the neurotic, obsessive, and self-regarding paraphernalia that attends the art of love these days. To the medieval poets, faith did not always mean fidelity to one's spouse or chivalric behavior spurning love's call. In fact, quite the opposite."

"But there is still pain." Michael's voice has become small.

"Oh yes," Adam replies, looking hard at Michael. "There is always pain. A deep, lifelong pain. A pain that goes to the very marrow. After all, these lovers are nearly always far apart from each other, sending their fevered longings into the dewy mists of morning, aching to be together but, I think we can say with some confidence, quietly reveling in the delicious agony of their separation. Pain is the purpose of courtly love, and longing—unrealized and unrealizable longing. Courtly love is about the *danger*—it is a word the poets use—of love, its disruption of order and calm in the face of the impermissible or unavoidable, even though every rule of polite society and well-crafted prosody is obeyed. Without the pain there is no quest, and that, in the end, Michael, is the point of it all. The pain is the making of the man..." he glances at me, "...and woman..." and then at no one "...apparently."

"It sounds very unfair," I interject, once more trying to keep things neutral. I move to sit beside Michael, feeling his need for some form of reassurance from me. I sense him breathing out, slowly.

"When has love or life ever been fair?" Adam replies. "The medievalists didn't invent adultery—they weren't even the first to make it into high art, although in the process they may have invented the tawdry and tearful world of romantic love we still wake up in. In my opinion, it is the Romans and Greeks who are the true geniuses. They constructed their entire civilizations out of a love for unattainable beauty and stolen kisses and forbidden embraces. Imagine that! Civilization merely the collective expression of an undeniable but unallowable love. No. The medievalists weren't the first, and they certainly weren't the last. It's all happened before and it will happen again." And he looks directly at me.

* * *

I asked him why we had to go to Iznik. Why didn't we go west to Canakkale, or south to Izmir? What was so special about Iznik that we had to waste a day there? He turned to me and said he was amazed I didn't know

that Iznik had once been Nicaea, where they had created the Nicene Creed. "I'm a painter, Adam, and an
agnostic. Why should I care about the Nicene Creed?"
He gave a melodramatic sigh. "What do you expect to
find there?" I asked. He turned away and said, "Faith."

He sits, staring into the water. He's been removed all
morning, wanting to think about a friend of his who
died; taking the opportunity (so he says) to feed off the
place that was once Nicaea in order to understand his
friend's death—someone who died twenty years ago! I
cannot understand why he has to bring this up now,
when he has his wife and children back home to be preoccupied about. Yet the ridiculous, maudlin tone he uni-
laterally established as soon as he arrived has been hard
to shake off. Perhaps that, and the women by the lake,
started me thinking about you, Mom, and how I needed
to try to say something about what had happened that
might make some sense to you.

* * *

"I thought it only rained in England," says Adam,
shaking his raincoat and umbrella at the entrance to the
gallery. "But it seems to have been wet every day I've
been in this city."

"It's November," I reply. "These things happen."

He walks over and kisses me on the cheek. "You have
a nice space here." He looks around appreciatively.

"It's not just mine. I have it on rotation with other
artists."

He smiles and pushes the hair back from his forehead. "I know, Marianne. God forbid you might be important enough to have a gallery dedicated *only* to your work! In any event, I am not interested in your being self-effacing." He walks over to a painting. "I want you to talk about your art. What about Ariadne?"

"Well, I have always been interested in the Ariadne story…"

"Really? I've never heard you mention her before." He looks soberly at me, and I try to suppress the worry that he has not come to talk about the art at all.

"There are some things, Adam, that I don't talk about."

"And some, no doubt, you've never talked about. Or written, for that matter." He smiles.

"Yes."

"You were always very formal. Never said how you felt."

"Words are not my chosen medium of expression, Adam." I wave an arm in the direction of my paintings. "They are."

He looks at me and I cannot read the expression on his face. But he lets the subject drop. "Back to Ariadne. What part of Ariadne fascinates you? The woman with the thread who helps the hapless Theseus, the betrayed woman on the shores of Naxos, the willing or unwilling bride of Dionysos?"

"All of them."

"Really? And why red? And, if I'm not mistaken, you seem to have quoted from de Chirico in this particular painting. Where does de Chirico fit in?"

I lean into the pleasure I feel, the warmth of being

understood, of my imagination being stimulated, of not having to try, and brush off the nagging sense that I am being patronized again.

"De Chirico created a number of paintings in 1912 on the theme of a sleeping Ariadne, and I've always been struck by them. Their sense of isolation, fragmentation—the desolation of the landscape around them, how denuded and stark and unrelated everything is: all of that resonated with me."

He nods.

"I had thought of using Titian's *Bacchus and Ariadne* as a template to work from." I do not tell him that I felt repulsed by its lushness and potency, how full the painting was with the bruisable fruits of happiness—how fearful Ariadne seems and yet how utterly she gives herself over to this god who does not care whether she wants him or not. And all for a constellation—for queenship, for power.

I continue: "But I kept returning to the emptiness of de Chirico. I think I once may have written to you about how the spaces between objects interested me more than the objects themselves or even the relations between them. That's definitely the case with de Chirico. While the individual objects may draw our attention, at least in his metaphysical period, it is the gaps between them, those open, empty spaces that, for me at least, hold the picture together, make it mean something.

"And as for red...well, over the last few years I have become fascinated with it: the color of pleasure and the shame that may go with it; the color of rashness, of passion, and yet the color a woman has to acknowledge every month as a sign of fertility and vulnerability; the color of war and the color of love. It is, for me, a tragic color—its spilling a sign both of the possibility of bringing life and of the ending of life. In this painting, for instance, I have placed de Chirico's sketch of the sleeping statue of Ariadne to the side of what I have imagined to be a rainshower of red sweeping over her. Ariadne seems at once so passive a victim of the whims of these powerful male figures—Theseus and Dionysos—who are impetuous and bloody, red with war and with wine. She is drowned by their redness. And yet she is also active—helping Theseus kill the Minotaur, her own brother—her own blood—and then, as some legends have it, leaving Theseus for Dionysos: her own lust, her own redness taking her over. So, I tried to show these two ideas in tension—redness and Ariadne."

He looks at me. I can see he is thinking. "The Roman poet Catullus's view of Ariadne—a scene depicted on the tapestry of the wedding feast of Peleus and Thetis—is of someone still crazy with longing for Theseus, and that is why perhaps she turns so readily to Dionysos when the god sees her. You're not alone seeing her that way."

I feel a spasm of irritation. "I am not trying to be original. I am merely painting what I feel."

He is apologetic. "I didn't mean to say that you weren't original." He pauses. "I am merely observing that you have tapped into something ancient and classical. Like 'fin amour,' if I may be so bold. Passion contained in tropes of art." He takes my arm and gives it a reassuring squeeze. "I think they're magnificent."

We walk around the gallery for a few moments, just looking. He says nothing, and nor do I, and I feel both close to him and vastly removed from him. Then he touches my shoulder and turns me to face him.

"Do you feel like Ariadne?" he asks quietly.

"Sometimes."

"Which one?"

I smile. "Sometimes all of them. I feel like all those women—Helen, Cressida, Clytemnestra, Iphigenia."

"All the women of Troy." Troy. Again, Troy.

"Yes. In spite of their different names, I think they are indivisible. *We* are indivisible."

He smiles back, but I can see that there is no mirth in his eyes. "You know, in spite of our sporadic, decorous correspondence over the years, I thought I would not see you again—talk to you again."

"Adam..."

"I thought it was all over then. Every time I saw your art I thought of you—and yet I could not say anything or call you."

"You could have," I reply unconvincingly. "It would have been OK. Better than this."

"And what is this, do you think?"

We stare at each other for a moment.

"You know, I pride myself on my words—my ability to speak. But anything I say, Marianne, seems wholly useless and trite and not what I mean at all. It's as if my tongue has been cut out."

We look at the paintings. Side by side—looking but not looking. The wordless writer and the blind painter. Blind with desire.

He speaks again. "I couldn't live with the thought that I might not at least see you again." He looks around the room, and his eyes flicker. "Absurd—for twenty years not to hear your voice or see your face. Just our words and polite questions about our spouses and our damned careers. Clippings from the newspapers; post-cards from exotic locales. And not a word that could hint at..." He seems close to tears. "Am I Theseus?"

"No," I laugh, without humor. "You are not."

*　*　*

There was nothing there then, still isn't. Troy. Truva. Twenty years ago. Michael and I are just married, on our honeymoon in fact, and my hair is dry and light with the sun on it, and Michael's body is firm and smooth beneath my fascinated, ignorant touch. We had spent time in Istanbul and wanted to go to Troy. Why? What we saw was just a little hillfort, covered with grass and a few bat-tered old signs, with the various levels of the city indicat-ed by Roman numerals. And the great Trojan plain? The river Scamander that Homer tells us about, rolling its bodies and helmets over in a red, boiling fury?

"Not very impressive, is it?"

We turn, startled. He is sitting about twenty feet away, his blue eyes visible at that distance, set in a tanned, intelligent, but not obviously handsome face. His accent is English. Michael speaks.

"Our guidebook had suggested something bigger, and I guess what little I know of Homer.... Well, it doesn't seem much like the Troy he writes about."

He lifts himself off the ground. He is tall against the cloudlessness of the sky. He begins to walk down the embankment.

"It probably isn't. After all, the Trojan War was, so the 'experts' say, a brief skirmish, or series of skirmishes, over trade to the Black Sea. Blind Homer—who could be a 'she' for all we know—made it all up."

"Are you an 'expert'?" I load the word like he did. For some reason, I want to tease this man. He has reached our level. He is better looking close up.

"I have an undergraduate degree in classics, if that makes any difference, and I'm working for a doctorate in Medieval Literature at Cambridge."

"Very impressive," says Michael dubiously. I can tell he wants to be a million miles away from this man. I confess that I find this person patronizing and annoying. But something about him makes me want to stay. Know more.

"A perpetual student," I grin.

"Perhaps," he grins back. A lovely smile.

"So, have you been here before?" Michael is finding this difficult.

"Oh, I come here every time I'm in Turkey. I visit all the usual places: Efes, Bodrum, Didym, you know."

"No, we don't." Michael's voice is clipped. "This is our first time. It's our honeymoon."

Adam's face breaks into a smile, but I remember thinking how his eyes seemed to narrow. "Congratulations." He shakes both our hands. There is mockery in the gesture. "You've picked a wonderful country for it. Very romantic."

"We've just come from Istanbul," I add, trying to sound impressive. "I thought it was romantic, didn't you?" I take Michael's hand and squeeze it, offering him some reassurance.

"And what about Truva?" asks Adam to both of us and to neither of us at the same time. "Do you find this place romantic?"

"Not really," mumbles Michael. "There's nothing here."

"Oh," exclaims Adam. "I don't think a place has to have picturesque ruins or that kind of thing to be romantic, do you?" He does not expect an answer. "There can be other attractions." He pauses. "Also, we bring our own conceptions to a place and let the place grow. It is, perhaps, the way a place flourishes inside the imagination and the heart that makes it romantic. Don't you think?"

"Perhaps.... I'm sorry, I don't know your name."

"Adam."

"And I'm Marianne, and this is Michael."

"Delighted to meet you." He thrusts out his arm at us again and shakes our hands portentously. "Now, I don't want to interrupt you two lovebirds on your honeymoon, so I'll let you go in peace."

He begins to walk off and I call after him. "Are you traveling with someone?" It is a strange question.

He turns back and smiles at me. "Oh no, I always travel alone. So many more surprises when you travel alone."

"Would you show us around, then?" I continue. I feel only a slight, regretful, resistant squeeze from Michael's hand. I squeeze back. Reassuringly? Defiantly? I can't remember which. Perhaps both.

"Well, I don't want to..." He looks at Michael, whose face is blank. "It would be my pleasure."

He unravels Troy but does not diminish it. He explains the digging, the reasons for it and the results of it—but what I remember most is how he unearthed what that place could mean.

"We arrive at a place, don't we, and expect it to reveal its secrets? Herr Schliemann, being the German Late Romantic that he was, certainly thought it would, so he dug, and, wounded and dissected, Troy revealed its historical layers. But are we any wiser, I wonder? You say you are interested in stones and fossils, Michael, but can we really get a sense of the time through them?"

"I think so. We have a sense of how the creatures looked, the stuff they ate, the eggs they laid. It gives us an idea."

"Yes, it gives us an *idea*," replies Adam. "But we'll never know what it was like to live in that world—to wake up to the sounds, the smells, the sensuousness of the place. Such feelings are always tinged with our own expectations."

"Perhaps. But the scientific endeavor is to minimize those expectations and try and put together the objective reality of that time."

Adam gives a dismissive laugh. "Ah, the quest for objective reality! Wouldn't it be nice to find *that* particular Holy Grail?"

Michael says nothing, but standing beside him I can feel his anger.

"Take Troy for instance," continues Adam, easily falling again into his academic voice. He was only in his mid-twenties then, only four years older than we were, but he sounded so much more self-assured than we felt. Already the lecturer, the professor. "It is not certain at all who these heroes and heroines were. There is a theory that Helen never made it to Troy, but was bought from Paris in Egypt."

"Do you mean to say the Trojans fought for nothing, then?" Michael's eyes widen.

"Literally, yes. The Greeks also. There may well have been no Helen to fight for, for all those men to suffer death upon the field of battle. Even in the *Iliad*, she is elusive. Every now and again the Trojans in the know presented a heavily veiled woman—an *eidolon*, she is called—or a look-alike to boost morale or taunt the enemy. Who could tell from the ground, looking up at those great battlements we're meant to be standing on, just who that woman was? All they needed were the vestiges of womanhood—the right shape, the veils, the sense of mystery." He looks at me.

"That makes it seem like a farce, or a tragedy."

"Perhaps both, Michael. But that in the end may have been the whole point of the game. In some ways, Helen was never really the issue. After all, abducting somebody else's wife is hardly reason enough to go to war, especially for ten years!"

"But isn't that part of the romance?"

"Marianne. Nobody, not even the ancient Greeks— even the idiot Ajax himself—is stupid enough to think adultery worth that level of misery or bloodshed. The

113

Greeks didn't even consider women important, anyway. Useful for sex of a certain kind, perhaps. A convenient bargaining chip and valuable property. But not *blood*. Helen was merely the excuse for a fight between the boys of Greece and the boys of Troy. But then, that again is not quite the point."

"Oh, really?" I can hear the frustration in Michael's voice, and I understand it. I too dislike Adam's insistence, his cleverness, the sense that he is teasing us, that we are missing his meaning. He, however, doesn't catch it, or pretends not to. "What *is* the point?"

"The point," says Adam, flicking a glance at Michael before looking at me, "is that you and I and Marianne are here, in Troy, and it could all happen again."

* * *

I asked him where he wanted to go.

"Nowhere in particular."

"Look," I said, annoyed at how quickly he had retreated into himself. "It was your idea to come here in the first place. What do you want to see especially?"

"I don't mind. Let's just wander."

"Where to?" I wasn't going to give in that easily.

"Oh, anywhere. Does it have to be somewhere specific?" He gave a "give-me-a-break-can't-you-see-I'm-suffering" sigh and loped off in the direction of somewhere.

An-ne. An-ne. Those little boys and girls. The women covered up in their black shawls, sweating and suffering

so that men will not desire them. A rule given them by
God. The Father. Pearls beyond price and yet a desperate
threat. What do they think about? What could they say,
if I could ask them if they felt trapped, diminished, if they
would rather not be free of their veils and shawls? There
would be the same incomprehension, even as generation,
civilization, and religion separate them from me. What
can you mean? It is right this way. This is the only way.
What would our men say? What would we do? We are
free from being victimized; no man bothers us as they
bother Western women such as you. To these women, I
am a whore, a lost soul: to them I have lost my value, my
dignity, my closeness to my own worth. Perhaps Adam's
friend would say the same—that I have betrayed the
spousal vows I took and I will be condemned to Hell. He
sounds as though he was a True Believer, which makes it
even stranger that Adam, who certainly isn't, should be
so obsessed with him, and coming to Iznik, or Nicaea, or
whatever its name is, should be such a pilgrimage.
Maybe they are all right—all these gatekeepers to eternity, with their views of what constitutes the Good Woman
as opposed to the Femme Fatale. Perhaps, after what has
happened, you think like them.

* * *

We end up in bed, inevitably, the evening after the
opening of Adam's show at the Library, full of conversation and humor and that charming, slightly intimidat-
ing, slightly ridiculous earnestness that Adam has, carrying all before it like a tidal wave. Michael cannot

attend the opening—a conference, he says—but all I can
think of is his face when he left the house for the airport:
reproachful, as if daring me to do it again, to dance the
dance one more time. And that is what I have done.

I fall into our lovemaking as if I were finally allowed
to grieve. He tells me I am beautiful and I believe him. He
tells me that Michael is not worthy of me and I do not
contradict him. He tells me how much he loves my art
and I convince myself that it is true. He tells me about his
wife, how bad it was, for him and for the children, how
it had never been good, even at the beginning—the easy,
lazy slide on his behalf and the intense need for stability
on hers. And I believe that, too. And he tells me that he
has never forgotten what happened that day and I say the
same, and we both believe each other. I watch him sleep,
his face toward me, and watch his eyes flicker behind his
eyelids. I wonder what he dreams about. I wonder about
the gift of desire—its undiscriminating urgency, what
Ariadne must have felt when Dionysos took her. Even the
word "took," so bland and yet so final, shocks me. Have
I been "taken"? I think of surrender, of not resisting,
and—in the night, lying beside him—I am overwhelmed
by how seductive seduction is: to give yourself so fully
that there is no turning back, to give yourself so fully that
there is no you at all.

I let my hand rest on his upturned cheek and feel it
grow warm at my touch. My fingers plane the curve of
his shoulder and circle the muscles of his arm. And all of
it seems like grief.

* * *

Not in Troy, not there.

Yes, we have drinks back at the hotel, and walk around town in the evening. We appreciate Adam's grasp of Turkish and resent it at the same time. That evening, in bed, Michael and I laugh at Adam's pretentiousness, and I feel almost as though I mean it. We meet with him the next day, briefly for lunch, and it is...well, I don't know what it is, except that we spend the rest of the day with him and leave each other with our addresses. Michael throws the paper with Adam's address away that night and I do nothing to stop him. But at that moment, I don't particularly care if I see Adam again. All is as it should be, and no more.

Not in Troy, but in Pamukkale. A week later, a week full of dreams and images of him. A week trying to avoid thinking of him, but seeing him everywhere—even though I was trying somehow to reconnect with this sweet, gentle young man whom I had just married and whose warmth and love of me I loved. In the hot calcium springs, with the broken Roman columns and friezes rippling beneath me, placed in the pools by some enterprising hotelier. Michael has gone for a nap in the heat of the afternoon. I am swimming, feeling the sun on my head and the thick, calcified water streaming around my body. And then suddenly and yet as if he has always been there, there is Adam, his brown shoulders rising out of the water, and his eyes even bluer for the shade thrown around him by a tree arching over the pool.

I cannot say anything, don't want to say anything. I somehow know he has followed us, but I don't care. All the indignation I should feel at him appearing like this floats away. He takes my hand underwater, out of sight of the others who are in the pool. The water sidles around and between us. I can feel the silken serrations of the columns in the water, sense the smoothness of the indentations under my feet, between my toes.

I kiss him.

"Isn't it meant to be me that does the stealing?" His eyes have deepened in the shadow, but water still glistens on his lashes.

"I don't know why I did that." And I don't. The moment weighs on me. Time slows.

He lifts my chin. "And on your honeymoon, too. That wasn't the plan, was it?"

"No."

"You can take some comfort in the fact that it was-n't Paris's either. But he saw the most beautiful woman in the world and had no option. There was no plan. Fortunately, Aphrodite's son does not make plans."

I look at him, and he is smiling, and I feel so open and already so wounded. I want to say something that would make him understand what is happening. Instead: "I thought you said there was no Helen, or that she wasn't the point."

"I said there *may* have been no Helen. This time there was." His fingers circle my lips. I move my body closer to his and my hand brushes against his thigh. "And what would you rather I have said in front of your husband? That I had been following you all day when we met at Troy? That I already loved you? That I wanted to take you away from him? That I would follow you until I could have a chance to explain to you what I felt?"

"No...but..."

"But nothing, Marianne. Your ring was shining too brightly in my eyes for me to act. I could not see." He takes my hands in his. "Now I see you are not wearing it."

"I was afraid I would lose it in the water."

Adam smiles. "Oh, the mythic significance of that!"

His laugh warms my face as he draws me closer to him, so that our faces just touch. And I can feel his arms slide down my back, and my back arching. His hands gently lift my body toward him and I feel his chest against my breasts. I close my eyes. And I don't know what I'm doing, what I want to do, don't feel I'm there somehow. Except that it seems, just then, right. That I want to.... Just want to....

"No, I can't. I can't."

I pull away, and swim, and I can see the columns mistily shimmering as I swim toward them, then shattering in the waves I make. I feel a constriction, something tightening behind my eyes as I force my body, all at once heavy and cumbersome, to get away from him.

"Did you have a good swim?" Michael is tousled and awake when I come in. He looks sweet. Like a little boy.

"Yes," I say.

He looks at me. Into my eyes. "And how was Adam?"

* * *

Michael says he wants to see the exhibition. It is an act of aggression, and we both know it. But this, I am discovering, is my time for indulgence. The spoils of happiness. We retreat to dinner and Adam soothes all worries with his solicitous, intelligent questioning of Michael and his work. I watch as Michael, briefly, flourishes like a wilting plant under a sunlamp, and wonder if I could have done more. I look at these men, so different from each other and yet so bound up in my life, and I do not understand what has brought us to this point where such a rearrangement has taken place. At the end of the evening we walk Adam back to the club. As we say our goodnights, Adam asks what he has wanted to ask all evening, but has waited in vain for Michael to ask.

"Did you enjoy the exhibition?"

"I was very impressed." I can see it. He is. Genuinely. "I now know all I ever need to know about adultery."

"Oh, I don't think one ever stops learning about anything," Adam smiles. "Especially adultery."

* * *

He arrives home early. I am still writing my note. For a moment he stands in the doorway, then throws his gray, generic raincoat on the chair, as he always does, and sits on the arm of the sofa. He has chalk stains on his jacket. His shoes are muddied, but I am not interested in clean carpets anymore. I look at him and he says nothing, but he awkwardly buries his hands in his pockets and cocks his head to one side. The posture is characteristic: the fury of resignation, the rage of defeat.

"Will you call?" he asks. "To tell me you're OK."

I look at him. "I'll be OK, Michael. Don't worry."

There is silence. I continue, unnecessarily, with the note.

"I suppose it wouldn't do any good to say that I don't want you to go."

No, I tell him. It would not.

He nods his head slowly. "I don't understand what went wrong," he says, addressing himself more than me. "I thought it was good." I look up at him. "Or at least tolerable, Marianne. I thought I was at least *tolerable*."

"Michael. Please."

"I know I am not as exciting or dynamic as Adam, or as good-looking," he continues, failing to contain the desperation in his voice. "But after all these years...."

"Michael, we've already had this conversation." I pause. "Sometimes I feel that conversation is all we have ever had."

His voice quivers, and he is near tears. I am almost overwhelmed by my wretchedness, but simultaneously I am shocked at how little I feel for his own. "If I only knew what I did wrong," he adds, redundantly, "or what I could do differently. I want to make it better, but I don't know how."

"Yes, Michael. I know."

"There must be *something*, Marianne. There must be *something* I, or we, could do that would make it worth being together." He runs his hands over his thinning hair, his body collapsed in on itself. At that moment, I try to feel something, anything, for this man, and all that I feel within me is contempt.

I smile at him, but there is nothing behind the smile. "No, Michael. There is nothing. Nothing to be done."

* * *

For some reason—an obligation perhaps, a challenge, rebellion against something I cannot articulate—I call you to tell you I have left him. You ask why.

"I have met someone else."

There is silence. I fill it. "I met him a long time ago and we fell out of touch, and then I saw him again recently and we just connected. It wasn't working with Michael and me. It was dead. Had been, for a long time."

I can hear you fighting the urge to ask me about this other man. Instead: "Michael is a good man, Marianne."

"I know."

"How will he cope?"

A flame of rage. "This is not about Michael, Mom. This is about me." Then my voice softens. "I thought you should know. I am going to Turkey for a few weeks."

"With this other man?"

"Yes."

"Do you mind if I talk to Michael? When you're away."

Of course I mind. "No."

"Perhaps I could help...."

"No. Please don't meddle. I know what I'm doing. This is for the best, Mom. Believe me. I have to go. I'll send you a postcard."

You say nothing. I hear the click of the receiver. Nothing is different. There is no hint of accusation, no intake of breath, no long sigh. Merely a thickening of the space between us, the phone suddenly hot against my ear, weighty in my hand. And there is a voice, one that itself may be only my own voice and no one else's— one calling to me so deeply that it doesn't sound like me, speaks in a way I do not understand, in a manner I cannot measure as to its seriousness or passion: There will be no child.

* * *

Adam's eyes are still blue, but there are lines around them now. We are in a hotel in Bursa, about to take the bus to Iznik. We have just made love—at least, this is what I call it—and I can still feel his imprint on my body. Feel him within me. I am sitting on the side of the bed, putting on my clothes. I turn to him, and see him lying back on the pillow, his arms behind his head, his eyes closed. In spite of what has happened he seems a stranger to me.

"A few months ago..." I begin. His eyes open. "A few months ago, I was on the subway going to the gallery. It was a Saturday and the train was half full of people like me, bleary-eyed, going to do something unnecessary. At one station, I can't remember which, a young couple got on. They can't have been more than twenty or twenty-one. And they were wrapped up in each other—completely oblivious to everyone else but themselves.

"I don't know why, but I couldn't keep my eyes off them. They weren't particularly good-looking; in fact, they had that gawkiness that goes with kids who have not quite grown into their bodies. But there was something fascinating about them. They sat down and the girl reached behind the back of the boy and began to stroke the hairs on the side of his neck with her fingers, very gently. They were looking directly at me, but they didn't see me—they were utterly *within* themselves, with just that connection of the hand stroking the hairs on his neck."

He reaches up and touches me underneath the ears. "Like this?"

I smile. "Yes, like that." I take his hand and lower it to the bed. "And yet, not like that at all. It was a gesture of such incredible tenderness, hope perhaps, that nothing in the world would change, that nothing else mattered. It made them so beautiful."

Adam sits up in the bed and removes his hand from mine and cups my chin. He can see I am near tears. "You don't know what they were thinking, Marianne," he says severely. "They were young, that's all. Young with all the glamour that unsagging bodies and minds with no responsibility have. Youth thinks it knows everything, has all the answers, needs no justification. That's what you saw in those kids on the subway. Like all things, it passes."

I stand up and pull myself away from the bed. "How

come I never had that insouciance? How come there was never a moment of surrender to the complete experience of being with someone?" I turn and look at him. "How come I pulled away?"

He smiles again. "It's a question I've asked myself for twenty years." He pauses. "Marianne. The possibility of living in the moment doesn't stop when you're young. Isn't what those kids had what we are looking for now?"

"Yes," I say, a little too passionately. "But it seems so forced with us. Those young people haven't had their disappointments, haven't made their compromises, haven't accepted something less, or some*one* less."

"But they will. They will grow up. Perhaps, like us, they will fail to take an opportunity and regret it. Or perhaps they will take it and regret it just the same. Or maybe, like my friend, they will be killed and never have to live to regret anything. But if they do live, believe me, there will be failures, and, if they remember the moment—which I doubt—it too will have the same tang of regret."

"I must seem awfully trite to you, Adam," I respond bitterly.

"I'm just trying to stop you from blaming yourself. It won't do you any good." He pauses. "Before I left with you, I got a call from Sarah threatening to commit suicide if I divorced her, even though we both know we had been drifting apart. I didn't tell you before, since I thought it might be a distraction."

"A distraction from what?"

"From us?"

"And why are you telling me now? I don't think I'm ever going to feel good about what we've done."

He closes his eyes briefly and exhales heavily. "I don't know why I told you, but I thought you should know, though I don't think you should worry. Although she has lost many things, Sarah has never lost her considerable flair for melodrama. She has also kindly informed me that our children cannot sleep at night— they miss their father, cannot understand what has happened, want to know who this other woman is who has so entranced me. This is how she phrases it. *This* is something that separates us from the kids on the subway train. Yet I *know* what *I* feel and I don't regret what I have done at all."

"That's what makes you different. Even though you talk about them, you seem to have no regrets."

He gives a shallow laugh. "Oh, I have *plenty* of regrets, Marianne. My life is one long catalogue of regrets. This is the first thing I have *not* regretted. Yet."

"What does that mean?" What was full is now hollow. What was connected is now broken. What was visible, if only for a moment, has gone. Broken columns— in the pool, in De Chirico, fractured memories of a beautiful past that never was. I can hear how harsh I sound, and it gives me no pleasure.

"It means that I am not placing any hope in this not being another moment that we pluck and then watch as it withers away in our hands." His voice becomes quiet. "Yet, at the same time, I want you to know how important you are to me, how much I am willing to give up for you."

"I gave up something too, you know."

"Yes...but..."

"Helen is not important in this story, hmm?" I walk into the bathroom. "The betrothed is not allowed to have her feelings honored?"

"I can't be held responsible for anything I said in your house after not seeing you for twenty years and having to talk to you and Michael about courtly love. I said a lot of stupid things."

"Including that you loved me?" The mirror returns my face to me apologetically, quizzically, wondering what I expect it to do with it. I imagine Michael, sitting at home, whiskey in his hand, staring miserably at the television. This is completely new to him—being alone. Rejection as well: utterly new. "And you didn't seem very reluctant to talk about it, I can tell you."

"Marianne. Dear Marianne." Adam comes into the bathroom and wraps his arms around my waist. He tries to kiss me and I pull away. His voice rises and coaxes. "Twenty years ago..."

"...I was a naïve and faintly ridiculous girl who had read too many knights-in-shining-armor stories and was impressed by your knowledge and charmed by your blue eyes. I cannot think what else I was thinking of, to do that—and on my *honeymoon*, for God's sake. Now I am...a *lot* older—an experienced, intelligent, well-respected painter..."

"Who regrets not taking a road in the past and has gone back to try that path again..."

"Who is now being *utterly* preposterous."

"What's preposterous about falling in love?"

"Oh, for Christ's sake, Adam. How could you even *know* what falling in love was? How could *any* of us?" I think of Michael and his unkempt, imploding grief and am annoyed at how much I have to force myself to care about him. Shouldn't it be more natural after all this time? "It was all in the head, some romantic notion that you concocted about Troy and me and Helen and some other cerebral shit. And then there was this exhibition and all that baloney about courtly love and selfless quests. What am I to understand from that? And Ariadne and her ridiculous claims on these treacherous, lovely men whom she seems to want to enable and who betray her or whom she betrays.... Now you tell me you want to go to Iznik because of a Christian friend of yours who died just after you met me in Turkey that first time, when you don't even believe in God."

"It's not that simple, Marianne, you know that," he mumbles.

"All right, Adam. Yet, somehow I feel as though I'm to blame for all of it—your friend, the 'seduction,' our absurd fantasy. All of it."

"Aphrodite doesn't pick her times, that's true."

I say nothing.

"Marianne. I am not claiming some kind of moral high ground here. I feel bad about Michael. I feel bad about your feeling bad about Michael. I even feel bad about Sarah; and I am definitely concerned for my children. But I cannot afford to regret this now, because we cannot go through our lives simply living in the gaps— if you want the de Chirico analogy..."

I glare at him.

"...which you probably don't. We have to make the connections. I don't know why you now seem to believe that you had no agency here—the abandoned Ariadne is also the treacherous Ariadne. So, you give up an admirable, attentive, if unromantic husband—a good man, a *mensch*, unexceptionable, all those things, who has been loyal to you, *faithful*, as far as we know, for twenty years—and take me up on my offer to tour Turkey again in various anonymous hotels. To you, suddenly, in spite of what we just...*transacted* on this bed, it all seems ridiculous. To me, it is...well, romantic, for want of a better word."

"You call what we did 'transacted'?"

"There was an exchange, I believe Marianne, a connection, a breaking down of borders—a displacement of some sort." He looks at me. "You seemed to enjoy it."

I am near tears. "You're right. I do think it's ridiculous."

Theatrically, he throws his arms in the air and sits down on the bed again. "Then, why, Marianne? Why come? Why throw your lot in with me?"

I look at him and am reminded of just how damned persuasive he can be. How he makes things not only sound right, but seem right.

"Would it be enough to say I preferred to be with you?"

"No. I see scant evidence of it, apart from what just happened."

"Or that this is the last fling before middle age finally sets in and my breasts sag and ass collapses and no one will want to fuck me?"

"Worse. Dishonest and trite and depressing and unworthy of someone who is moved to tears by the touch of a finger on neck hair. You don't have to coarsen what we have."

"True. It's coarse enough as it is."

He pauses. "Is that all you really think this is? A menopausal flight, a last gasp at some fecund lost youth, an attempt to stop time, 'Alas, poor Yorick, *carpe diem*?' "

"How about, I don't know why I am here?"

Adam takes a deep breath and begins to pace the room. "I am, in spite of my highly expensive education..." he spits the words out, "...not the most sophisticated reader of the female soul. Who is it that you want to be with: the Adam of Troy or the Adam of 'fin amour'?"

"Do I have to choose?"

"It would help."

"Help whom?"

"Who knows? Perhaps both of us."

"I'm not sure if the choices are clearly distinguishable."

"And that is my point exactly." He looks triumphant. I run over the reasons why I am with this man and fail to settle on any of them. It seemed clear when I walked out the door and left Michael standing there. But was it clear because reason wasn't involved? That it was merely sensual, the delicious possibility of abandon, the fear of abandoning possibilities, the movement beyond the sensual into the mythic? The risk of riding in a ship away from the labyrinths of a marriage where I had no way out? I don't know. And now there are his kids and this other woman, his wife, threatening to kill herself. What must she be going through now—knowing that it was all a fraud, that all the moments she thought were absolutely hers were always shared with another? His blue eyes looked through her at me. And was it the same with Michael? Had our relationship always been unreal, a youthful phantasm, an expectation that we were meant to be together simply because we *liked* one another? That *liking* was enough?

He is speaking. "One is always reliving the past. Gawain must always carry the mark of his brief infidelity around with him."

"Don't lecture me, Adam."

"I was merely saying..."

"In any event, that exhibition was months ago."

"Months of brief interludes in shabby hotel rooms; months of candlelit dinners and sleepy breakfasts; months filled with emails and furtive phone calls; months of, 'I think about you all the time...' 'I find myself thinking about when...' "

"You said that as well, Adam."

"Oh, I'm not denying that we are equally guilty of a shamefully formulaic courtship. Courtly love is nothing if not formulaic. What I am saying is that neither of us can be pious about this."

"And yet that is what you *are* being. Why are you making me feel guilty about your wife? Or your friend?"

"That was not my intention. I'm sorry if you saw it that way."

"Then what was the intention?"

"To show you how high the stakes are, and how large a gesture this is. To uncover the real Helen."

"There is no real Helen. What about your wife, and your kids? Don't you owe something to them?"

He pauses. I can see I have wounded him. I realize I know nothing about these people, about Adam and whatever unspoken or spoken contract he had with his wife—what she did or did not give and what she did or did not take, and what and how it had broken down. It is as if everyone has no depth, that we are shadows on a screen or figures in a painting, our postures set, our attitudes fixed. I do not want to know anything about them and don't want him to know anything about me. I want what we have to be removed from time and its erosions. A finger traced on a neck.

His voice is cold. "They will be well cared for. I will not abandon them completely." He looks at me. "I do not need to justify myself to her."

"I'm sorry. That was unfair." I walk over to him and take his face in my hands. "But, Adam. There is no real Helen."

"All right, then. To make you see the pattern," he whispers, drawing me closer to him. His eyes are blue. I can feel his shoulders beneath his white shirt. I remember swimming away from him. The broken columns. How his body was, and how my body was. And twenty years at once become meaningful to me, as measurable and solid as the suitcases and shoes by the door. Twenty years of broken columns covered by the gentle opacity of soothing, lukewarm water. I think of Helen. I think of his wife. What does she count now, now that her years, like mine, have collapsed into a mere hiatus, an absence? Can she see the real woman behind the deception?

I look at Adam, and lie.

"There is no pattern."

* * *

"Where would you like to go?"

"Wherever you want."

"But I want to go everywhere."

"Well, then let's go there!"

I have my arms around his neck. "Why don't we open the atlas at any page and go there?"

"We can't do that! What if it's the Sahara Desert?"

"Or Antarctica?"

"Or somewhere in the middle of the sea?" We laugh. He smiles his funny, crooked smile. I like it best when he shows his teeth when he smiles. His face seems so giving then.

"Why don't we use the index to pick a page, and the first thing that sounds sensible..."

"Not sensible, Michael. Anything but sensible."

"All right. Something that is reachable."

"Yes." My voice flattens. "We've got to be able to get there."

It opens on Turkey, and something seems right about it. I don't know why. He looks at me. "What do you think?"

"I think it looks great."

I sit down beside him. We are in the kitchen and it is evening. That I remember. His hair was so long and dark then, and so fine. It would always fall over his face and he would shake it back, not knowing that he did it. He smoothes out the double page of the atlas and starts to trace the places we can go. I look at his hands. They are young hands, with long, fine fingers. I can see the veins through the translucent, soft skin. He is caressing the page, spanning it, encompassing it, lovingly stroking a journey through history for us. I remember how I felt that even then. I remember thinking how beautiful his hands were, how I suddenly felt they were revealing their full beauty to me for the first time. I remember what that feeling was like—how sweet and welcoming it was—and how I wanted to hold his hands and have them touch me. Forever.

The Treachery of the Eye

The eyes are the organs of treachery. They beseech and they stare. They narrow and they weep. They fall shut when they should be open. And, as I discover more and more at night, they do not close when they should.

They say the eyes are the gateway to the soul. They may be correct. But the eyes I have seen are fathomless pits. They say that character is revealed in the eyes. It may be indeed. But I have only seen the shadows of appetites and the rigidity of the mask. They say that one falls in love through the eyes. For some this may be true. But I say love is never revealed through the eyes. But then, nor is love offered through gesture or touch or a kiss—and all of these I have known in my life.

My father visited them upon me when he sold me as a bride of fifteen to the heir to Byzantium. They were bestowed upon me by my husband, your father, who had no interest in me and what I wanted for myself, but except for the nights in the marriage bed looked at me as one would an unwelcome stranger. They were lavished upon me by the eunuchs and the generals who ultimately had no wish to see me rule except as a substitute

135

for you. You, my son, gave me them in your false promises to let me reign alongside you when you came of age. Never once have I known comfort or tenderness from these gestures or touches or kisses. Never once have I known them true.

Yet, after many years, I have become comfortable with the lies of the hands—the open palm of friendship that turns into the fist of defiance, the sensual touch of fingers that becomes the grip around the throat. I have become inured to the lies of the tongue—the soothing words that turn to cries of hate, the expression of hope shaped into an undeserved denunciation. I have myself licked the lies of the lips—the loyal kiss and the irresistible seduction. But I can never be accustomed to the lies of the eyes, for they are the organs of treachery.

In the immediacy of the pain and the unrelieved, baffling darkness in which you will hear this letter, I do not expect you to understand the deepest reasons why I had you imprisoned, beaten, and then blinded. Of course, at more superficial levels, the reasons are obvious and known to you, for you did the same with those you considered threats to the throne. Your imperfection, your unworthiness for kingship, now makes you able to hear without the noise of false adulation the truth about things you never understood, my son, in your childishness: the meaning of loyalty and the horror of treachery.

I say this without anger or bitterness, although you may choose to believe, through the inflections or intonation of your reader, that the case is otherwise. I also say it without pride—for I took no pleasure in doing any of this, even though you may think I did. Instead I speak to you from my own darkness—both figurative and literal. For this letter comes to you from a cell on Lesbos where I, the Empress Eirene, like you am deposed, imprisoned, and awaiting my death.

In truth, I believe your blindness will be a blessing for you, for the world will cease to age in front of you. You may hear familiar voices grow frailer, less certain. The skin of those you love may become rougher and less tender. You may more exquisitely smell and even taste the approach of death. But you will not see your own or your contemporaries' white hair or stooped bodies—nor the sly evil or accumulated failures of life expressed in the eyes. Those whom you knew before you lost your eyes will remain as they were the last time you saw them. Those who are new to you will appear to you only as you wish them to be.

I, on the other hand, have been given a cell with a window that overlooks the sea Aegeus named—weighed down by the lightness that reflects off the waves and the intensity of the blues and whites in comparison with the gray shadows of my prison. Like the ancient king, I await the black sails of my executioners to throw me to my own particular doom, swallowed by the blue indifference of the water. I am sure the waters of the Aegean will cure me of the curse of my blood, just as the waters of Pege did when you were a child and I could not stop my bleeding. Unlike you in your blindness, I can see what is coming. Unlike you, I still scan for signs of hope.

To while away my time in this jail, my captors have allowed me to spin threads of wool in my cell. I am to

be Penelope waiting for her hero to rescue her from her
tormentors; I am a Fate waiting for the other two sisters
to determine my lifespan and apply the cut. I do not
expect the former, and expect the other soon. But I never
harbored any regrets about anything I did, and I am not
about to do so now. Regret and love are weaknesses that
men expect of women. Your blindness, my son, is, I
repeat, a blessing, a condition of innocence as well as
ignorance—paradisal, even, because nothing can betray
you except your own imagination.

In the beginning you will have searched out the
darkness for light. You will have believed that, if you
just studied the black world that surrounds you with
more acuity, more resilience, more patience, perhaps, a
shard of a shape might flicker into view. It is, you will
by now be coming finally to understand, only an illusion. In fact, all sight will have become a memory—a
turning inward to the stored light from before you were
blinded. This was also my intent. For we can spend our
whole lives looking outward, my son—searching horizons, marking the limits of our territories, in quest of
signs and interpreting their meaning, reaching the top
of one range to see another we have to climb. It never
ends, this moving forward, propelled by our desperate,
yearning eyes, always seeing in front of us the possibilities of displacing ourselves in favor of a greater equilibrium elsewhere.

And yet, do we ever see what we are meant to see?
Aegeus himself was deluded—for black was really
white, despair was really hope, and his son was alive—
and it was not he, the father, who needed to search the

seas for a ship, but the abandoned Ariadne, who had lost her boy-king when duty to his father called him away from the woman who had given him everything.

This is why I understand the treachery of the eyes all too well. For they see what they will see. I looked at you and saw you in me, and I loved you, Constantine. I wanted the best for you, thought I could shape my vision of what you could be out of the matter of what you were. Yet you were not what I needed you to be. I had an icon in my mind of what you might be—perfect, virtuous, the contours of your face and your hand raised in blessing, sharply defined and facing foursquare towards me. Everything was proportioned, all was in place, each element of the design encrusted with the heritage and history of the throne of the first Constantine. And you were to be the continuation of that image, the palimpsest of his glory.

Instead, you plotted against me, rearranged every delicate tile of the mosaic I had laid out for your eventual triumph. Even when I struck you and poured hot tears of rage and despair over you, as you—a traitor—kneeled before me, supposedly repentant and remorseful, you did not change. You destroyed the icon. You defiled the image.

All this, however, has now changed. In blindness, you have no need to see beyond—to plot the coordinates, measure the terrain, position or reposition the probabilities for success or failure. Where you are is where you will have to be, because there is no vision of where you could be. All life will, from now on, be a permanent nostalgia, a present in the past—comforting, already experienced, the failure already known, the triumph already tasted.

I foresee—for that is my lot now and no longer yours—that you will be puzzled at my decision. Not because I did not hate you as you me; not because you sought the throne that I had no wish to relinquish; not because I had no time for your foolish irresponsibility, your failure to be a man. All this is known between us and is now unimportant. You will be puzzled—and rightly so, perhaps—that I chose to use blinding to rid me of your threat when together we had loved and worshiped icons. This is the heart of my letter to you, an attempt to explain this, my greatest achievement at Nicaea and to tell you the distinction between the treachery of the eyes and the visualization of God.

Our love of icons is perhaps the only thing we have ever shared. For you, it is a reflex devotion; for me, it is a poison and its cure. Fifteen years ago the iconoclasts were defeated because of me. With the help of your father they were mindlessly destroying everything that was beautiful and true—all that expressed the divine and spoke of what could not be spoken. And I stopped them. At Nicaea I recalled another heresy that had been brought to an end during the reign of another Constantine, and I stopped them. At Nicaea I declared that henceforth there would be no more destruction of the means of reaching God. At Nicaea I achieved more than countless emperors before me had failed to achieve: I listened to God's wishes.

Yet, even there at Nicaea, even then, I was aware of the treachery of the eyes: the devotional always verging

on blasphemy; the depiction always on the cusp of idol-
atry or, worse, caricature; the expectation of reverence
only a step away from a celebration of the art of the fall-
en and not the perfect divine. This is why I understood
why the iconoclasts wanted to destroy the icons and
why I could convince them otherwise.

But treachery is treachery. Even though I am old and
have no use for desire and its satisfaction, the eyes still
search out the curves and welcoming lines of the body.
They are still pleased by the beauty of familiar shapes
and place themselves too readily at the disposal of the
suggestive. They still rest too long upon the sweep of the
shoulder, the tangent of an arm against the hip. They
want to linger where the index finger and thumb arc
around the nape of the neck and brush the tiny hairs
that cluster around the ear. And they are not content.
They seek out perfection where there is none; they
search the faces of those they wish loved them and
whom they love, urging a softening of the frown or a
relenting of the stare. They attempt to gather all the
minute signs that do not speak of indifference through
the lines around the eyes or on the forehead, the contours of the cheeks or the strength of the chin. They
insist on the possibility of connection where there are
only colored tesserae, broken threads, and scattered
brushstrokes. And, when all the other parts of our body
have accepted the mortality and imperfection of our
being human, the eyes—although they may cloud or
dim—never settle for less.

I have come to understand deeply and fully that the
eyes are never more treacherous than when you are a

woman. Even though I came to the throne at a time when your father and the court had endorsed iconoclasm, and banishment awaited those who worshiped icons, I knew that men understood that women were different. We were, and still are, expected to respond to icons because of our predilection for the superficial, the wayward, the fanciful, the artful. We are expected to be deceived by appearances, for through such deceits of art are we ourselves meant to attract men, who can then blame us for their own supposed entrapment.

Yet the men know that we hold the truth. They know that the veils they throw over our bodies, the clothing they give us to adorn ourselves with, the optical illusions of an eye underlined in kohl, or a lid smeared with aquamarine, a lip or a cheek enhanced with copper dust, the scent of musk—all are a function of their fear of what we might reveal. And more: not only do we hold the truth, but, if we are unveiled, if we reveal our nakedness and truth's nakedness before them, they are not able to bear it. They see us for what we are—the bearers and barers of infinity, the virgins and mothers of God, the raw and vulnerable and yet supremely powerful sensuous expression of all that must be contained yet continued, inhered and put forth. They look at us, our full breasts and our open vaginas, our wide hips and tapered waists, all that gives and all that takes, and see how much they need us to break through to the *logos spermatikos*—the creative and procreative force of the universe that is barren without us. Without which they are nothing, inert. Speechless. Blind.

The men know this energy is expressed in the icon, and they are fearful of it. They know that we women understand its power and are not threatened by it, because we know the penury of the artifice when confronted with the rich coloration of the truth. We know that the anarchy of emotion and the mess of the real are too much for men to take, and therefore understand why they must contain it in proportion and balance within the icon. And we hate the icon and we love it. We love it because we know that it is the only place where we can be seen, where the delineations of the female are finally expressed. Yet we hate it because, in the end, icons and women are measured by the same criteria.

When my father brought me to be married I had already been chosen. Old men with long beards and gray faces stood silently and appraised me. My head, they noted, was correctly balanced with my body, my feet were small and my fingers long, my hair was suitably pomaded and of requisite cut. I was, in sum, ready to receive the seed of the king, to be the vessel of continuation. And I later did this for you when I chose your bride—a frail young thing with anxious eyes and the smoothest skin. I regret my determination to make sure that what happened to me should not be unique, for she did not deserve to be chosen by me to be loathed by you. But she was not the first woman hated by a man and she will not be the last. She is merely one more.

I do not expect you to understand any of this—for to my mind you are as superficial as men have for centuries accused women of being. When you had eyes, you always gave yourself over to the glittering surface of life that your blindness will now force you to abandon—a superficiality that only the loss of your eyes could force you beyond. You will thank me for this, for you will no longer be seduced by what *seems*, even though you will also not know what *is*.

* * *

The men have come with news. They tell me you are dead, indeed that you have been dead these many months, withered away. They tell me this now because they thought I would not have been able to handle the grief. "It is not good for a mother to have her son die before her," they say. They do not understand that I died many years before you were even born.

They tell me I am to pack my things—as if there is anything to pack!—for we are to go to Athens. I tell them it is a journey I will never make, and they seem disinclined to tell me otherwise. They ask me to whom I am writing. I tell them no one, because I do not want to be thought insane in communicating with someone who is dead, even though I thought I did not care what anyone thought of me anymore. I have decided to continue the letter, for reasons I cannot quite fathom. I ask myself whether I have a need to confess or justify my life to you. I ask myself whether I feel compelled to apologize. You wished for all of this, and yet, even now, I am not able to give you what you want.

They tell me you died in no pain. That is good.

You must understand: I was not born cruel. I did not want fame. I did not seek power. I did not seek out

empires, or thrones, or gold. None of these things concerned me when my father married me, still a child, to
the Emperor. I did not even know my body then. I had
not even begun to bleed. I had no feelings for men, or
even boys. I was a child, simply a child, in awe of the
power of the throne and the Church and the attention
paid to me. My son, do you not understand that I did
not even *know* myself—what I was capable of? I did not
know the lengths men will go to in order to have their
hands on young flesh. I have not forgotten what my
father did to me and I have not forgotten what your
father did to me. I was sold and bought as chattel, a
mere transaction for the purpose of carrying you. I cannot describe to you my feelings of revulsion on the night
your father took me as a bride.

So I hardened my heart—consciously, deliberately,
absolutely. I resolved that I would never give in, never
show what I knew they wanted me to show. They tested
me: appealed to my better nature, my sensibility as a
wife, as a mother, as the leader of the state, as a human
being. They cajoled and coaxed and intimidated and
pleaded. But I did not relent. I resolved that everyone
would fear me—and you were to fear me the most. I
watched you grow—a sickly, vacillating child, constantly looking for my approval, searching my face for a
glimmer of love, of attention, and then of weakness. I
did not give it to you because I knew two things: the first
that they would make you betray me; the second, that
they would then betray you. I wanted to make you
strong, to train you not to seek the approval of the eyes.
And now you need never worry about that again.

You accused me of being a monster. I heard you call out in the night for me and I did not come. Then you called for your nurses, and they came running, cursing me. When you were grown, you spat in my face and told me of your sexual exploits with unsuitable women and that you would defile the decencies of our church. And I did not budge. I saw you plot against me with my enemies and overthrow me, and then I saw you beg me to come back. And I was immovable. I saw you try for one last time to claim what was, I will admit, rightfully yours by the ridiculous, fearful prerogatives of masculinity. And you could not displace me. All your life you struggled to claim my affection. You begged and wept like a woman before me. You amassed the soldiers against me and plotted with the eunuchs. And you failed.

But, I repeat, I take no joy in that. I merely state the facts. Joy would mean the presence of emotions I exiled long ago. The emotions make you weak, distracted, easily betrayed. Once my father betrayed me I decided I would tolerate no more betrayal. I decided that if I could not expect love or tenderness then I would have everything else—glory, power, wealth. And if I could not expect to be loved, then I would not give any in return. And I never did.

Yet there was one facet of my life where there was no betrayal and where love was given without expectation of return or a demand for power, and that was the love given through icons. I was never in any doubt when I knelt in front of them that I was receiving a different kind of love than the fumbling, physical folly we mortals call love. This love emerges from a body that expresses none of our fevered urges. The palm is open not for ours to take and place on the breast or inside the thigh; but it offers a space in which we might truly live. The eyes stare at us, not to trick or examine, but to inquire whether our life is dedicated to God. But, ultimately, the icon enables me to understand the distance I have created between observer and observed.

This is the meaning for me of God—the space that opens up between my own eyes and the eyes of the icon, between the gesture of my hand and that of the Mother of God. Her hand is paint, mere tincture, ineffable and undemonstrative; my hand is flesh, merely blood-brimmed skin, mortal, decaying, expressive of so many things, none of them ultimate. Yet, in the incarnation of Christ, the distance is bridged between the silent mouth and my lips, between the frozen limbs and the deliquescence of my frail, bleeding body. Christ—of the body but not confined in the body; Christ among us but removed from us. The iconoclasts saw only the human in the interaction. They always returned to their flesh because they could not see the icon as a pathway to the divine but as a mirror. I, however, who knew the betrayal of the flesh, did not stop at the flesh. I went further and I did not go back. I moved beyond the tawdry display and the proportionate delineation. And I will never regret it.

For what I did at Nicaea they will revere me as a saint. I returned the Church to the true faith, restored the incarnation to the disembodied, the flesh to the spirit. They will sing praises to me for my miraculous life, for the inspiration of my vision and the virtue of my life. Yet they will not know the price I had to pay, how much of my own body and blood I lost in the preservation of the soul of our faith. They will not know how unsure we were of success—even as they gaze upon the faces of our Lord, his mother, and the saints staring out at them in questioning benediction. They will not know what I had to do with you—you, my forgotten, hapless, inconstant Constantine, silent companion in prayer and treacherous fruit of my loins.

Yes, you will be forgotten, passed over.

Like a pause in a sentence.

Karagöz and the Sultan

In the time when the old empire of Byzantium was threatened from every side, and the little that remained of its former strength was but Constantinople and its surrounds, when the Seljuk lords and the great sons of Khan were no more and Timur the Lame not yet upon this earth, Sultan Orhan, great warrior and leader of men, noble successor to Osman, commander of the four hundred tents, fighter against the Turkmen for the glory of the Seljuks, himself son of Ertogrul, first of the line of the Kayi tribe of ghazis, upholders of the true faith and leaders of the Holy War, strode in triumph through Anatolia and that part of the country known as Ottoman. With his conquering army, and his dying father's last exhortations for glory deep in his thoughts, Orhan marched into Bursa and made it his capital, bringing under the rule of Dar al-Islam those of the unconverted who wished to be protected. In Bursa he established order and commanded that his progenitors be honored by all. Then, after the passage of seven years, and sufficiently mighty again in arms, his courageous generals at his side and the courage of God in his heart, Orhan marched his army toward the east, where both were welcomed by its citizens into the town of Iznik, ancient capital of the area once called Bithynia, and known to the Romans as Nicaea.

* * *

Now, Allah be praised, *that's* what I call an opening! Tarantara tarantara; lots of snare and kettle, big and brassy; the once strong and decisive hands of wine-soaked generals quivering in lachrymose pride as they polish the richly undeserved medals splashed across their sunken chests; unsoiled lilywhites dabbing a lacy tear off the flushed and downy. Red carpet stuff. But, of course, that's Hajivat's thing: the periphrastic, the Ciceronian. His demeanor, you'll have noticed, is one of delicious disappointment, elegantly Epictetal, with the well-modulated, après déjeuner la-di-dah accent. Always goes down well when the occasion demands a revisionist recollection of heritage and homeland.

But I jump ahead. Let me introduce myself: my name is Karagöz. Unlike Hajivat, I smack more of Aristophanes than Aristotle. I unbutton the bored businessman for his maddening maidservant. I drag the covers off the half-cocked holy man and his slim-buttocked, uninflected scribe. I am the narrative graffitist, verbal tattooist, lubricious laureate for all the tosspots and piss-artistes who ever spilled their effusions on the sweaty bedsheets of literary history. Court jester, all-licensed fool, trickster—I am the unavoidable plunge into the tasteless. I am the vaticinator of the entrails for the disaffected, toaster of the talentless bohemian, arouser of the cowardly rebel, psychopomp for the pervert and the peacock. And I lie, cheat, trump, and in the process compile my incorrigible adjectives, blasphemies, entendres, and bavardisms to punctuate any narrative, including my own, with egregious vulgarities.

Unlike Hajivat—content as he is with the self-effacing if paradoxically self-aggrandizing third-person singular—I begin, as ever, with a particularly polymorphously perverse first-person plural. In short, each show demands that I retell *our* history—how we became the literal shadow of our former selves, confined to the tatty corners of this diminished, ordinary land within the puppet-theater tradition. It is, I might add, a history of betrayal, of opportunities lost, of jokes misunderstood, of truth perverted, and (since this is, after all, a comedy) hope regained.

So, as Hajivat suggested, let us don our Osmanli garb and regress six centuries. Yours truly and Hajivat (even then shameless stereotypes of sodomite and sophisticate) are one of those itinerant doubleacts who are at once beloved by the unwashed and loathed by the bourgeoisie. Our act is unremarkable: I fart and Hajivat wrinkles his solid roman; I get caught on the job with some oily merchant's fat sack of goods and Hajivat excuses my depravity to the appalled authorities with rhetorical flourishes of a carbuncular palm; I ball some fat burgher's illgotten and Hajivat ties the sheets around the knobbed bedpost and we shimmy—wind billowing the white nightgowns around our hairy thighs—to safety and rounds of applause and raki.

You get the idea: bags of corn, scads of suds, ample dimples and pimples, and, for the audience apparently, the seductive surprise of shocked—*shocked!*—satisfaction. And let me tell you, our audience's glee is unrestrained—mouths open in gummy laughter, oily gobbets of tobacco-y phlegm spewing from between tartary ivories. Orhan hears of this and demands an audience of one. Incautiously, uninhibitedly, Hajivat and I do our thing, and soon we're puffing and blowing for him on a regular basis and making the whole court gasp in appreciation and wet their delicate underthingies at the sharp ends of our shtick.

But what is this? Orhan is filled with the remorse of the repressed. The State, he determines, calls for restraint. God, he senses, demands a less disordered tone. The universe, he surmises, requests order. In short, he decides a mosque needs to be built and that Hajivat and I should cease all pratfalls and lay our hands on stone and brick for the glory of God. Needless to say, Hajivat and I have never worked with our hands except to grab a tit, or pinch a bottom, or slip a wad of cash into a sweaty palm. So we do what we do best: pulling the foreman's pisser, ducking swinging planks of wood and walking under unfortunately placed ladders. Orhan hears of it, and before you can utter "Ottoman" we are grabbed by the short and curlies and left shorter by a head.

No sooner are the frayed curtains drawn across the dirty windows of our souls, but Orhan the great, the almighty Sultan who brooks no weakness and dispels all doubt, feels an unfamiliar emotion—the dewy, fluttering pit-a-pat pit-a-pat of remorse. Open-eyed in the early hours, distracted in the act of congress, a palpable pall in the palace. And what else to do, except to build us a pair of tombs in the center of town? And how else to repair the damage except by enlarging our fame, with three-inch headlines proclaiming us the perfect pranksters for this part of the empire? And how else to preserve our posterity except by engendering a shadow-puppet theatrical tradition that is as popular and wickedly licensed as ever we were in life? We become the pressure gauges for the engine of state, as we drive the well-oiled pistons of expansion and contraction through the up and down, in and out of the centuries.

So, here we are. Ready to begin. Except our puppeteer has taken it upon himself to indulge in the water of life to such an extent that until someone knocks him on the head or he sobers up, I can't get lucky, or change sex, or cap a cop, or whatever ribaldry's shadowed for today. So, it'll just have to be Hajivat and his storytelling to keep you ugly bastards happy. Let us, therefore, return to the plot. Orhan's in Nicaea and, as Hajivat would have it, "at the very height of his fortune."

* * *

The Sultan's celebrations were as lavish as long. For five days and nights the festivities continued, with dancers and music following each other in seemingly endless, glittering displays. Just before dawn, when the party had begun to wane, the musicians were conjuring up the pangs of lost love and not the sugar of victory, and the generals and courtiers were reclining dreamily in the soft arms of sweet-smelling concubines, the Sultan arose from the reluctant arms of his favorite and, on leaving his tent, lifted his face to the fresh air and his recently conquered territory. Soon he found himself by the lake, the sun curling its light over the horizon and the early morning mist floating above the waters, which were as still as the mirrors into which the Sultan stared every evening.

The Sultan was appreciating this tranquility when he saw a young woman carrying a large amphora, moving silently towards the water's edge. The Sultan had always trusted in his own eyes, but his confidence in them was tested to the limit by the vision of her. For she was the most beautiful woman he had ever seen and, what's more, as naked as the day she was born. Yet she seemed oblivious to the coolness of the morning air and the intruder's gaze upon her. When she had reached the water, she strode in to her waist—not pausing for a moment to register how cold the water must have been. Then, dipping the amphora into the water, she raised it above her head and poured the contents over her. After doing this three times, she filled the amphora with water and walked toward the land. She emerged, glistening wet and covered only in the fine mist of morning, the amphora filled to the brim. She then strode away, vanishing into the mist. All this without uttering a sound.

The Sultan prided himself on being a man of action, able to make lightning decisions and act on them immediately. However, at the sight of this girl, all his limbs seemed to lose their power and his faculties their precision. He didn't know whether to follow her or remain behind. He wasn't sure if she was real or simply the result of too much celebration. All he could be sure of was that he had never seen anything or anyone so beautiful, and not only did he have to see her again, but he would have to have her as his own.

The Sultan hurried back and called his advisor to him, who appeared with his long-learned silence and swiftness and asked the Sultan if he could be of assistance. The Sultan told him what had occurred, dwelling on the woman's beauty and adding that if he didn't have her before five days were out the advisor would lose his head.

The advisor, who also happened to be the Sultan's distant cousin and went by the name of Suleiman, was not at all perturbed, for he had heard this threat before. The Sultan had had many such women in his life, and all of them had been acquired at the risk of Suleiman's head. In the past, Suleiman had simply approached the women in question and offered them a chance to be in the Sultan's favor or otherwise be beheaded. He had never yet failed, as he reminded himself, rubbing his neck, to secure their agreement to these reasonable requests. He saw no reason why this lady should be any different—although her habits, he admitted, were not such as to inspire confidence in a sane decision.

The next day, therefore, Suleiman rose slightly before dawn and went down to the spot where the Sultan had said he had seen the serving-girl. Sure enough, as the sun was rising above the horizon, she appeared again, carrying an amphora as before and naked as the jay. As the Sultan had said, she strode down to the lakeside and straight into the water, filled the amphora, poured the contents over herself three times, filled the amphora again, and walked back to the lakeside. As she emerged from the water, Suleiman stepped out of the shadows and without a pause told her that the Sultan demanded to see her. The girl turned to him, neither showing fear that he should suddenly emerge from the shadows nor embarrassment at her nakedness.

"Let the Sultan tell me himself," she said. She then turned and walked away. Suleiman wanted to follow her but found his limbs overcome by the same mysterious powerlessness that the Sultan had experienced the day before. Moreover, he was too astonished by the girl's unusual reaction to his order to pursue her. Suleiman then returned to his master's tent, where he found the Sultan waiting impatiently for the details of what had happened.

"Well?" said the Sultan.

"She appeared to me as she did to you, O Sultan," said Suleiman.

"And did you tell her?"

"I did, my lord."

"And what did she say?"

Suleiman paused. "She said she would speak only to you."

"Only to me?!" exploded the Sultan.

"I'm afraid so," said Suleiman, rubbing his neck anxiously.

The Sultan flew into a furious rage. "How dare this paltry serving-girl defy the wishes of a sultan?!" he thundered. The Sultan began, as (Suleiman had noted long ago) he did when his will was thwarted, to devise terrible punishments for the unwitting victim of his rage. In order to recompense his frustration, the Sultan proceeded to list his many possessions and numerous victories, both on the battlefield and in the bedroom. Finally, and somewhat soothed by his recollection of past and present glories, the Sultan summarily dismissed the serving-girl as someone not worth the glory of his consideration. Yet, as the darkness closed in upon his encamped army, Orhan found himself unable to sleep. For, as he closed his eyes, this beautiful and naked girl walked across his mind—her soft, olive flesh inviting his caresses, her hair urging him to bury his face within the jasmine-scented strands. At the very point of the first bird's call for dawn to begin, Orhan called for his advisor and told him that he had decided to speak to the girl himself. Yet, he acknowledged, he had no idea what to say.

"Make it plain you are the most desirable man in the world," said Suleiman.

"This is self-evident, you fool. I am the Sultan."

"True, O Sultan," replied Suleiman, cursing himself for the misstep. "But you must make her aware of how honored and privileged she would be to be in your favor," he continued, pleased at how swiftly he had gathered himself together. "And how rich," he added for good measure.

"Rich?" asked the Sultan, baffled by his advisor's swiftness of thought.

"Rich," affirmed Suleiman. "Women cannot resist the thought of being wealthy. Promise her everything you have. Then, once you have her in your grasp, deny her everything she asks for. In this way you may gain your prize, exert your authority over her, and punish her for being so haughty in the winning."

"This is the correct plan," exclaimed the Sultan. "I shall do it."

Sure enough, at the lake the same curious sequence occurred. The naked woman appeared with the amphora, washed, and filled her amphora again. The Sultan, crouching behind a bush with less dignity than he was entirely comfortable with, was startled again by just how beautiful and unashamed she was. As she emerged from the water, the Sultan stepped forward, and, walking boldly up to her, stood in front of her, his great hands resting on his hips in as imposing a fashion as he could muster.

"Stop!" he bellowed. "I am the Sultan."

"I know," replied the woman calmly, looking up at him. The Sultan then found himself staring into a pair of the blackest eyes he had ever seen: blacker than the blackest night and deeper than the deepest lake. "What do you want?" she said.

"My servant didn't tell you what I wanted?"

"He did. But I want to hear *you* tell me what you want."

"I...I," stammered the Sultan, again lost in the bottomless wells of her pupils. He then recollected both who he was and what Suleiman had told him. "I wish to have you as my own."

"And do you think this is what I wish?" responded the girl immediately.

"What do you mean?" said the Sultan, with a mixture of rage and bafflement.

"I mean what I say. Have you considered what I may want?"

"It doesn't matter what you want. You are only a serving-girl. I am the Sultan. I am the lord of this entire region. I am the son of Osman, and our family will one day rule the world. If you become my wife, you will be honored beyond measure and wealthy beyond your wildest dreams. And, should you be lucky enough to bear me a son, you will be the most powerful woman in the land, with servants at your command and princes paying court."

"And if I refuse?"

"If you are foolish enough to refuse, I will have you executed forthwith, and your body will be thrown out for the wild dogs to eat."

"I see," said the girl, without emotion. "How long do I have before I must decide?"

"How long?" stormed the Sultan, who had never had to converse this much with any woman he had ever courted, let alone a mere serving-girl. He glared down at her, but was met only by her velvet eyes. Almost against his wishes he found himself weakening. "Three days."

"Very well," answered the serving-girl. "In three days I shall give you what you truly desire. But on one condition."

"How dare you talk to me of conditions," shouted the Sultan. "You wretched woman, consider that I could have you killed on the spot." Even for a man of sudden irascibility, the Sultan had never been so out of temper.

But still the girl remained as calm and as still as the lake from which she had just emerged.

"But you won't, will you?" she said, looking up at him, half in scorn and half, it might have been heard, in despair. The Sultan could not sustain his fury.

"What are these 'conditions,' then?"

"There is only one, Sultan. Every morning at this hour I come down to the lakeside to fill my amphora with water. You must meet me here at dawn for the next three days. Each day I shall tell you a story, and you must listen and not say one word until I have finished. At the end of each story I shall ask you the same question. If you listen well, the answer will be easy. If you do not, the answer will be very hard. If you answer correctly, then I shall give you what you truly desire. If you do not, then I shall die at your hands. That is my only condition."

The Sultan, who had not been used to conditions, either in war or love, was thoroughly confused by what the girl had requested, too confused even to be angry. However, before he could reply, the girl had vanished, leaving not even a trace of her presence. The grass, now shining with the sun-reflected dew, seemed untouched where she must have walked, and the lake was without a ripple. The Sultan then hurried back to his advisor to ask Suleiman what all of this meant.

"Ah," murmured Suleiman sagely. "I see."

"What do you see?" asked the Sultan impatiently.

"Very interesting," said his advisor again, as ignorant of what to do as the Sultan. "Very interesting indeed."

"What's interesting, in the name of God? Stop fooling around and tell me what you think, or I shall have you executed."

Suleiman knew that he had bought all the time he was able to afford.

"She is a very clever woman, this serving-girl."

"Is she?" The Sultan did not think this. He considered it stupidity of unprecedented proportions to deny him in favor of decapitation and wild dogs.

"Indeed she is, O Sultan."

"Perhaps you would grace me with a reason why she is clever, you fool."

"Well, my lord," gulped Suleiman. "Did you in any way make clear the exact nature of the wealth she would get when she became your wife?"

"No. I promised her greater riches than she could imagine. Isn't that enough?"

"No, my lord," said Suleiman, summoning up as much gravity as he could. "Such women are used to dire poverty. They will not believe vague promises about wealth. They must have details and exact assurances."

"Is she so stupid," shouted the Sultan, "that she denies the word of the Sultan?"

"Not denies, my Sultan. Merely does not believe."

Orhan, who didn't see what the difference was between the two, let it pass. "Well, I shall go out tomorrow and tell her exactly what she can expect. And more, I shall take some of what I own as well."

"An extremely wise course, if I may say so, O Sultan." Suleiman, convinced that appealing to the girl's vanity—which he knew was something all women possessed—would work, was pleased with the turn of events, especially since he had not suggested the idea and therefore might be able to escape the blame if it didn't work.

The next morning the Sultan rose early and went to the lake and, as always, the girl arrived with her amphora and carried out her routine. The Sultan emerged from the bushes at the appointed time and walked toward her, emboldened by his confidence in winning her over.

She stood in front of him, dauntingly beautiful and naked. The Sultan then proceeded to lay out on the dewy ground the finest assortment of plunder he could possibly have mustered. There was gold and ivory from the sultanate of Muhammad ibn Tughlaq in far-off India. He produced silk from the Empire of the Great Khan and huge carbuncles of green and red from Mogok. He displayed for her great furs from the Kara-Khitai, ermine and sable from beyond Kazakhstan, and threw onto these furs piles of the most precious stones—topaz and amethyst from the Khanate of the Golden Horde, jasper and onyx from the deserts to the south. He then drew from his pockets delicate vials filled with exotic sweetmeats and studded with diamonds, slim-necked vases hewn from marble looted from the palaces of ruined kings from Samarkand to Karakorum, and fruits and flowers soft and lush on the tongue and the cheek. As he displayed to the girl these unparalleled riches, the Sultan sprinkled from translucent dishes, each with his intricate cipher inscribed in gold within, perfumes of indescribable aroma from Turkestan and Persia; he scattered exquisitely wrought bracelets created lovingly by craftsmen from Kashmir and Ladakh; and presented cloths of miraculous design from Kwangtung and Fukien. These, and more, he promised would be hers if she would agree to be his.

The woman looked at this wealth and then up at the Sultan, with eyes on fire.

"Did you not listen to what I said?" she said. "I asked you to listen to my stories and answer my question, and not interrupt me in any way. How dare you insult me with these things?"

The Sultan went bright red with a mixture of shame and rage; but as he looked at her he realized how much he did not want to lose her. He swallowed his anger and apologized, as meekly as he was able.

"You must listen to my stories," she continued. "Never again offer me anything. Do not appeal to what you believe I want. Listen carefully, and then you will be able to answer my question."

The Sultan was lost for words at the girl's boldness. His anger diffused in the wan morning sunlight. Without more ado, he sat on one of his precious rugs while the girl sat on the ground, her amphora by her side, and began.

There was once and there was not, in no place and no time, a sheikh of enormous wealth, whose followers numbered a thousand and whose camels were the most numerous in the region. He was renowned for his hospitality, and no sheikh, no matter how wealthy or well-meaning, could outdo him in his generosity to strangers.

One day, a caliph, returning with his victorious army from a far-off war, passed through the region where the sheikh was encamped. The caliph had heard of the sheikh's generosity and decided to test it. He told the guards who he was and they escorted him to the sheikh's tent. The sheikh welcomed the caliph as his own brother, and bade him sit down and tell him his story.

"No," said the caliph. "This I cannot do. My men are hungry and I cannot allow them to go without food for a few hours of idle talk. Can you tell us the nearest place where we can find sustenance?"

"Of course I can," exclaimed the sheikh. "You and your army shall eat here."

"That is impossible, O sheikh," answered the caliph. "My army numbers many thousands."

"If they numbered a hundred thousand, O caliph, I should still feed them," replied the sheikh.

The caliph agreed to the sheikh's offer, still unable to believe that there could be enough food. He went back to his army, and the sheikh commanded his men to arrange the feast. It was the greatest banquet the world had ever known. As the caliph had been promised, there was enough food to feed ten times the number, so each man could more than eat to the full. The caliph was astounded and asked the sheikh how he could possibly have so much food.

"God is good," the sheikh answered. "He always provides when you are most needy."

The caliph thanked the sheikh. The next morning when all had rested from their feast, the caliph came to the sheikh to bid him farewell.

"*You are indeed the most generous man in the world,*" *said the caliph.* "*What can I do that can possibly repay you for your kindness?*"

"*Give me the hand of your youngest daughter in marriage,*" *said the sheikh without hesitation.* "*That I consider is just payment.*"

Now the caliph's youngest daughter was his most treasured possession. She was the most beautiful girl in the whole region, and many a prince had been her suitor. But the caliph, because he was an honorable man, agreed with sorrow in his heart to the sheikh's request, for he loved his daughter very much.

"*I shall send her to you with a special gift. She will arrive before the moon begins to wane.*"

With that, the caliph and his army marched away until they were nothing but a cloud of dust on the horizon. As the caliph had promised, within the changing of the moon, his youngest daughter arrived, dressed in a simple white gown. Wrapped within her long jet-black hair was a feather, and tied to the feather was a message from the caliph. And this is what the message said:

> This princess who is born so true
> Comes penniless to marry you.
> This princess who is born so fair
> Has but one feather in her hair.
> If you wish to keep your gold
> Listen to what you are told;
> Keep the feather in her hair;
> Never let it stray from there.
> If you do not do these things,

> *All your friends and diamond rings*
> *Will vanish before you are old.*
> *Listen to what you are told.*

Yet so overwhelmed was the sheikh by the beauty of
the girl that he did not read the caliph's message and
ordered the wedding ceremony to begin without delay.
As for the feather, it was thrown to the ground, along
with the paper on which the caliph had written his message, when the sheikh took his new wife in his arms that
night. As he did so, a breeze wafted the feather and the
paper out of the tent. Then, a few hours later, as the
sheikh and the girl slept, a sandstorm parted message
and feather and carried both far away.

Time passed, and in due course the princess gave
birth to a daughter. The sheikh loved this daughter more
than anything in the world. He praised God for his
bounty and the many blessings given to him by the
Merciful One. But fate is never secure, and things began
to go badly for the sheikh. A terrible disease killed many
of his camels, and his wealth began to wane. The sheikh
cursed fate for his misfortune, but, because of his reputation, continued to spend more than he owned. As
times became harder, so he neglected his duties within
the tribe and among his followers; he spent his money
recklessly and soon had neither money nor retainers,
both having withered like flowers in the unwatered
desert.

One day, the caliph and his army passed by, this time
marching to a far-distant war, and the caliph decided to
visit the sheikh and his youngest daughter. When he

arrived where the sheikh had previously been, how different was the sight greeting him! Where there had been a thousand tents there were now but two; where there had been three thousand camels, there was but one emaciated beast; where there had been the joyous sounds of festivity and welcome, there was a terrible silence broken only by the wailing of the caliph's daughter and his granddaughter.

The caliph entered the sheikh's tent and demanded to know what had happened. The sheikh told him about his misfortune, how he loved his wife and daughter but had no money to keep them in the glory they deserved, and how he had neglected the duties befitting his position as a sheikh. The caliph was furious with the sheikh and commanded him to return his daughter and granddaughter so they might go back to the splendor of courtly living. The sheikh wept and pleaded with the caliph to be allowed at least to keep his daughter. Finally, the caliph relented and agreed. Grabbing his own daughter, he took her away with him, never to be heard from again.

The sheikh was utterly bereft by this and began to blame his daughter for everything that had happened; for, he said, if he hadn't had to impress her with his wealth and maintain her in luxury, he would not now be impoverished. Soon his deep love for her turned into an equally deep hate, and as he had lavished presents on her when he had been wealthy, so he threw upon her all the contempt and despair he now possessed in such abundance. He cut off her hair and spat in her beautiful face. He locked her in a cage and fed her scraps of food that even he, in his wretchedness, could not bear to eat. All this time, his daughter said nothing, but cried great tears as she witnessed the terrible state to which her father had declined. One day, the sheikh could bear the sight of his daughter no more. Leaving her barely enough food for a day, he left his tent and walked into the desert to die. His daughter pleaded with him not to go, but he was deaf to her protestations. Not looking back, he stumbled away until his daughter could see him no longer.

Then how truly alone and afraid did the girl feel! She cried and cried for what had come to pass and prayed earnestly for someone to release her. In spite of everything that happens in this world, God is good and everything works out for the best. As the girl was about to give up hope, there by chance rode by a young man who noticed this solitary girl weeping in a cage. He drew in his reins and brought his horse to a standstill. He asked the girl how she had come to be in the cage, and she told him her story. Cursing the sheikh beyond measure, the young man released her, noticing how beautiful she was in spite of her hunger and her sadness. He lifted her up onto his horse and they sped away faster than the wind.

"Where are you taking me?" whispered the sheikh's daughter weakly.

"To a magical place," said the young man, telling her not to worry.

For ten days and ten nights they traveled, the horse's hooves barely touching the ground, so fast did it run. During the journey, the young man fed the sheikh's daughter and cared for her. Her spirits began to revive.

Eventually they reached a huge cave. The young man dismounted and took the girl into the cave with him.

"This is my underground palace," said the young man. "Here we will be alone."

The cave was very dark and the girl was afraid. And well she might have been, for when they emerged into a hall filled with lighted candles, the young man who had rescued her had turned into a monstrous ghoul; warts covered his face, and his huge, hairy arms scraped the ground.

"Get into this cage," growled the ghoul. "You shall be my partner before the day is out."

What choice had the girl? She got into the cage and began to cry, lamenting what had come to pass. But one cannot cry forever, and eventually, when the tears had dried, she began to look around the cave. In the dim light, she could just discern treasures which, she thought, must have been pillaged from places near and far or stolen from strangers accosted on the road. At the edge of these spoils she saw a brightly colored feather. The cage was in the center of the room, and she discovered that by stretching out her hand she could just reach the feather. She drew the feather into the cage and marveled at its array of colors and exquisite plumage. But what use was a feather to her now, when she was to be in a ghoul's bed before the sun had set?

She began to cry and shouted out, "Oh, that I was free!"

At this, the feather suddenly flung itself out of her grasp. Before she could reach it again, it burst into flame and in a puff of smoke disappeared. The girl was too

*shocked to cry out, for in its place was a brilliantly col-
ored bird, with brighter feathers than she had ever
known on any creature.*

*"What is your command?" asked the bird. The girl
was so stunned by what had happened that all she could
ask was what the bird was doing there.*

*"You said the words spoken to me by your mother,"
said the bird. "Many years ago, your grandfather gave
one of my feathers as a dowry from your mother to your
father, with the warning that it was never to be taken
from your mother's hair. On his wedding night your
father ignored this, and threw the feather away. A sandstorm carried it many miles until it was picked up by the
very scavenging ghoul who threatens to marry you. I am
a phoenix: when a woman asks to be free, I am born of
the feather. This was the gift your father refused when he
threw me away."*

*The girl asked the phoenix to release her. The
phoenix flew off and, finding the monster asleep, quietly stole his keys with his beak. The bird then opened the
cage, let the girl out, and guided her to the entrance of
the cave. But the girl did not know which way to turn.*

"But where shall I go from here?" she said.

*"That is your decision," said the phoenix, dropping
another feather into the girl's hand. "But remember this:
trust in God always, and if you find yourself in need,
call out for me holding one of my feathers and I shall be
there."*

*"But what about the ghoul? What if he follows
me?"*

"It is now near dusk," said the phoenix. "He will

sleep until midnight. He is unable to ride his horse unless he is a young man; and when he is a young man, he does not intend to harm you. It is only in his cave that he becomes a ghoul."

Having comforted the girl, the phoenix disappeared. The girl decided to walk to the nearest town. Days became weeks and weeks became months as she walked until her reserves of strength were nearly at an end.

Finally, she saw a town and, stumbling into an inn, asked for some food. Because she seemed in such a sorry state, the landlord took pity on her and gave her what she desired and allowed her to have a room for the night. After a meal and some sleep the girl felt much better, and, thanking the landlord for his hospitality, she stepped outside the inn, still wondering with some trepidation where she would go next. Huddled against the wall on the other side of the road she saw a beggar, dressed in filth and rags, which covered his emaciated bones and face. She took pity on the beggar and approached him.

"I have no money, my friend," she said gently. "But like you I am lost, and perhaps we might help each other find comfort and security."

The beggar lifted his head, and, in spite of the dirt on the man's face, the girl at once recognized her father.

All her father's cruelties were forgotten by his daughter in the moment of joy at seeing him again. They embraced and wept, and he told her how he had wandered for days in the desert, seeking only death for his misfortune and the unhappiness he had caused her. But God had not allowed him to die, and he had survived to arrive in this town where he, the man known through-

out the world as the most generous of sheikhs, had been forced to beg and be treated as less than a worm for so many months. His daughter told him what had happened to her, and he wept again for his thoughtlessness toward her and her mother.

After she had finished her story, the girl called out for the phoenix, and, as it had promised, the bird appeared. The girl asked it to build a little house on the edge of the town for herself and her father, which it did in the twinkling of an eye. The two lived in joyful happiness all their lives, the man caring for his daughter and she looking after him. They never told anybody of their past, or ever thought of returning to the caliph who had so cruelly taken the sheikh's wife.

She kept the feather at her side
Until she and her father died.

When she had finished, the girl turned her great black eyes to the Sultan and asked him the question she had threatened to ask at the beginning, the question the Sultan had been dreading as he had attempted with difficulty to follow this story that seemed to have more fathers and feathers than he had thought possible.

"What is it that I want?" asked the girl.

It wasn't the money, thought the Sultan, nor could it be the power he'd offered her. He wished his advisor was there to help him, since he was unused to thinking for himself. What could she possibly want that he hadn't already offered her? It came to him in a blinding flash of light.

"You want me to find your father?"

The girl said nothing, picked up her amphora, and vanished.

The Sultan felt humiliated, and as shortly as ever was boiling with fury. He stormed back to the town, summoned Suleiman his advisor and, after a jumbled rendition of the story, full of expletives and cries of anguish, asked him what he would have said.

"Ah," said Suleiman. "Very interesting."

The Sultan was not impressed. "There's nothing interesting at all, confound you. Tell me what you would have said."

Suleiman knew that it was a question of the truth or pleasing the Sultan's vanity. He chose the latter.

"I would have said exactly what you said, O Sultan."

The Sultan snorted in exasperation, but also, Suleiman detected with relief, with a certain pleasure, thus vindicating his own and his advisor's decision.

"Well, I will go again tomorrow," said the Sultan emphatically, "and tell this girl that you, the cleverest man in the empire apart from me, thought the same."

"I would not advise that, if I were you," said Suleiman equally emphatically. "That would, if you don't mind my saying so, be playing into her hands. It would also, if you pardon the liberty, be verging on petulance. And that is not a noble trait in a sultan, as I think you would agree."

"Very well," replied the Sultan. "What would you suggest?"

"I suggest being your usual noble self. Be kind to her.

Show her how high, how great you are in comparison to her. She will be impressed by your bearing if nothing else. Wear your most magnificent clothes; deck yourself in the regalia due to a sultan. This cannot fail to move her."

The Sultan was, as you might imagine, delighted by the advisor's counsel, as he considered himself particularly splendid in uniform, and the thought of this impudent girl, on seeing him in full dress, his huge masculine chest barely contained within the rich and astounding costume, falling upon her knees and pleading for mercy, was very pleasing to him, and allowed him to pass the night in untroubled rest.

The next morning the Sultan rose especially early and for a full hour adorned himself with his most magnificent finery, replete with winking jewels and glinting scimitar, polished helmet and sparkling breastplate. He went down to the lakeside, where, as on all other days, the girl appeared as naked as the dawn itself, with the same amphora. As she emerged from the lake, the Sultan strode up to her, his battledress glowing in the early morning sun.

The girl, seemingly unmoved by the radiant light reflected from the metal, turned her eyes as large as moons on him, more in pity than in anger. "Why do you try to impress me," she said, "when I come to you as naked as when I was born? All your gifts and trappings mean nothing to me. All I ask, and have ever asked, is that you listen to my stories and answer my one question. You can come with the full might of your army, but I will not be content until you have answered the question."

The Sultan was thunderstruck, and ran through his limited gamut of emotions before settling uncomfortably on the ground. The girl also sat and, with no thought for the coolness of the dawn, began her next tale.

There was and there was not, in no place and no time, a king. He was a great warrior and a just ruler, and his people loved him. One day he took the daughter of a neighboring king as his wife, a match that made him the most powerful and, after a few years, the happiest man in the region. His wife was beautiful and kind, and tended his wounds after battle and bore him six children, all boys and handsome in their turn, each with his own special skill.

The first child was a warrior, who grew up strong and sturdy and the very image of his father. The second was a great poet who dazzled and delighted the court with the brilliance of his words and the refinement of his wit. The third son was a magical musician who played such sounds as charmed all who listened to them. Every time his father came home from battle, his son would soothe his anger with sweet music. The fourth child possessed the ability to create tapestries of great design and sublime beauty, which depicted the triumphs of his father interwoven with colors that recalled the beauty of his mother. The fifth child was learned and thoughtful. Soon he became his father's counselor, reining in his father's impetuosity with his considered knowledge. He was renowned for his wisdom, and princes from far and wide paid just homage to his sagacity, so far beyond his years. Through his maintenance of the household and finances, the king became the richest man in the whole continent. The sixth child was a healer, and through the power of his touch cured many of the sick who came to the land from far and wide to seek relief from their ailments.

The king and his wife felt themselves blessed in their sons, and praised God for his beneficence. Then, one day when all of her six sons were fully grown, the king's wife gave birth to another child. The king was delighted at this, and wondered what special gifts the child would possess. He marched into the room where his wife lay resting and demanded to see his son.

"You do not have a son," said his wife.

"What do you mean?" asked the king angrily.

"You have a daughter," she replied.

The king was beside himself with anger and stormed out of the room. He retired to a far part of the palace and vowed never to speak to his wife again. Shortly afterwards, he announced he was going on a long march to wage war against a distant enemy. Taking his army and all his sons with him, he departed the next day, never to return.

The king's wife was distraught at the loss of her husband and sons, and commanded her handmaidens to take her daughter to the highest tower of the palace and from the uppermost turret throw the sleeping child onto the stone battlements below. The handmaidens did as the king's wife ordered. They bundled the child up and took her to the highest tower in the palace. As they were about to throw the child off the balcony, she woke and opened her mouth as if to scream. But, instead of a baby's cry, out of her mouth poured flowers of every description: auriculas and roses, daffodils and clematis, delphiniums and artemisia, of a multitude of colors and smelling more sweetly than the most aromatic perfumes. The flowers floated gently to the battlements below, forming a bed of soft petals where the child would have died. The handmaidens were so amazed at this that they could not bring themselves to kill the infant. They decided to keep her secretly beneath the turret, in a room where no one ever went.

For sixteen years the handmaidens kept their secret. They fed the girl each day and she grew up in their care, wholly ignorant of the world beyond her room. All this while the king's wife mourned the loss of her husband and sons, and cursed the day she had given birth to her daughter. She began to sicken and pine. She took to her bed and would not move.

She did, however, notice that her bedroom was always filled with flowers of the most beautiful kind— jasmine and forget-me-nots, orchids and lilies, chrysanthemums and honeysuckle, irises and asters—and that her room smelled, even in the depths of winter, as though all of nature was budding there. She asked her handmaidens how it was possible for her to have flowers all the year round, and of such variety and aroma. They said nothing but that God had provided them.

Soon the king's wife lived only for the flowers that arrived each day to ornament her otherwise dark and desolate bedchamber. The flowers seemed to become more beautiful and more various as time went on. Colors she did not think possible, from flowers she had *never seen and had not thought existed, filled the chamber from wall to wall. Her handmaidens walked over petals that fashioned a tapestry lovelier than any her son had made—petals of ocher, indigo, crimson, and peach, of mauve, azure, and aquamarine. Where did they come from? Why, they came from her unknown daughter, who, every time she opened her mouth, produced not one sound, but a cascade of opalescent blooms.*

One day, the girl was looking from her tower through the thin aperture that was her only view of the outside world, when she saw a horseman appearing over the horizon. Nobody had passed that way for many years, and she watched astonished as the horseman came closer. As he did so, her eyes beheld a handsome soldier, dressed in the livery of a prince, and on a proud white steed. She called out to him. But out of her mouth came only a single rose, which floated slowly down through the air and landed on the ground just in front of the gates to the castle as the young man drew up. The young man, who was indeed a prince, wondered what this could possibly mean. He stepped back from the gate and looked up at the battlements, but saw no one, for the girl had drawn back into the room, blushing at her audacity.

The king's wife, desperate for news of her husband, commanded the young man to come to her chamber and asked him if he knew of the king. The young man did indeed know of him and reported that he was an emissary from her husband's captor. He himself had been a member of the king's army but had been captured after they had lost a great battle. For sixteen years her husband's army had fought the army of his eventual captor.

As *much as they won on one day they lost on the next,
and it was only the exhaustion of the king's soldiers after
so much fighting that had led to their surrender. So her
husband and her six sons had all been captured, and he
had been sent to gain a ransom.*

"What *proof do I have that my husband and sons
are being held by this tyrant?" said the king's wife.*

"Wife *to that brave man," said the young man,
beginning to weep. "The things I must give you as proof
are terrible in the extreme. Do not force me to show you
them."*

But *the king's wife was adamant. So, trembling in
horror and fear, the young man drew from his bag the
following: "This is the right arm of your eldest son," he
said. "No longer will he be able to defend his honor and
the honor of his father and forefathers in battle. This is
the tongue of your second son. No longer will he be able
to dazzle all mankind with the beauty of his language.
These are the fingers of your third son. No longer will
he bring you delight with his playing of the lute and the
harp. These are the eyes of your fourth son. He too will
no longer weave beautiful tapestries of exquisite design.
These are the ears of your fifth son, whose wisdom will
now be unpraised and whose counsel will be lost. And
these are the hands of your sixth son, who will no longer
be able to heal the sick as he did in the past."*

The *king's wife cried out aloud and wept and tore
her hair. "And what of my husband?" she said at last.*

"That *is the most terrible object of all. I bring you
the head of your husband. If you do not submit the most
precious thing you own within six days, then in six more*

days all your sons will likewise be dead. This is the message I am forced to bring. I do so with great sorrow, for your husband was brave, and went to death like the great king he was."

The king's wife was overcome with sorrow and rage as she beheld the severed head of her husband. Furiously, she dismissed the young man from her presence, commanding him never to approach her again, for he had brought her wretched luck in coming there that day. The young man sadly went to where his horse was being kept for him, thanked the stable boys for feeding his charger, and, with his head downcast, left the castle.

As she saw the young man riding away from her castle, the king's daughter began to cry out after him from the tower. This time streams of roses poured from her mouth, so that the young man found himself riding through a multicolored rain of ravishing flowers with intoxicating smells. Astonished, he turned to see a rainbow of color and perfume behind him, and its source a thin cleft at the top of the highest tower in the castle. Not for a moment fearing the wrath of the king's wife, so transfixed was he by the vision of this arc of flowers, he turned his horse back to the castle to seek an explanation.

The king's wife meanwhile climbed out of her bed and began to pace about her room, forgetting her illness in her desperation to find something of value in a castle stripped bare of ornamentation when her husband and sons had set off for battle. She went down to the throne room, seeing once again the great halls where so many years ago she had been part of the most glittering court *the world had ever known. She wept more tears both in memory of the past and in sorrow for the future. She summoned all her servants and commanded them to bring her everything in the castle so she could decide what was of greatest worth. Her servants went off in different directions to search out all that could possibly be of value.*

The handmaidens of the king's wife, who were still the only ones to know the source of all the flowers, were at a loss as to what to do. One of them advised that they should not tell the king's wife about the girl because she would be angry with them and have them all executed. Another thought they should keep the girl's presence a secret because one day her magic might prove useful to them. And the third said they should not reveal the existence of the girl because her producing the flowers had made their lives easy and would continue to do so. So they all resolved to keep quiet and brought to the hall only the items they found scattered within the empty palace.

After a brief but desultory search, the servants of the king's wife had gathered all she possessed in the whole world. A sorry sight it was indeed. All that she had was piled in a small mound in front of her. There were a few battered pots and burned pans, bronze jewelry that had lost any sheen it had once had, and some worn carpets that had frayed through many years of neglect. When she saw how little was hers to give, the king's wife wept again at the poverty of her ransom. At that moment, the young man burst into the throne room, pushing the guards aside.

"*Wife of our leader, I must speak with you.*"

The king's wife woke from the daze of her sorrow.

"*How dare you have the effrontery to return so soon after I warned you never to appear in front of my eyes again!*" she stormed. "*I give you one last warning to go or face my anger.*"

"*But you have in your castle something beyond price,*" protested the young man.

The king's wife laughed through her tears. "*All I have is here, you young fool. How can I possibly pay the ransom?*"

"*All you have to do is look in your tallest tower. There you will find all that you need,*" said the young man.

"*There is nothing in that tower,*" answered the king's wife with the greatest contempt. "*Guards! Take him away and put him for his impudence in the deepest dungeon.*"

So the guards took him away and threw him into a dungeon where no light shone and no roses ever fell.

The king's wife, however, looked at her miserable hoard on the floor and began to lament her fortune again. She tore her clothes and threw herself on the cold, stone floor, not caring for her dignity now that all hope had gone. Soon, however, she began to reflect on what the young man had said. Was there indeed something in her tower? How had he known? Curious to know the answer, the king's wife commanded her guards to go and fetch whatever was in the tower and bring it to her. The guards did so, and brought the frightened young girl into her presence.

The girl had never been told about her mother. All the handmaidens had related was that she was the daughter of a queen and king who had abandoned her a long time ago and in a country far away. The girl had thus mourned a queen who did not exist, and knew nothing of her mother who lived so near to her. How cruel indeed is Fate that it should play tricks on our minds, so that what is farthest away seems most desirable even when it does not exist, and that which we truly need the most is closest at hand! Man is indeed blind to his true desires!

The girl stood before the king's wife in awe at her severe brow and in pity for the red rims around her eyes.

"What is your name, child?"

The young girl tried to speak, but out of her mouth came nothing but the blooms with which the king's wife had been surrounded for sixteen years. These blooms were, if imaginable, more sweet-smelling than anything the king's wife had smelled before, and she found her heart blossoming in response to the half-remembered fragrance of the past. The king's wife ordered the guards to bring her handmaidens to her, and the three trembling women found themselves in front of her.

"So this is where you get the flowers," said the king's wife sternly.

"Yes indeed, O spouse of the mighty one. It is surely a wonder of God, is it not?"

"Undoubtedly," she said uncertainly. "Who is this girl? Where does she come from?"

Then the three women began to cry and blame each other, all shouting and pointing at the same time. The king's wife commanded them to be silent and asked the eldest of them to tell her the story. Then, unable to hold back the truth and her tears, the woman sobbingly told her that the young woman standing in front of her was in fact her daughter, whom they had been commanded to kill all those years ago but had found that every time the girl tried to speak, flowers of great beauty and aroma replaced words. Both fearful of killing something so clearly miraculous and full of hope that they might use the child to advantage, they had kept her locked up and had brought the flowers to give solace to the king's wife in her sorrow.

The king's wife was astonished at the story. Confusion reigned in her soul, for she did not know whether to be grateful to the women for not destroying her child or angry that they had disobeyed her orders. Furthermore, she was unsure if she was happy now that she knew her daughter was alive or sad because she had brought so much suffering upon the girl. So greatly did guilt and happiness, anger and fear rage through her body that, as she was embracing her daughter, she collapsed in a dead stupor. Try as they might, neither the handmaidens nor the servants, nor the flowers of her daughter, could wake her from her swoon. Finally, the handmaidens decided that the young prince, who seemed to them to have been told by God of the presence of the king's daughter in the tower, should be released to give advice. So he arrived shortly in the bedchamber of the king's wife, to where she had been taken, and saw with sorrow and joy the woman sleeping on the bed and her daughter sitting quietly beside it.

When he was told of what had happened, the young
man understood what should be done. He warned the
handmaidens that only the touch of each of her six sons
would wake their mistress, and that unless someone
decided that day what in the castle was most valuable,
she would never see her sons again. He then turned to
the king's daughter and, looking deep into her eyes,
spoke thus:

"You are the most precious thing your mother has.
Only you can save her by bringing back her sons. Do
you consent to be the ransom?"

She looked at the young prince and nodded. As she
opened her mouth to say she would go, another single
red rose fell onto the sheets, a rose redder than blood
and with a perfume that filled the room. And then soft
tears rolled down her cheeks and onto the rose, so that
it glistened in the darkness of the bedchamber.

"Very well," said the young man. "You must come
with me."

The young girl obediently got up and followed the
young man back to his horse.

"Hold on tight," said the prince, "for this horse
travels faster than the wind."

The king's daughter did as she was told, and the
young man spurred on his steed. Before she knew where
she was, she saw her father's castle as only a spot in the
distance, and before the day was spent, the great
fortress of her father's and brothers' captor rose up in
front of her.

The young man rode straight up to the castle door
and knocked three times. The door was opened by a

huge ghoul, the like of which the young girl had, of course, never seen, and she fainted. She woke to find herself alone on the floor in front of this ghoul, so ugly she could scarcely look at him without shuddering. The ghoul surveyed the young woman lying on the floor and, with a voice as loud as thunder, spoke:

"So you are to be the ransom for your six brothers. You had indeed better be of similar worth to them, for they are talented and worthy men all. Indeed, it would be fitting that you were six times more talented than they, for how else should you compensate for the loss of them?"

The young woman rose to her feet and bowed three times. She dared not speak lest her flowers betray her secret—for no one, not even the prince, had bothered to tell her what gifts she had.

"What is your talent, my little one?" said the ghoul, as quietly as he could so as not to frighten her.

The girl shook her head. It would be folly, she thought, to open her mouth and pour forth the very things that, to her mind, had caused her to be locked away for so many years.

"Why do you not answer me?" he continued, more stridently.

Again she shook her head.

"This is impudence," shrieked the monster. "How dare you come to this court and pretend to be a suitable ransom for your six brothers?" He turned to his guards and ordered them to throw the king's daughter into the deepest and darkest dungeon in the palace. As she was being dragged away, he shouted: "If you do not prove

your worth for me by tomorrow, then I shall have you for my morning meal."

The girl cried silent tears, but these did not move the ghoul. He stormed out of the room, and for many hours he was heard thundering around the palace. The king's daughter, meanwhile, was taken to the deepest and darkest dungeon and abandoned, without bread or water. In the total darkness she could see nothing. She began to bewail her fortune, and lamented having agreed to be the ransom when she was so worthless. After all, she thought, what had she to offer in return for the great talents of her six brothers?

She began to sing to herself, songs telling of her hopes of a young prince rescuing her from her imprisonment, songs of finding her father alive again, songs of being reconciled with her mother and being folded once more in loving arms as she had so briefly been before. And, rustling in the darkness, emerged rivers of flowers, a bouquet so mixed and varied that it soothed her own heart and made her begin to feel drowsy. Soon she fell asleep on the bed of flowers of her own songs.

The smell of the flowers, however, knew no prison walls, but wafted through the dank passages, up through the cracks in the stone and the grates in the wooden doors and along the marble corridors. It slid up the ancient banisters of the curved staircases and lingered in the hallways. It finally reached the chamber of the ghoul, who still stomped around his bedroom, furious at having been cheated. At first he didn't notice the captivating smell, but nevertheless he found himself inexplicably becoming calmer. He ceased his impatient *pacing and sat on the bed, wondering what was causing the exquisite fragrance. Soon, he forgot all about the girl and determined to find out where the aroma was coming from. In a trance, the ghoul followed the scent. He walked down the corridors and then descended into the dungeons, until he arrived at the cell where the young girl lay asleep. It was so dark, however, that he was unable to make out the girl with his one lantern.*

The ghoul was by now overcome, like the young girl, by the heady aroma of the countless number of flowers. He fell asleep and that night dreamed the sweetest dreams he had ever had, dreams of rivers and trees, fields and flowers, millions of them. He slept so long and deeply that the next morning his guards began to wonder where he was. They looked high and low for him, through every part of the castle, until, with flambeaus and lanterns, they arrived in the dungeon to find him asleep outside the girl's cell. They shouted to the ghoul to wake, who did so, not with his usual anguished roar, but slowly and gently. Then they all stared in amazement at the sight which greeted them, glimmering in the flickering light of their lanterns.

The girl was so embedded in a cloud of flowers that she was almost invisible. There were flowers of all the colors God gave us. Complete serenity sat on her brow, and she seemed to be unaware of her imprisonment and her sorrow. The ghoul found tears springing to his eyes and he began to cry. Great wails of sorrow soon tore themselves from his mouth and stirred up the petals encircling the girl. When moved, these petals seemed to whisper words. Astonished, the ghoul stopped crying, and commanded his men to blow on the petals. This they did, and were amazed to find that the petals did indeed talk. For an hour the men blew on the petals, which echoed in a confused and uncertain manner the sorrowful songs the king's daughter had sung the previous day.

The ghoul learned of the tragic desertion of her father and her six brothers, how her mother had commanded that she be killed, and how she had been saved through the greed of the handmaidens of the king's wife. He listened in wonder as the flowers whispered how the young prince—murdered at the ghoul's command—had discovered where she was hidden, and how the king's wife had fallen into a swoon, perhaps never to awake.

Again the ghoul wept. So loud was his weeping this time that the king's daughter woke up and, terrified, found herself surrounded by the whispering petals and the howls of the ghoul. Fearing she was going to be killed, she called out. But out of her mouth came only more petals that mixed with the other whisperings, making them bewildered and unintelligible. The ghoul, however, saw these flowers and crashed to his knees, so that the whole castle shook, and pleaded for forgiveness.

"Name your price. You have indeed suffered, and right it is you should be released."

The young girl could only weep silently in return.

"I shall give you and your brothers freedom and safe passage back to your land. Alas, I have had the young prince killed. For that I am cursed by God. I shall never wage war or hold hostages again. Is there anything else I can do?"

The king's daughter, still bemused by the sudden awakening from sleep, shook her head.

Soon, her six brothers, all white-haired through their ordeal and blind after years in the dark dungeons, were brought to the sister they had never seen. She kissed each one of them in turn, and gave them names so each had a different flower to hold. And, when they understood the depth of their sister's love, they fell upon their knees and begged in their own ways to be forgiven, and their sister touched their lips once as a sign of her forgiving them. Then they set off, the ghoul himself giving them safe passage, until she saw her father's castle in the distance. At this point the ghoul, with tears in his eyes, turned back to his own land, repeating his vows never to harm or hold anyone. These vows he kept until the day he died.

Nobody was there to greet the six brothers and their sister, for all the servants and the handmaidens were in the bedchamber of the king's wife. She had not moved since the departure of her daughter with the young man, and nor had they. The girl rushed up to her mother's room, and there was great rejoicing tempered with sorrow when she brought her brothers into the room. The servants and handmaidens saw how old the brothers had become, and that they were all blind; the one with no eyes at all. The brothers one by one were brought to their mother's bedside, where they each placed a kiss on her lips.

But the king's wife did not awake as the prince had promised. In desperation, the king's daughter rushed to the bedside and shook her mother. But the more she

*shook, the more deeply did her mother seem to sleep.
Finally, as her soul began to despair, she cried out, and,
instead of flowers, there came the desperate plea:*

"Please, please wake up for me."

At this, the mother's eyes opened and she saw her
daughter and her six sons, and then many a tear fell in
joy at her sons being home and her daughter being able
to speak, and in sadness at the loss of her husband and
the lost manhood of her sons. But most of all, the king's
wife shed tears of joy for the love of her daughter, who
had suffered so much, and yet retained such love for her.

> *They celebrated all the morrow*
> *I left them filled with joy and sorrow.*

As on the previous day, the serving-girl asked the
Sultan the question. "What is it that I want?"

"To speak?" asked the Sultan tentatively.

The girl once more looked at him and vanished.

The Sultan was desolate. His anger had vanished a
long time ago through sheer frustration at not being able
to find the answer to her question. He returned to his
rooms and began to brood. Suleiman had never seen the
Sultan so subdued and asked him what the matter was.

"I cannot find the answer to the girl's question.
What can I do?"

Suleiman thought long and hard, and then had a
brilliant idea.

"Tomorrow is your last chance, is it not, O Sultan?"

"It is," said the Sultan miserably.

"No doubt she will have another story for you. Do

not let her tell you the story she has planned for you. Ask her to tell you the story of herself. Have you not wondered at her strange behavior? Surely in her past will lie the clue to the answer she desires. Plus, women love to talk—especially about themselves. This will allow her to trust you."

The Sultan was delighted at this, and began to cheer up enormously. He promised Suleiman riches beyond all his wildest imaginings if he were proved right. That night, the Sultan slept a contented sleep, convinced that the next night he would be lying in the arms of this most beautiful but incessantly taxing girl.

The next morning, the Sultan rose and hurried down to the lakeside. Sure enough, the young woman came and washed herself; she filled her amphora, met him at the lakeside, and they both sat down. Before she could begin, however, the Sultan asked her to tell him the story of herself. "For your behavior is most strange," he said, "and, since I may have to kill you, I would like to know why you are naked, and why you fill your amphora, and who your master is."

The girl again turned her great black eyes towards him.

"O Sultan, you shall hear both my story and my history, for I was going to tell it to you anyway."

The Sultan inwardly cursed Suleiman, but settled himself down and tried to concentrate.

"I am, like the girl in my second story, the only daughter of a great and noble man who is no more. He was my master, and, although he is dead, it is him I serve. My mother was abandoned by my father when I was young, and she blamed me for this. Out of wickedness, she betrothed me to a man I did not love. He was one of the soldiers killed in your last battle, O Sultan, and his name will remain secret. He took away all the clothes my father had given to me before he died, and now I walk naked throughout Iznik in memory of his cruelty. For the shame of my nakedness, I come down to the lakeside and wash myself three times in the water. Once is for the death of my father. Twice is for the sadness of my mother. And the third time is for the cruelty of my husband."

"But why do you fill the amphora, and where do you go with the water?" asked the Sultan.

"This I shall tell you. You must not be impatient. The amphora is my well of tears. These tears are the tears of all the daughters and all the mothers abandoned by their husbands and their fathers, O Sultan. With these tears I water the ground where I live. It has created beautiful flowers and nutritious plants by which I live, for the former fill the heart and the latter the stomach. Before I ask you your question, let me give you a warning. You are no longer young, and the indiscretion of youth is no longer a justifiable excuse. You will soon take to yourself a wife in marriage who will extend your power and your honor throughout the whole region. She will give you the right to the throne of an empire, and through this will be the foundation of a dynasty that will rule for many ages. But, remember the fate of the sheikh and the king, and remember the amphora full of tears. So, now I ask you. What is it that I want?"

Before he had time to think, the Sultan found the answer on his lips.

"Freedom."

The serving-girl looked at him, and, to his surprise, instead of walking away, stayed exactly where she was.

"That is correct. You may now do with me as you wish."

Then the Sultan understood how foolish he had been, how great had been his blindness, and how he could never have this serving-girl as his own. He turned to her, and with his most magnificent gesture began.

"Since freedom is what you most desire, then freedom is what you shall have. You are right to give me what I most desire, for what I desire is not you, but what I thought you were. Therefore, go, and take this money for clothes. You need not atone for being innocent."

At this the young woman smiled sweetly, and kissed his hand. And then she vanished, leaving no mark, as though she had never been there. This time, however, she left her amphora behind. The Sultan looked inside, and there he saw priceless jewels and ornaments of great beauty and value. Barely able to lift the amphora, he staggered back to the town where he told an amazed Suleiman (amazed not least because of the Sultan's decision) what had happened. That night there was a great feast in celebration of this wealth, but the Sultan found himself again walking by the lakeside at dawn as the sun rose above the horizon. This time, however, the serving-girl did not appear.

* * *

And that, my friends, is that—and, I will add with particularly personal emphasis, in the nick of time. For my fleshless buttocks were also shifting uncomfortably at these altogether too decorous and sexless displays of courtly love. However, for those who prefer a coarser thread in their yarns, I bring joyful news from backstage that our esteemed owner has apparently imbibed some of our particularly rich brand of coffee and is in moderate control of his diminished faculties. I am also delighted to say that the rest of the cast, without whom we are mere shadows of shadows, as it were, has arrived. Ah, Jenem, my succulent sweet; Chelebi, my tumescent friend—now we can inject a seditious touch of delicious depravity into the proceedings. Do you remember that trip to the brothel in Bursa we made the other night, Chelebi? If I remember rightly, it was my turn for Fatima with the magnificent mangoes, and you wouldn't let me chow down. You do? Great!

And as for this amble of a preamble: well, what can we say? Undoubtedly, like a dust mite in a warm marriage bed, there is some moral hidden deep in what has gone before. But I have no wish to search for it. Personally, I crave only amusement—of impossible seductions and unlikely repentances—but amusement above all. I would leave it to Hajivat to apologize for what has transpired while our owner sobered up, but, given his beginning, we can only shudder at the prospect of his end. Instead, let me offer a deep apology if we have in any way offended and an even deeper one if we have not.

The Dervish at Iznik Remembers God

Sometimes

Bismillah irrahman irrahim

Sometimes he found that in spite of everything, when he was mired in despair and sin, his body would force his soul to turn and face God; suddenly his knees would buckle and his head would bow and he had no idea why he was doing what he was doing, but that he was nothing before God. At moments like these he saw the idiocies of his life—the paltry considerations of fear, pride, anger, and jealousy—vanish in the simplicity of his prostration. Yet they always returned, these incontinent graspers of his soul, to hold him down and hold him back. It was his greatest struggle.

At these times, his long black cloak was truly his grave and his hat his tombstone; he felt inert and without spirit. And God was distant to him, an echo of a once all-embracing song that was now merely the vapor of a great breath. Ha. He was terrified that he could die at any moment and not have the name of God on his lips. Allah. Allah. The name itself filled him with dread and comfort. This was before the Master had taken his position and those whom he loved had begun to circle.

Sometimes, when the Turn began, he felt this place alive with the memory of God. Time, which tied all the knots of constraint around him, became insignificant as he was set free to be the flute for God's breath and saw and felt things from the past and the people who had lived here. It was not as if he stood behind their eyes or moved their strings like puppets. No. He became them, his body shaping itself into theirs, filling their bodies with his breath as God exhaled their stories and the history of this place into his soul. He kept this to himself, aware that what he saw and became would to others seem a loss of direction, perhaps a turning away rather than a turning within, or simply a misplacing of his devotion. Yet these people were real to him, and he trusted that their reality was given him by God.

So, slowly at first, with his hands on his brothers' shoulders and the fullness of the breath of God starting to expand in him, he began to turn. And this is what he was.

He was a boy when the Greeks first came, fishing in the fertile waters of the lake, so excited when a fish swam near that he kept shouting out and frightening the fish away with his leaping shadow. His father had told him of a huge army that had passed by to the south, led by a great leader whose light eyes had been so focused on the East that he had not bothered to rest his troops amid these orange-groves or near the water.

One of his generals, however, returned years later, after his leader, known across the sea as Alexander of Macedon, had died. The boy was now a young man, strong in mind and will, but still impatient, careless with his line and carefree with his time. His mind did not empty itself of intent or desire, as his father had said was necessary for a fisherman, but wandered to thoughts of the women he loved or wished to love and the glory that would one day be his, and his alone.

He saw this general, Antigonus the One-Eyed, march into the scattered houses and huts that constituted a nameless village and watched as Antigonus's son, Demetrius—a young man, graceful and tall for his age, on the brink of manhood—strolled to the side of the Ascanian lake. Demetrius tipped his body forward, pivoted on his hip, balancing himself on his right leg by stretching out his left behind him, and picked up the oval pebble that had winked at his passing eye as he lifted his head to look across the lake. Antigonus observed how Demetrius took the pebble between his finger and thumb, reflecting on how, because of his one eye, such a judgment was much harder, much more a question of calculation and less of instinct, than what Demetrius could achieve. Demetrius raised the pebble to his eye, examined the subtle smoothness of its patina, and brushed off the few grains of sand that clung to its surface.

Antigonus the One-Eyed stared intently at his son as Demetrius leaned back, uncoiled his right arm behind him, lifted his left leg like a colt in front of him, and for a moment balanced himself in perfect equilibrium. In an instant he had brought his right arm forward, clipping the side of his head, brushing past the hair that curled over the tops of his ears, and then stretched his arm out before him as the stone fled from his grasp. For a fraction of time, Demetrius kept his arm straight, the sun spreading over the fine hairs on his arm, as soft as wind-blown grasses in a field, his tender muscles rolling toward his sleek fingers, which pointed, yearning, into the sky. His body swung around and he jerked his head back toward the trajectory of the stone to try to see where it fell.

For a second, it seemed to Antigonus that it would not fall, that Demetrius's stone would be the same as the stones of Alexander, when he had stood at other expanses of water and thrown pebbles so far that they had vanished from sight before they fell, so far that the inevitable brief eruption of the smooth surface of the water or the minuscule diversion of the running current was never seen.

But then Antigonus saw it fall, saw it fail suddenly of its energy, hang briefly in imploring space, and then plummet into the indifferent lake. And he saw that, like Alexander, he too would fail, that both his and his golden boy's attempts to define space and time with their momentary markers, projected from their own hands and no one else's, would fail, fall, and cause merely a distant, contemptible splash in the unfathomable lake of history. And Antigonus saw Demetrius as he turned back toward him, fresh from the triumph of a far-flung stone, and he felt his army behind him, waiting for the word to begin building. And he had nothing to say to either his army or his boy—nothing of any consolation or approval—for he knew, with the sharp savor of failure, with the bitter recognition that any name or action was meaningless, what he should call this place. Antigonia.

Years later, when Antigonus and Demetrius had been defeated at Ipsus, and the victor, Lysimachus, King of Thrace, another of the generals of Alexander of Macedon, had renamed the place Nicaea after his wife, the fisherman, no longer young, his hair flecked with gray, his shoulders bent with the patient resignation of an experienced angler, his head full of thoughts of his family and his life, saw Lysimachus also come to the side of the lake. Lysimachus knew the stories about this place. Antigonus, his defeat full in his mind, had died muttering curses against their one leader. Absurdly confident that Demetrius would save him from the melée of lance and sword, Antigonus had fallen from his horse and had railed against the stones of the city of Nicaea.

The fisherman saw Lysimachus lift up his arms in the open air and dedicate this place to the gods. Then and there the king determined that here at least the name of Lysimachus would not be forgotten, nor would the name of Nicaea ever be ignored. Yet, twenty years later, Lysimachus had died and his kingdom had come under the control of Nicomedes I, King of Bithynia, who made Nicaea the capital of Bithynia until nine years before his death, when a new capital was named. It was one that carried the echo of a previous attempt to stop time's erasing of the person. It was called Nicomedia.

The day Nicomedes left Nicaea for good, an old man was seen casting his line slowly into the still lake where he had fished for sixty years. He knew the tow and pull of the current beneath the placid surface; he understood why the fish did not fight against the pulse of the water but diverted it, angled themselves into it, let its force guide them. No longer did he care to catch a fish for his evening meal; no longer did he care for family and life; his actions were all that remained. Purposeless, without desire for food or victory, the old man cast and pulled in, pulled in and cast. He felt instinctively the projection of his line into the water, saw it only as an extension of his hand. He knew it could be recalled; but only when it told him that the time was right for him to draw the line to the side of the boat.

He smiled as he remembered his youth, his intemperateness and his agonies over what were always fetters to his real purpose. Of course, he had no idea what his real purpose was, only that there was a purpose and that he could only know it by entering fully into it, without anxiety or lamentation. As he looked around him he saw how the great sky bent gently towards the yielding lake, merging with it and yet swallowed up in it. He had seen the pebbles smoothed into sand, the grass decay into mud and sedge, the waters ebb and flow, the sun move through the sky, the seasons pass. Now each cast he made had become one single arc; each withdrawal had become another cast; each destabilizing flick of his wrist had become simply another form of balance. He saw how the town stood before him on the other side of the lake, and he laughed out loud at how these warriors, so powerful and so ambitious and all dead, had tried to claim it as their own. And, then, with the warmth of the embrace of a loved one, he understood: it was Nicaea.

And this was the first turn.

* * *

Sometimes

Ishq Allah Ma'abud l'illah

Sometimes he felt that although he possessed only a prayer mat and his clothes of wool—tokens themselves of his having nothing—even these were too much. He wondered whether he invested these items with too great a significance, and he feared they were too important for him to let go, as he had to do if he wasn't to lose focus on God. Life became a battle between his understanding of what poverty was and simply being poor. He feared that if he thought about his poverty too much, a love or pride or fierce attachment to it might rush into the vacuum that should have held a genuine lack of interest in material things. But if he accepted it as his way of life and forgot about it, he would fall into complacency or an ignorance of suffering. His prayer mat was there to remind him that everything he possessed was to be used for worship—and worship alone. It was to be the sounding board for his love of God, the shell in which the effortless sound of God could be heard and repeated, the tablet on which God would write himself over and over again.

The drums and flute began to play. He turned to his fellow dervish and looked at him. Sometimes he could see between his companions' eyes a pearl that seemed to him another eye, a shining point of inner reflection, inspecting the very deepest parts of the soul.

This time, however, there was a mirror, and in it he saw a man sitting at his desk, occasionally brushing away the dust that settled on his scroll, dust caused by the incessant work on the amphitheater and other buildings in Nicaea. "It is nearly finished," thought the man, being of an age when the thoughts of the past and the present merge and separate continually and the mind thinks of completion at all costs.

There was, the man thought dryly, so much to say. The citizens of Nicaea, as well as other towns in Bithynia, had taken too literally his people's proclamations of the infinite riches of the Roman Empire and had built a gymnasium and amphitheater that had already cost far too much—the latter now more than ten million sesterces—and they were either half-built, with cracks already appearing, or disappearing into the mud. It wasn't really their fault, he thought; after all, Rome *was* the whole world, and, moreover, they were undoubtedly impressive projects (the theater alone would seat fifteen thousand people). But why in the name of the gods hadn't the engineers surveyed the ground beforehand and made sensible estimates of cost? He had hoped that his governorship of Bithynia would have been seen by the people in this province, and, more importantly, in Rome, as one of satisfactory order and not a little triumph in the area of administration and construction. He sat back in his chair, tapped his fingers on the table, and smiled quietly to himself. He had always had too strong a sense of history in the making to do anything daring. It was all, to say the least, very unfortunate. But at least the Nicaeans had enthusiasm.

And now because of the absurd claims of a Jewish rebel in Judea during the reign of...who? Claudius? Tiberius?—one of them.... In any event, because of this one rabble-rouser—one, he remembered reading, among many during those turbulent days—the people of Bithynia were deserting the temples and not providing food for the sacrificial animals. And it wasn't the peasants, either, who could usually be counted on to toe the line if they were fed enough and given enough entertainments. It was the ones with some education, something to lose. Even women! Young or old, it didn't matter. All on behalf of a degenerate Jewish cult that had begun as an apocalyptic sect in Palestine and now had become this hugely troublesome *thing* that he had to deal with.

Yet, he had to admit ruefully, these Christians undoubtedly had some kind of passion. Some time ago, he remembered his father telling him, there had been a Jew from Tarsus, a Roman citizen, a tentmaker—Paul is what his father had said his name was. Responsible for spreading these ideas throughout Asia Minor, Thrace, Macedonia, even to Rome itself. Had taken the Mithraic cults and turned them on their heads, so his father had said.

The man leaned forward and looked again at the blank scroll in front of him. He really had little time for fractious religious activity—if he was honest, it all struck him as absurd, anyway. Yet this region seemed obsessed with it, besotted with the idea of divine callings, magic tricks, and all sorts of ritualistic barbarism that was simply—well, *irrational* was the only word for it. Of course, people clearly felt some need to believe in things beyond this world, and if they had ridiculous rites then that was their concern. But his responsibility was to keep the peace and guard the Roman state, and for that to happen there had to be order. And for order to be maintained people needed to sacrifice and keep the economy going. It was as simple as that. People didn't have to believe in what they were doing, they just had to do it.

But not the Christians. He knew it was always problematic to try to control sects—it was best done absolutely and without mercy at the very beginning. That way it could be stopped before too many of the credulous or the foolish began to believe and thus more had to die than necessary. Domitian's massacres twenty years ago had done something—but it was all too late. The Christians were starting to become as pestilential a problem as the Jews were in Palestine.

Of course, he thought, urging himself to feel some sense of resolution, he didn't *need* the mandate of the Emperor to try to deal with the Christians. They were undoubtedly stubborn and had, quite simply, refused to obey the simple instructions of sacrificing to the gods and disclaiming their one god. He had put some on trial and, without much enthusiasm, had executed those who had refused to offer sacrifice. He had carefully put aside considerations of whether they were Roman citizens or not and had sent two to Rome. He had even had two slave-women, whom the Christians called "deaconesses," examined—a word he knew barely disguised its true meaning—to see just what it was they believed.

This had seemed to work at first; people were sacrificing again and making offerings to the temples. Yet others seemed to be hardening in their beliefs. Those whom he had tried to make examples of had tediously become what the Christians called "martyrs." At times he felt he was beginning to see Christians everywhere;

even those who made a show of sacrificing he was unsure of. People laughing in the street, or talking at the forum, or going about their business, saluting him, maybe—how did he know they were not engaged in this preposterous worship of a man dead over seventy years and who was actually meant to have risen from the dead and appeared in the flesh again? Somehow it was all so difficult to square with this town's ragbag collection of theater and sport enthusiasts who had rushed headlong into trying to make Nicaea as grand a city as Nicomedia. Everybody had become suspicious, either because they were too Roman or not Roman enough. He couldn't tell, that was what was so frustrating—things were just not certain anymore. It was a wretched way to end a career in public service, overrun with a kind of jealousy for peace in an area he had thought never to have been at risk from this scourge of passionate, ordinary believers.

It was not as if the Christians were as easily or as justifiably a force to be crushed as a foreign people's rebellion. While they refused to worship the true gods, all they did, instead, was to rise at dawn and offer hymns to their Christ as a divine being and at dusk do the same thing. They also utterly disavowed such crimes as murder or adultery and demanded of their followers that they follow the law in all other ways as long as it did not contravene their belief. This was hardly the stuff of revolution; therefore, what was he, their rightful governor, to do, when he was in the peculiar position of disagreeing with their motives but applauding their outcome? He stared at the paper and found that he didn't believe a word of it—the need for "decisiveness," the stern claims for "something to be done," this confidence that the Christians were just a sect and could be dealt with as long as the correct measures were taken. There was in these people's earnestness, their commitment in the face of so much suffering, that which made anything he or Rome might do the mere tired, violent whimperings of bitter old men. He had never imagined that he might be forced to be as pathetically violent toward them as Nero had been. Yet he was—and so was no better than that poisonous degenerate, torturing and sending off to execution these average, unimportant, unthreatening people, who simply and silently believed in ideas different from his.

And then, with a fear that filled him with warmth and stifled his breath, he discovered that he already knew, perhaps had always known in his heart, that the Christians would triumph, that he would be in history— like Nero—just another character going through the motions that had to be gone through for the new values of the Christians to silence the final, drawn-out cry of a dying people. He felt infinitely tired, tired down to his marrow. Slowly, he found himself listening to the sounds of the building again, and realized that his world, which he had thought was a magnificent work always being renewed, was itself subsiding, cracking under the strain of old ideas and an old sensibility. He would die and another governor would try to stop it, defray the expense or employ more slaves, torture and cajole, and he would fail as well. It would crack and crumble and return to nothing.

Nevertheless, the Emperor would expect some action, or rather some confirmation of action being seen to be taken. It would be enough to soothe the Emperor with some form of specious reasonableness. He looked at the quill in his hand, and smiled wryly at how easily it sat there and how expectant his hand was. He had trusted in his skill before in times as bad; his writing would not let him down. And so he began his empty address. "Gaius Plinius Caecilius Secundus to Marcus Ulpius Traianus Maximus Augustus, greetings."

And this was the second turn.

* * *

Sometimes

Allahu akbar

Sometimes he felt so grateful to God that he was almost overwhelmed by his dependence. He was grateful if God gave him his blessing and grateful if he didn't. He was grateful for the fact of being grateful, and above all grateful for being endowed with patience—patience to bear the separation that sometimes occurred between him and God and caused him such pain. God's gift of patience offset the passion of his longing for God; and gratitude magnified that patience and steadied the love so that it did not consume him.

And then, as if breaking out of the quietness of his patience and gratitude, he sometimes felt total joy, the bonds of the grave loosening as he threw off his black cloak to reveal his white skirt—his shroud beyond death—and began to swirl beneath the girdle of cloth.

And as he turned, he started to hear God in every movement he and his circle made and in every sound that came from their mouths and the mouths of the flute and drums.

He felt his eyes close as the circle dipped and bobbed with him. Inside him he felt his eyes open, and he saw the earth move and the walls crumble and the buildings shudder and the lake's waves spread out. He heard the shocked cries of women, the frantic shouts of men, the screams and wailing of babies and children. The axis of this town itself seemed to break as tower collapsed on tower, roof on roof, person upon person. And it was as if his whole body was torn apart like the earth, each bone broken, each sinew snapped, each vein punctured, each muscle torn. The cracks that ran down the city walls became cracks in his heart; the mortar that fell from the walls were spasms of pain pulsating along each artery and meridian. Every cobble and stone, every joint of every body broke within him and he died a thousand deaths, each one filled with a unique pain and a reaching out to hold onto him, tugging at his sleeve, grasping his leg, a hand slipping away from his neck. How hard, he felt, it was to surrender! How hard it was to let go of fear, of hope for the future, of the love of our family, the terrified grip we hold on our individual lives!

And then, as suddenly as it had happened, there was silence, and he felt complete stillness. Occasionally he heard a quiet whimper, the sound of a mother—no longer desperate but instead weak with resignation— calling one last time for a child she knew was no longer alive. He saw the broken patterns of mosaic and the shattered glass of the churches, and yet within the desolation he felt peace. Because slowly, emerging from the rubble, he saw people pull themselves to their feet, covered in dust and soil, and then lift up their arms and thank God that they were still alive. He understood then God's love of him and humankind—that there would always be mercy amid tragedy, hope from despair. And he heard the sound of hammering and sawing and knew that Nicaea would return, would be rebuilt.

And this was the third turn.

* * *

Sometimes

La

Sometimes he felt like a leaf in the wind, blown by the breath of God. And he had complete trust that God would keep him safe, and that he could rest in his arms and his will and know that faith was all that was necessary. Sometimes the knowledge that God loved him reduced him to tears because he knew he could never return the love of God with anything approaching the amount of love that God had for him, and that his whole life would be spent trying to show God his devotion and he would always fall short. But then, at other times, he realized that that falling short was itself God's love allowing him the opportunity to celebrate once more the depth of his love for God and God's for him; and it calmed him and he found himself once more experiencing the joy of absolute surrender to the will of God.

And as the circle turned he felt his head filled with

the noise of God's name and he was present at the crowning of Theodore Lascaris II by the Patriarch Michael IV four years after the defeated emperor, his army and empire in tatters, encamped in Nicaea. And he loved Theodore, as he stood on one of the hundred walls of the city and addressed his people.

"Fellow Christians, true Hellenes all. This is indeed a great day, for here, in this magnificent city—one made famous over four hundred years ago by Empress Eirene as a center where truth in Christianity was restored, just as it was when Constantine spoke here four hundred years before her—now we can say that the true Christian Empire has begun again. For it is from here that we will retake the city that was named after that great Emperor himself, the city that has fallen to those whom we had thought to have trusted, those who worship the same God and came as the defenders of Jerusalem—the false Baldwin of Flanders and his fake empire of Romania. Instead of turning their wrath upon the warriors of Islam who beat at our gates, for the love of gold and the plunder that they will offer to the rich charlatans of the West, it is these so-called Christians—the same who even now accuse us of degeneracy and of betraying the true spirit of the Church—it is these who have destroyed our icons, raped nuns in their convents, left women and children dying in the streets, torn down the silk hangings and ripped up the sacred books, sacked our houses and palaces, and ruined us all. It is they who have sat a whore, singing barbarous and profane songs, on the throne in our great Cathedral, all in the name of the King of France and the Pope.

"It is to the people of this great city that I must dedicate this coronation, for when myself, the Empress Anna, my three daughters, and my brother Constantine were at our lowest ebb, with the forces of the barbaric Latins surrounding us on every side, you, Nicaeans, after serious deliberation and deep thought, offered to take us in. When we were justified in coming here in sorrow, and with bitterness in our hearts, you filled us with hope, so that we are neither sad nor bitter, for Constantinople has been downtrodden before, and we regained her.

"A mere hundred years ago, my forebear Alexius I Comnenus came with an army and drove Islam from Nicaea through the light of his faith, and in so doing brought great glory upon himself and his soldiers. Our task is no less urgent and many times as hard—for the armies we must beat bear our own banners and seem our own brothers. Once we ruled together and worshiped together, and now they stand at the very heart of all we hold dear and desecrate it. Our thoughts turn to the people of the South, who respect our works and Jesus as a prophet. For many years now we have sought an understanding of their beliefs and have waged many bitter struggles against them. We would do well to heed their judgments upon our believers in the lost lands and reflect on how we, as Christians, might seek to emulate their behavior. But we cannot simply rush back into battle with our forces shattered and our might weakened. We must wait and quietly regain our strength and then strike, as Samson brought down the temple after being blinded and imprisoned by the Philistines.

"Here we will rebuild. Here we will begin the task of recapturing the Empire and Constantinople. We will add another hundred towers to the many that glorify Nicaea, and in the building of each tower we send out a beacon of light to those who believe in Nicaea as a center of art and faith, of grace and truth. We will acquire wealth through the practice of prudence and caution, so that no matter how much the enemy spends in order to expand its vainglory, we will have ten times the amount to disburse to bring the sound of the language of God back to Constantinople.

"It may take five years, or ten, or twenty, or even perhaps fifty. Nevertheless, when the time is right we will march in triumph back into the city that truly belongs to us, and which the West in its perversion and hatred will never take from us again. And Nicaea will be honored by all of us as the home of the new order, the place where true faith is sounded out in trumpet and song, because Nicaea received and nurtured us when there was nothing left. Truly this city is a city of God."

And as he turned he saw an army march away from the city, powerful and mighty, with the banner of the Byzantines fluttering in the wind. And he marveled at all of this, for he felt the emptiness of everything, the illusion of these ignorant armies with their pointless battles and inconsequential victories. He felt within him the nothingness of the flags, the walls, the great speeches of the mighty. The lake was no lake; the sky was no sky; the sun and the dark were simply the same, which was nothing. As he turned once more, everything that there was and everything that was not became shape and color; and then even shape and color dissolved until the great mind itself emerged—filling all space, yet compassionate for the beings who lived out their illusions in the expectation of permanence. And as this mind occupied everywhere with sorrow, he turned again, and the mind itself disappeared and was no more.

And this was the fourth turn.

* * *

Sometimes

illaha

Sometimes when he turned he felt he was no longer a man, but that his features softened and his hips widened, and his waist became cinched and his breasts swelled, and God entered him as a man would a woman. Sometimes he became a man, and his love for God was as a man for a woman. Sometimes he was both; filled with desire he was the union of the two and yet man and woman separately. When he felt these ways it seemed to him that his body glowed and his heart raced, and he couldn't distinguish anymore between the passion of the body and the passion of the soul. But when he danced there was nothing more joyful than to feel his body swing and turn and swivel. And his turn was like a planet and the Master was like the sun, and the sun's light gave off the light of God. The circle replenished the turn of the heavens and the turn of Time and the return of all things to their source.

Sometimes, however, he felt absolutely alone, alone with nothing beyond him. He knew, perhaps more deeply than he dared admit, that God was testing him to understand that he was in the presence of God and that there were no intercessors who would plead for him. He felt himself in these moments almost crushed by the weight of his aloneness, deserted by his fellow turners, lost in the sea of insignificance. He stopped turning and sat down. His black cloak was placed upon him, and he closed his eyes.

And this time he was Theodora, the wife of the old Sultan Orhan, daughter of Emperor John VI, walking silently before sunrise through Iznik. This was the only time the young woman could be alone, when the rest of the town and her husband—all of whom turned to the south to face the *kaaba*—were asleep, awaiting the morning call to prayer. As she walked she would recite her prayers to God through the intercession of Christ, prayers which—because they were memories of the palace in Constantinople from which, barely more than a child, she had been taken to be the bride of the Sultan— had become increasingly hard to remember and say with any conviction as to the rightness of phrase or choice of word. She had talked sometimes to her husband about her beliefs, childish as they still were, and he, like all the people of Nicaea and the lands under the rule of the Ottomans, had bowed and offered his respects—as if feeling nothing but the sympathy of those whose religion was simply complete, whereas hers was not.

At birth she had been called a gift from God— Theodora—and had become, she knew without arrogance, a beauty, one possessed with intelligence and curiosity. Her marriage to the Sultan had at first been an attempt by her father to stave off the ambitions of the Ottomans by allying her with their leader, and Orhan had agreed to this and behaved towards her like a gruff and slightly embarrassed uncle. As she had grown older, she had watched him with an attentive caution she had masked in shyness. And he had slowly begun to fall in love in front of her, his love like a cat that stretched itself out after being awakened from a long sleep. His burned-out eyes had regained their fire beneath his graying eyebrows, and more and more he would turn to her and ask with urgency for her opinions and her counsel.

She had asked herself what she felt about this man who was so much older than she, who had spoken a different language then and sometimes, it seemed to her, still did, and who, she occasionally felt, worshiped a different God. He had intrigued her with his decisiveness, and with his ability to be so irascible with others and so tender with her. She could not say she loved him, although he asked her every day. Instead, she would take his still surprisingly soft-featured face in her hands and then put her ringed index finger on his lips and tell him gently to be quiet.

She knew she cared for him, was concerned when he told her that he could not sleep because of her, appreciated his solicitousness and sympathy when her father died. But...love? Love was too complex a word for her. She knew the word for it in her own language and had learned it in his. But somehow the translation was not the same: her love had been learned when she was a child, and his was the love of an older man. She tried not to think about it.

She walked past the hospice she had founded for the wandering mystics who had come to the region. This was the nearest she came to love—these people who knew their God so fully that they at times seemed mad with joy. In her private moments, alone in the chamber that overlooked the hospice, she had cried out loud to Christ—whose face stared impassively at her from the icon by the window—that she might feel the ecstasy these men did, that she might be consumed in the same fire they shouted for, that she might be overwhelmed by the love they felt as they sang and danced around and around. But she had waited and been left with the silence of Christ's eyes and the blessing of his long fingers. She had stared at the icon and remembered how when she was a child she had gazed at it for hours, fascinated by the colors and the texture of the work. But Christ's fingers now seemed to her more admonitory than dedicatory, and when she had looked into his eyes, without understanding why, they seemed to her inconsolably sad.

Her life was not incomplete. She had given Orhan an alliance, which was what he wanted. Orhan trusted her with the running of his lands when he was away, more often as not fighting the very battles their marriage had been meant to stop. It was true she was glad of the responsibility, but she felt in her every action that there was a schism between who she was and what she was expected to be. She remained impartial, scrupulous, and considerate only to stop herself from shouting out for everything to stop, for the senseless fighting between the two worlds she lived in and which owned equal parts of her soul to cease. But she knew they wouldn't until another prophet announced the arrival of the end or Constantinople finally became her home—and neither one to her seemed possible.

She heard the muezzin give the call to prayer—a distant, high sound reaching into the still, thin air of morning, a sound that always bit into her and filled her ears with its passion and its celebration. God is great. She had known that once, childishly perhaps but truly, without question or puzzlement; perhaps, somewhere within her, she knew it still. But then, at that moment, it seemed as though she heard it for the first time. She thought of her icon and of the starkness of Christ's features. This distant God, his forbidding stare coming from eyes that were rounded and softened by something intangible, unfathomable.

She stopped, wheeled around, and, in tears, walked back towards the palace of old Nicaea.

And this was the fifth turn.

* * *

Sometimes
ill'
Sometimes when he thought of the names of God, he was filled with an immeasurable love. It was an ache that made his head spin and forced his body to dance. The uncreated sounds filled his head. In each of the ninety-nine names God exploded, was destroyed and recreated and preserved in the unmistakable, unmispronounceable sound of the perfect God. The names disap-

peared and reappeared, merged and separated, joined and splintered, increasing in subtlety in the head until there was no singer and nothing said or sung, but all was one great indivisible essence of sound, one great breath of joy.

And as he breathed and the sound surrounded and filled him, he thought of the lines and curves of language, the unwritten Word of God; each dip and loop his body made as he turned became part of the great words of God that sounded in his head. He tried to imagine God, tried to see the figure as distinct from his love, but found himself dazzled by his own joy at simply being with God, unable to turn himself away from God. How could he look at God when God was behind his eyes? How could he depict God when God was in every gesture of his hand?

And it seemed to him as though he was nothing but the very breath of God and the very sight of God and the very hearing of God and the very touch of God and the very taste of God. Yet it also seemed to him he was nothing, less than an ant, less than the ground on which he turned.

And he was Yusuf the Tiler, working on the tiles he had brought from Tabriz in Persia to paint for Sultan Selim. It was noon and the sun was high over Iznik, bearing down on the dust and the pale grass around the Mahmud Chelebi Jami. Yusuf was tired, for he had already that day carefully inscribed in delicate arabesque whorls the flowers and leaves upon the ninety-eighth tile so that the name of God was subtly woven into the texture of the tree and plants. He could hear the kiln being prepared for firing and the sounds of other craftsmen at work.

As he began the ninety-ninth tile his eyes were pulled skyward by the flap of wings, and he saw two storks flying through the sky. Yusuf found himself fascinated as the storks' long wings undulated through the deep blue and across the silver lake and into the distance. His eyes followed them as they flew further and further away until, just as they were to disappear from sight, the black dots wheeled on the edge of the horizon and began to turn back. Soon he could make out the gray and white of their plumage and their long, smooth necks and bills. They came to rest on the top of the minaret of the mosque until, disturbed by the sound of workmen, they flew off again in the same direction, this time sailing over the edge of the horizon out of sight.

Yusuf's eyes turned down to look at his tile and he found them, to his surprise, full of tears. For he knew that his lines and strokes, no matter how artfully conceived and no matter how deeply dedicated in his heart, could not emulate the prayers these birds made to God in their flight across the sky. There was an effortlessness and a uniformity his art never had; there was a refinement in their coloration he could not achieve. For where their wings were like waves at the sea's heart—connected one with the other, forming and reforming constantly—his hand movements were like waves upon the rocks, splintering the motion of the wave violently and finitely. Even the mosque, built by those like him who loved and worshiped God, was, he felt, unable to replicate the smoothness of the storks' flight or the ease with which they saw the world beneath them. He knew in his heart also that the birds were waiting to build a nest in the minaret, and he knew that it was merely a matter of time before they would have the peace to do so. They had no use for tiles, or books, or for knowledge in the way he and his fellow humans had; they simply were alive in their devotion, possessing neither expectation nor anxiety, and thus fully rewarded.

When Yusuf had finished the ninety-ninth tile he stared at it for a long time, lost in the lines that no longer formed words. And at that moment he understood Nicaea, and began again.

And this was the sixth turn.

* * *

Sometimes
'llah
Sometimes after reciting the first sura of the Holy Book, after he had kissed the floor and risen, he had felt the presence of God in the circle with him. He had heard the Master say "Hu"—bringing together all of the names of God in one sound—and, suddenly, had felt himself die through the overwhelming power of God's love. God had molded into one his closeness and his fear, and had destroyed those chains that had stopped him from experiencing the fullness of God. It was not that he could not recollect where he was when this happened or where he was at that time; instead it was a loss of self, a dispersal of his identity in the ocean of God's love. And then God had gathered him together again and let him

return to himself, with the fire of God in him, but not too great, lest he never recover. He had opened his eyes and found himself back with his fellow worshipers by the lake of Nicaea, the grass smoothed underneath their feet by their turning.

And as the very word "Hu" was on all their lips he became a soldier walking through Iznik. Like the town around him, the soldier was shattered by the ravages of war, a war that had brought down an empire and forged a country, but had also destroyed the hope of history. The soldier would be the leader of his country—indeed, his people would call him their father—and his actions would change the face of their country forever. Yet, at that moment, the soldier stalked the ruined city, its walls destroyed by fighting between two faiths, two civilizations, two old empires, its places of faith empty and desolate, its walls laid waste by the same people who, over two thousand years, had built them.

He shook his head and, leaving the town, walked towards the lake, stopping at its edge. The lake stared back at him, impassive as always. Then the soldier bent down and kissed the ground. As his lips touched the soil, pebbles, sand, and grass at the side of the lake, he experienced truly for the first time the smell and feel of his homeland. He knew its contours and its texture and the shape it made in his imagination every time he thought of what it had been, was, and could be, and now this patch of soil had made it not just a rallying call or a way of controlling his forces, but a reality to be grasped with all its sharp edges, grain, and softness.

He had seen the soldier in his mind and had loved

him, even though the soldier would banish their order and deny them their rights to gather and celebrate the greatness of God—even though the soldier had done and would do terrible things. At that moment, however, all he felt was love.

Yet, at the end of the dance, when God had been remembered, when it was all over and he had to return to his home and the world that God had created; when he had opened his eyes and seen in the fact of this place a perpetuation of acts of faith that could never be denied and that no soldier, through any act, could destroy or avoid; when he had known that God was with them and in this place, and would be so through any turn that history might afford—he heard the sound of Nicaea and that was enough.

Similar Endings

Karagöz's Last Sentence

By blowing on the still but still unflattering surface of the guilt-edged mirror of his soul, and in the brief bloom of steam writing with perfumed paw his judgment upon me, and in that judgment offering me one last sentence in order (as he would be too dull of wits to conceive it) with quivering tongue to justify myself, collapse as a careworn caryatid and beg for mercy, salve my soiled soul in my penitent secretions, or through whatever plan he so designs to vindicate his vindictiveness so that his murder of a man whom he was too obtuse to know he needs most may be seen as less of an evisceration, evacuation, or amputation and more the decisive action of a wrathful father avenging his favorite daughter, the State's, untimely deflowering; by breathing so, in one halitosic huff, this pneumatic peacock—who only comes face to face with himself when he brings his blotchy chin close to the mirror to examine the revolting outbreaks across his psyche and in the nimbus of his own wheezy respiration mistakes the glow surrounding

his stubble for the aura of divinity: this man, our lord
and master the Sultan, has deemed me too foolish (my
words too barbarous a blend of obscene truth and elaborate falsehood and my metaphors too mixed for mixed
company) for the elegant patination of his nascent glory
and yet (as the price for perpetuating his petty princi-
pality) has stupidly allowed me to stretch his sentence
out with my own, that my punctuation may delay for as
long as I wish the point of my departure and extend in
deep breaths (deeper than any that squeezed between his
pearly whites or filtered through his mucus-flecked mustache) the expiration and inspiration of my being in the
construction (yes, construction, damn it!—I who never
did anything but defoliate, deflate, deprecate, defecate)
of a heretical, byzantine palace of words for those who
have just cause to revolt at my presence and revel in my
departure:—with this scribbled on your *tabula rasa*,
therefore, I call upon you to stay the sweet blade, O executioner, inhaling as I do the green aroma of the chop-
ping block, imagining as I shall that fraction of time
when the clean coolness of the disinterested metal
against the flushed heat of my ruddy neck insists on a
brutal forgiveness before it effortlessly shaves its way to
and through the bone; ask you to stay your brawny arms
by lifting them (remember?) the way you did on the hal-
cyon nights when my furtive fingers dove over the con-
cave rim of your hairy, pitching chest to the smooth pool
of your rippling belly and onward to where the swell of
your passion rose and fell in time to my susurrations in
your shell-like; remember me when you return to your
comrades and lovers, telling them how I cried and died

the same way as I did when your arms embraced another with more to take and less to give—for (and each breath circulated through pore and capillary seems shorter and more precious) I can see from the podium those who gave me license to be licentious, and I wish them to know I know my executioner, that they might understand the existential balance between that caught moment of unconsciousness when time ceases to tick its irresistible tock—moments from which I have forged my life—and the great plans of Orhan that will reach beyond their generation and blossom (in some unimaginable and intangible beauty) when all the unmoved shakers and unshaken movers are forgotten: and in that knowledge recall how I straddled two worlds, how I taxed and exercised their minds and bodies, my tongue teasing the very roots of their reasoning, my riddles creeping into the apertures of their silks, to places where their logic was no match for my probe and thrust; and (breathe, Karagöz, breathe) ah yes, and now the anthem plays, and the people stand to attention as I talk through it, talk above and below it, offer my blasphemous cacophonies, my syncopated caterwaul, my flat expectorations to counterpoint the bars and staves with which the officers and lawgivers have beaten the rhythm out of me, who offers a richer melody than found in their martial medleys; and I offer you my foul-smelling wind for your well-blown, blue-veined nostrils to expand in disgust to, I offer my lapses of taste, my barfs during the court banquets, my dribbling in the toasts, my unacceptable itches in unmentionable places, my unmissable excitations among the eunuchs, my sudden exposures to the holy—I offer these to you all now because at the moment of my death I refuse to entertain being entertaining by being entertaining, decline to allow you the pleasure of one last performance, resist letting you take the praise at my expense, for (breathe, Karagöz, breathe) I have known the mysterious bottom, the unfathomable hole, have landed on the floor of the pit of the unknown and recognized the effluence of mortality and smelled its realness, have known more than you will ever admit the stark pleasure of a life without apology, have heaved and sweated more than any to reach the unreachable goal, and I have sucked it in through my teeth, washed in it, swallowed it whole; so you can laugh your bronchitic laughs, and cough your consumptive snickers at my execution; but I will breathe, breathe, breathe, and go on breathing in my life from the smell of all of your orifices, from the areas where your cries of pleasure were most acute and which you have all denied in the act of sanctioning my death; but I will breathe, breathe, breathe, and permit no stopping, that you will hear me out as your whoops drowned me out when all of us, and sometimes more than all of us, joined our bodies and our minds in play; breathe, breathe, breathe—not with the silent, measured shallowness of the yogi or pandit, but with the restless pants, the reflex intakes, the deep sighs, the sudden convulsions, the exhausted but excited gasps, the unresisting giggles of lovers here and now, near and far; and as I do so bless the degenerate and the desperate in whose snores, snorts, and belches lie the unexpurgated life I have always believed and lived in—for (breathe, Karagöz, breathe) each breath is shorter, each drawing up of the flexed intercostals less convincing, less magnificently muscular; my shoulders huddle now too close to my ears for comfort, and the lungs ache, my lords and ladies, flunkeys and floozies, the lungs ache; with each breath my eyes and underclothes grow wetter, with each breath your smiles and lies grow broader, with each breath the poisonous phlegm in my mouth becomes less easy to channel down my gammy tongue, out through my moued mouth, and onto the mudlarked faces below me; yet each breath presents a challenge and a triumph, each breath remains a dangerous intent, each breath could deliver anything from a curse to a blessing, for it is from Karagöz, prince of fools and jester to the world; and yet each breath is shorter and more fretful, each breathing-in harder than the relieved breathing-out, each breath more whining and less melodic than the last; and I have no energy to fool, only my unvoiceable memories to foster and tickle into a weak, tear-diluted life; no energy, no breath, only the possible joy that comes from seeing the end of the (breathe, Karagöz, breathe); and it seems a joy, you know, suddenly a joy that I could stop at the end of the (breathe, Karagöz, breathe); I would almost welcome it, and with the delicacy of a young girl's acceptance of her first kiss, ask you to grip the handle of your axe tighter (breathe, breathe); and bring it down, in a flash, on a sudden inbreath, that I might end it all even as I reach the end of the (breathe), end of the (breathe), end of the (breathe), end of the (breathe), end of the sentence.

* * *

Soner or Later

The day Soner the Cook jumped into the hole dug by the Post Office outside his lokanta, Death, who had been trailing Soner for twenty years and had even then been rippling with his breath the hairs on Soner's neck, flew up Mount Olympus and angrily demanded of Zeus that he do something.

"Like what?" said Zeus.

"Like getting him out of that hole, for a start," replied Death.

"I'm afraid that the workings of the Post Office are beyond even the gods' understanding," responded Zeus magisterially. "You will just have to wait."

Death blanched—as only Death can—and fluttered away furiously on the breeze. And well you might imagine his anger, for Soner the Cook was the prize he had always desired. Whereas other cooks in Bursa had supplied Death with a constant feast of customers to diet upon through their unclean pots, or unscrubbed tables, or undercooked food, Soner had maintained an impeccable lokanta and an even more spotless cuisine. His tahinli pide had exactly the right amount of sugar and peanuts, and the perfect combination of spice, herb, and vegetable furnished his pizzas. His bread was always warm and soft, his meat delicate and tender, his zebzeli kebab succulent and aromatic. His preparations of fish were the pride of the west coast. Local and regional celebrities were not ashamed to have the table by the window in Soner's lokanta, and Elma the Grocer swears—as he often does—that the Great Leader, on a secret visit to Bursa near the end of his life, tasted the young Soner's fare and then and there renewed his commitment to God and his country.

As to the hole itself, scabrous rumors began to spread—mostly from those lazy layabouts Ali and Suleyman, who do nothing but chew tobacco and play backgammon all day—that the Post Office (or the PTT, as it was anonymously and mysteriously called) had dug a hole outside the lokanta at the behest of one Doner Bey, a jealous and probably foreign restaurateur who wished to have Soner done away with. These rumors were, of course, refuted wholeheartedly by Doner's cousin Metin Bey, the controller; but as Jenem the beautiful daughter of Iyi Kirmirzi, the town communist, argued in the Kultur Park's most fashionable tea-rooms to a crowd of admiring young men from the University, flicking her ebony hair contemptuously away from her rouged cheeks, banging her bejeweled fist on the worn and ash-strewn formica, and pointing her manicured nails in the direction of the glinting town, the indisputable fact remained that on the evening of March the twenty-fourth the hole wasn't there and on the morning of the twenty-fifth it was.

That morning Soner had complained to the soldier who stood nonchalantly guarding the hole that not only was the hole an eyesore and a danger to his customers, who were beginning to stay away as a result, but that there was no reason for the hole to be there in the first place. "There are no mains or cables or anything beneath my pavement," said Soner sensibly. "So why is there a hole outside my lokanta?"

The soldier said he'd refer the matter to the sergeant. The sergeant referred it to the captain. The captain referred it to the colonel. The colonel referred it to the general, who said it was a civilian matter and referred it to the commissioner. The commissioner referred it to the magistrate, and the magistrate referred it to the mayor. The mayor, raising his perspiring eyebrows to the great mountain that snored above the city in the sun, sighed through his pendulous mustache that the workings of the Post Office were beyond his understanding, but said he'd look into it. He did, the next day, as he was passing by the lokanta on the way to his beloved Inji, pearl of the Bedestan, and for a reasonable price in turn beloved by all.

"It's deep, isn't it?" admired the mayor, leaning cautiously over his stomach.

"Is that all you're going to say?" replied Soner, with the justifiable contempt of a man who could baste a salmon to make the dawn blush.

"I shall look into it," said the mayor again, once more setting off on his quixotic pursuit of a final decision. As it turned out, the mayor had no chance to do anything about the hole, for, just one hour later, Soner jumped into it.

But the day Soner the Cook jumped into the hole to escape Death, he thanked God that the PTT had chosen his lokanta outside of which to dig their hole. He silently blessed the hand that had held the spade that had been placed in the hand by the hand that had been greased by the hand that had served a pizza that failed to emulate the special pizzas that Soner's hands could toss and swivel like the hands in the finest pizzerias of Italy. And yet, even as he reflected on his luck, Soner pondered with dejection the life that remained to him in his hole, where he had to stay if he wanted to avoid Death's skeletal fingers tapping him on the shoulder.

He need not have worried, however, about the bleakness of his hole, because before the week was out he was being offered gifts from citizens from all levels of Bursa's society. The old beggars, outlaws in their own land, who day in, day out stood in front of their broken scales, asking to weigh passersby for a spare lira, gathered together the money they weren't being forced to pay to the local Mafia and bought Soner a threadbare, secondhand rug to sit on. "For," as Yok, the eldest and most desperate of their number, said, in a voice halting with emotion, "many of our friends and colleagues have been victims of Death's hatred of the poor and needy, and we admire somebody who can refuse its ravenous appetite and yet still retain his humility."

The town widows and widowers came and offered him cups of tea and a year's supply of raki because, they said with tears in their eyes, having no one to love because of Death's cruelty, it was the least they could do to offer succor to that man who had in his lokanta not only lighted the candles over which they had held each other's hands, but who even now was fighting the ultimate battle of the heart with the slayer of all passion.

Although initially many of the aristocrats and parvenus in Bursa resented the new hero because he tended to take the crowds away from their frequently indulged walkabouts, soon they began to see that

Soner's being there had considerable advantages. Soner had become something of a tourist attraction. Parties from the Western lands passing through on their way to the pleasure beaches on the coast would make a special stop to visit the facilities, as their guides would delicately put it, and wave at Soner in his hole. Soon, dignitaries and notables from the town and the locale came to visit him. The minister of tourism spent one night in Bursa on his way to Bodrum from Istanbul in order to congratulate Soner on his contribution to that most vital of industries. Stalls began to cluster around the hole, selling mementoes of the man who was rapidly becoming Bursa's most famous citizen. The local Motherland Party chief had the bright idea of starting a competition to see who could make Soner the finest carpet, and politicians from Ankara and Izmir came to Bursa to canvass Soner's opinion on important social issues. The police commissioner made Soner a special constable due to his conviction that the streets were safe if one of the public was buried in them, and the commander-in-chief of the army was reputed to have asked Soner to construct an effective ground battle-plan because of his proximity to it.

Soner's unusual situation quickly became folklore: the great Arabesque singer, Sen Seviyorum, composed a passionate and patriotic tune likening Soner to the Great Leader in his defiance of Death. It was an instant hit among all the young rich who skied and played on the mountaintop in winter; it became an anthem to an audacious life under the stars for the gypsies in the shacks along the slopes; it even softened into a love song among the inamorata on Tophane, and a chant for the young hopscotchers of School Street. With Sen's song in their hearts, Bursa's basketball team began to win, and even the soccer team turned up for training. The young film star Chokchok Güzel sang it in his next film, and the cinemas were awash with the tears and laughter of old and young alike as they recognized and applauded the sentiments.

But what of Soner? Well, he was as aware of all the ruckus as a man can be when he is ten feet beneath the surface of the ground. While his friends, colleagues, and other malicious gossips did come and tell him the latest news, he couldn't help feeling that while he was out of the hands of Death, life was nevertheless passing him by. He missed his wife, even though every day she would come out of his lokanta, which she ran with her usual efficiency and dedication, and blow him kisses. His beautiful daughters would each week present their new boyfriends, whose hairless faces would redden at being presented to such an important personality. He was not happy, but then nor was he unhappy: jumping into the hole had left him in...well, a hole, which not even the presentation of the keys to the city could allay. After all, Soner reflected, what door could he use them on?

Throughout the years, Death looked on all of this, perched atop the magnificent dome of the Great Mosque, occasionally dipping his wings to fly off towards the road to Istanbul, or the hospital in Chekirge. But more and more he found himself returning to the Great Mosque, his heart full of dark contempt and revenge. About ten years after Soner had made that leap into the hole, Death could take it no longer. He lifted the mantle of his wings and flew to the summit of Mount Olympus, and insisted that Zeus send a flood to drown Soner out of his hole.

Zeus had quite forgotten about Soner and the hole. He found it astonishing that Death, who really had quite a good time of it generally, should be bothered about one man, even if he was becoming famous throughout Western Anatolia. Yet, as a god whose own fortunes had declined and whose reputation had diminished until he was now, by his and others' estimation, a mere demiurge, a cluster of energy lines, a genius loci—and not much of one at that—Zeus found himself sympathizing with Death's situation. Recalling the curses he had heaped for millennia on Abraham and his children every time the lame and flea-ridden horses of the sun left their dilapidated stables, Zeus understood how sharp were the pangs of nostalgia for a golden age when one was insuperable. Lowering his eyelids in ancient understanding and shaking his hoary locks, Zeus agreed to Death's request, confident that Soner would not survive the storm he would unleash.

A tempest of unspeakable ferocity it was. Clouds from Erzurum in the east blew rapidly over the central plains, and the winds howled through the ancient caves at Göreme. Sunlovers at Yalova in the north ran screaming with laughter into their expensive seaside villas as the sky thickened. The great cliffs of the Dardanelles were blackened by a muddy pall darker than those crags had ever known. And Antalya in the south shook in fear as the close infernal heat simmered the storm. All these elements Zeus collected in his mighty palms and crushed them together to mold a flood to resurrect Noah.

Down came the rain, cascading down the muddy tracks and past the Green Mosque where Orhan slept. It saturated the back streets and alleys. It streamed past the proud and erect statue of the Great Leader, whose magnificent nose dripped with equally substantial raindrops. It flooded Six-Finger Street, overfilling the boating lake in the Kultur Park, so that the wretched animals in the zoo suddenly found their cages buckled and bent and their lives their own at last. The old city walls became a waterfall, and the dusty soccer fields mudbaths; the bazaar turned into rapids, and the buses in the bus station jostled together like gondolas. But more than anything, the rain gushed into Soner's hole, filling it to the brim, soaking his beautiful carpets and vases of flowers, pouring onto his ancient gramophone and even older brass trumpet, splashing his finely carved table and drenching his freshly baked bread.

But Soner the Cook was not only a superb chef, with a delicious recipe for smoked mackerel that surprised and delighted gourmets with its daring use of marjoram and garlic, but he was a highly resourceful man as well. He took a single amaryllis from the vase and, snapping off its head, breathed through its stem as the water rose rapidly over his neck, chin, nose, eyes, forehead, and crown. Zeus emptied half of the Black Sea and Mediterranean on Soner. The townspeople, all meteorologists of considerable prowess, as they would frequently inform you, swore they had never known a time when there had been so much rain. Even Merkedes, the indomitable wife of old Okyanus the bus driver, who went shopping in all weathers, didn't venture out this time. All stayed indoors, looking out for leaky roofs and overflowing drainpipes. None of them thought of Soner, who all this while continued to breathe through the amaryllis stem, blowing out the occasional salty rain-drops that slipped into the slender tube. Eventually, when it had been raining for forty days and nights— which Zeus considered a suitably ironic length of time— he called Death to him and said:

"Soner the Cook cannot be drowned. The man is more clever than I thought."

"Then what am I going to do?" Death whimpered.

Zeus settled back to disperse the clouds. "We shall just have to try and burn him out."

As quickly as the skies had darkened before, they cleared. The remorseless sun shone down on the rapidly caking mud, wilting the flowers and warping the records and blistering the table and bleaching the carpet and all the while beating down on Soner's hole with a glaring white light that burned his skin and dried up his tear ducts. Despite the loan of a large hat from the town undertaker, Soner gained no comfort from the shade, as sweaty nights gave way to bone-dry days, and his soaked shirts hardened and froze, only to be wringing wet as soon as the sun arose to torment him again.

At first, the people of Bursa welcomed the sun, and it brought out promenader and tea-drinker, teenager and pimp, all to enjoy the weather and comment to Soner on what a beautiful day it was. Soner, whose eyes were sore from the sun, could only nod at hearing their voices, and

croak—for there soon was little water left in the city—
that indeed it was. As the days went by, the river that
had once been a gushing torrent became no more than a
trickle in a cracked bed, and the townspeople took to
staying indoors. Work stopped at the huge car factory,
and the cherries rotted on their trees. The roots of the
plants that hung perilously from the walls of Tophane
dug deeper in their search for water, while ice cream
vans from a hundred miles around clogged the highways
from Izmir, Ankara, and Istanbul. But in spite of Death's
frequent visits to the vans and his surfeiting on the buses
to the beaches, he could not forget Soner, who did not
move from his hole. Zeus sighed to Death when he
protested again: "I cannot do anything against Soner's
will. Moreover, I am hurting the innocent townsfolk of
Bursa with this drought. Let him be. He will come out
eventually. What about a game of chess, instead?"

So Soner grew old and poor in vision. His hair fell
out, as did his teeth. Soon he could no longer lift up his
head to look at the stars that shone with never-ending
brightness on the city he loved so much. His wife died,
and the lokanta was sold. His daughters married and
moved away, and more and more infrequently came to
show their less and less interested children their extraordinary grandfather. Soner was ignored more than
noticed, and the citizens even began to protest that Soner
was a relic of the past who should be persuaded to climb
out of his hole so that everybody could get on with their
business. The songs that had graced Soner's defiance
soon became ribald jokes about holes, and Soner was
mocked as a figure both arrogant and cowardly. Children

prayed at night against the bogeyman Soner, and it became local legend that to walk past his hole before noon was bad luck. Soon everybody avoided Soner, except one figure who with his great black wings flew down every day from where he perched on the top of the Great Mosque and offered him food. And Soner, despite weakening all the time, refused, content merely to eat the grass and fruit that miraculously flowered in his hole.

One day, as Death looked at the wizened old man blinking in his direction, he experienced a sudden surge of an unfamiliar emotion: pity. "Soner. Soner. Climb out of the hole. What is the point in continuing this defiance of me?"

"No," croaked Soner, arthritically pulling himself upright and thrusting forward his sunken chest as best he could. "I have my self-respect."

"Respect is nothing but what other people make of you, Soner," said Death vehemently, his red eyes softening slightly as they caught sight of Soner's weather-beaten neck and the spreading moles that clustered on his chest. "And nobody respects you anymore. I admit, there was once a time when your cheap trick fooled everyone into believing that Death was invincible. But no one can resist me. Here, look in this mirror and see how pathetic you are."

Soner squinted at the hunched winged figure that perched at the rim of his hole. "You have offered me this mirror every day for more years than I can remember," he scoffed, "and every time I have refused to take it. I have no use for it. I am too old to wonder what I look like."

"Soner. Trust me. Just look," said Death.

"How can I trust you? You want to kill me!"

"True," said Death. "But I can't force you out of that hole. If you take the mirror you will understand."

"What do I need to understand?" replied Soner.

However, Death said nothing but held out the mirror toward him. And Soner, who had never been tempted before, suddenly felt compelled to take the mirror. He reached out and felt its weight in his hands, and with closed eyes ran his fingers over the surface. Then, slowly, he opened his eyes.

What greeted him was a face that had undergone decades of solitary resistance. The lips were chapped, the cheeks sallow, the lines deep gorges in a deserted face. Age had taken up comfortable habitation in him and had spread like luxuriant ivy into every crevice and along every surface of his body. Before he knew what he was doing, he began to cry. For the first time in the countless numbers of years he had spent down the hole, he cried. He cried for his wife, and his children and grandchildren; he cried for his lokanta and for the ragged carpet the beggars had given him, for the carpet that had never recovered from the rain and the sun. He cried for all of those who had told him their news and had gone on to live their lives—with all their failures and triumphs, betrayals and acts of total selflessness. But, above all, he cried for himself, because for all of his defiance of Death and the fame and infamy that had attended his life down the hole, what washed over him in a wave that no amaryllis stem could stop was the sense that, ultimately, none of it mattered. His tears were no longer tears of sorrow at what had passed and what he had missed, but tears of relief, as he understood that the burden of his life could finally be released. He understood, even as Death's eyes narrowed and hardened into a stare, how great and fleeting were life's mysteries, how attenuated its promises and hopes, and how fragile was his hold on it in spite of his leap into the hole. But, more than anything, he saw that it had not been Death who had been his closest companion. It was Time—invisible and undemonstrative, neither vindictive nor forgiving, insistent on its dues and exact in its punishments—that had been with him all along. And no jump, whether across the marriage threshold or into a hole or across ten thousand fathoms, could leave it behind.

So, taking what few possessions he could carry in his frail arms, Soner the Cook wearily and with much effort climbed out of the hole. And as he did, he felt Time release his hand, the sun warm his back, and the icy fingers of Death tighten around his heart. Soner's hole was rapidly filled in by the PTT, whose memory is everlasting, and all there is now to mark the spot is a cluster of amaryllis flowers that, in their season, wave their delicate blooms in the breeze that descends like a mist from the mountain above the town.

* * *

The Belletrist

The caravans have ceased their restless wandering for the night; the owls have finished their admonishments and fly towards the East where, like me, an aged fool lies in the bed of a warm and ever-youthful beauty whose long fingers stroke his feverish head and who has now left his sagging arms to light up the world. But, unlike the raddled lover of the dawn, I am not content and have not made my peace; for my face—painted white by the unblinking moon that breaks through the slats of my litter's window with a half-indifferent, half-sorrowing pallor—is the face of an old man, unprepared for death.

Mademoiselle Latriste is my confidante, my aging confessor. Similarly white-faced (although in this case with the delicate touch of the sculptor's art) she stands as my arthritic Erato holding aloft—perhaps contemptuously, perhaps pityingly—the thyrsus and the lyre as testaments to the power I thought my mind once possessed to gather from the deep or breathe into the clay. Mademoiselle Latriste has not aged well, but she has been a mademoiselle for so long that it no longer seems risible to address her so. I once called her by her first name—Belle—in a flash of sudden, unwanted and unwarranted intimacy. It was but an instant of intemperance and overconfidence, when the words that lay before me, at once so familiar and so alien, seemed almost what I had imagined they should be. I looked up at her, posed marmoreally on her pedestal: "Belle, my Belle," I said. "Look. At last. Perhaps this might atone. Perhaps we might call this the beginning." But no. She dipped her frozen gaze and I found myself rebuffed by her stern, finely drawn eyebrows arching into a frown of contempt. I knew then that we were never to be friends, and I kept my art hidden from her. Mademoiselle Latriste has done the same to me.

Mademoiselle Latriste. I have tried, you must believe me, to pity her sorrow. I have tried, more times than I can even think, to salvage from her perpetual disappointment some remnant of the talent with which I courted her on the mountain and in the pantheon when I was younger and bolder and had not been so vulgar as to commit an offense on, or anything to, paper. But every time a work emerged—trivial, unnecessary, importunate, with title and subject vacuous even for those vacuous days—the disillusionment was etched that little bit more firmly on her patient visage.

It was not always so. In her youth, indeed, she had not been Latriste, but an unnameable nymph or dryad, chaste of mortal touch and chased by all. But the years deepened the lines around her eyes and darkened the shadows under them; her unblushed cheeks hollowed and her lips thinned and froze. Or perhaps those lines and shadows, depressions and pinches were simply imagined by me in the failing light of countless, unyielding nights of flickering candles and guttering fires. It is too late to ask.

Yet it is to her that I offer these, my last words, written down not in the looping arc of my irresponsible youth, but the corvine scratching of my decrepitude. My beautiful girl, my nurse and embalmer, whose throat warbles unknown sounds as she weaves her soft fingers over my sallow cheeks, has gone. I can only guess at which distant land she directs the slow curve of her eyelashes when she suspects my dim old eyes are closed. For when I ask my urgent questions—urgent with the fear of what the answer might be—in the primitive language of a sophisticated European country she has never been to but whose elaborate tongue she envelops and yet understands so little, she offers merely platitudes of homeland and family, of enslaved peoples and desolate villages, of a lost love and the hope of restoration.

Mademoiselle Latriste knows, with the cold discernment of art, why my girl ministers to me so. Mademoiselle Latriste understands why the child every night gently removes her soft hand from my emaciated clutch, slides soundlessly from beneath my sweat-soaked sheets, gathers up her vivid satin robes (my pathetic gifts to her) and retires to other vans, richer and more populous than mine. Mademoiselle Latriste recognizes the epiglottal lamentations my companion offers at dawn and dusk and the pendulous tears that hesitate on the sweet thing's cheeks. But Mademoiselle Latriste has even denied me words to offer any literary consolation to this tender creature. Instead, for my last years, she has commanded silence, bid me throw down the pen and go eastward. For in the East, she has said to me in the fever-ridden nights, I will find absolution; in a pristine dawn I will burn myself in the fire of an ascendant sun and die in peace.

So have I traveled, across a cocksure, bankrupt continent, thick with the preparations for a mad war; I have crossed the Bosphorus into a new land, a different set of expectations, a continent that for so long cultivated enemies who taught us everything. And I can go no further. Nor, incidentally, will my train. The drivers and their associates—the disconsolate local servants hired before we lost sight of the Golden Horn—have asked in various dialects but with uniform bafflement where Effendi is going, and, more insidiously, what he is leaving behind. And I have waved a scrawny, dismissive hand in the direction of the sunset, and pointed a bony forefinger towards the Caspian. But now I do not care any more to see Samarkand or the Kush, or to dip my weary feet into the rivers Alexander crossed. I have arrived at Nicaea, and this is where I will end.

Once I would have welcomed the chance to compose some broken verses on an eloquent death and paint in— by way of background or chiaroscuro—perhaps for Nicaea a ruinous wall or two, the half-eroded ivy-covered Roman inscription, a disreputable yet picturesque band of swarthy, nomadic camel-drivers gathered around a broken-down gate before the long march at sunrise. But I have not the palette and Mademoiselle Latriste certainly has not the palate for such local color—not that this place lends itself to much in the way of pastoral or sonnet. So what I have left is this brief death rattle, the grubby apologia of a disappointed and uneminent Victorian.

But, and this is where irony wakes from its shallow nap to bark and wag its tail at me, I knew them all—the distinguished gentlemen of letters who composed for God and Country—Tennyson, Browning, Swinburne, even that fatuous bore Arnold. I published them all in best India on vellum, with silk markers and the most illustrious, apposite typefaces. I gave their fevered imaginings the respectability they—lickerish, barely bearded, wild-haired, sparkling-eyed—all craved, a respectability that crushed what life and spontaneity they once could have claimed to have owned. While none became as hoary as Wordsworth—archaically crumpled on the front bench of the Upper House, grunting in approval at anything the aquiline and cantankerous Wellington snorted, composing wretched sonnets for the half-cocked amusement of a philistine queen and her pompous German consort—they, all the rest of the glorious Nineteenth Century, became fat, or bald, or repetitive, or sentimental, or suffered from gout, or grew long beards, or cut their hair. In short, they were successful, while I, who never suffered from that particular ailment, had to spend my days gathering together their essays, meditations, reflections, thoughts, and the other clap-trap they regaled the Reading Public with, and establish them for posterity so I might earn enough to publish my own *rimes brûleés*.

There are a few volumes of my poetry, endorsed in error by Patmore and with forewords tricked from Jowett and Pater, but read by no one except bored relatives and uninterested lovers. I did not strike martial enough a chord for the phalanx of severe aunts and catatonic uncles, sober nephews and consumptive nieces, whose dedication to Queen and Empire grew in inverse proportion to their sense of humor. I was, for them, only a step or two on the evolutionary ladder above the savages they were so interested in civilizing, and overly concerned with perfumed feuilletons and not enough with imperial reams for their taste. But then, I was neither unbuttoned nor, I might add, devoted enough to all those hirsute women who lounged with exquisite resignation for Rossetti and Millais, or those farouche entrancers Terry and Bernhardt, or the frightfully serious suffrage-seekers who gathered around Elizabeth Browning, née Barrett, or Mary Ann Cross, née Evans.

I cannot lie and say I particularly cared at the time, since most of my days and nights were spent in the wine-dark sea of my own or some fellow sot's bibulousness. Yet now, when even a sip of dry white is enough for me to greet Morpheus with a welcoming embrace, the failure washes saltily behind my fading eyes. Even when, with me at an age when my sideburns had turned a respectable white, the Aesthetes swept in with their studied disdain for anything vaguely moralistic, and I hoped I might pass myself off as an elderly roué, a salutary Silenus, I still remained not quite bold enough for Beardsley or Wilde, or expressive enough for Symons. I was too precise to be precieux; trop père and not enough the faun. I also did not care for boys, which it seemed was, and still is, de rigueur for the True Artist.

But I do not want bitterness to cloud my last missive, Mademoiselle Latriste. You were generous to them—as you always are to those with a talent the cultivation of which is less self-regarding or more disciplined than mine—as you have been patient and unrewarded with me. I did not begrudge you then, and will not do so now, when although more of a matron of honor than a laughing girl you sat so obviously at their table, occasionally glancing across at me from over their feasts. I see you now, laughing with open throat and glistening eyes at their jokes, your fine-boned hand cupping your ivory chin as the well-tailored and fine-fingered captains of literature set sail on another stirring saga, or launched a brilliant monologue, or floated a precocious idea. My jottings were on the napkins and kerchiefs you used to dab your dewy eye or slightly retroussé nose with when, yet again, I had promised you an evening to remember and had let you down by turning up intoxicated, or the show was closed, or I had been somehow inappropriate. How were you to know that on these scraps I had dedicated my soul to you?

Yet, here I am, in my mid-eighties, alive when the others are long dead, or in prison, broken by debt or a woman or a boy, or simply in colder climes, possessed of what I ever had of my wits and most of my bodily functions, and the sharer of a bed with a sloe-eyed lovely who caters to my every fading caprice. Is this not the very end of life for the poet, the closure that all of us wish for: another new dawn, the lingering scent of a fragrant young body, the knowledge that we have tried our best, that when we are gone someone may find (mistakenly perhaps, miscatalogued possibly, mispriced no doubt) on a dusty shelf in some secondhand bookshop somewhere in the civilized world a collection of our work and be surprised by the sanctioned pleasure of words once more? One can only dream of it—and I would for many more days do such a thing were it not for Mademoiselle Latriste and Nicaea.

For, put another way, the dawn has begun its tired resurrection and I am alone in my bed again, left with only the distant memory of the aroma of her softness and the sack of my bedraggled bones. In the corner of my wagon I see Mademoiselle Latriste, her hair full-bodied yet white, her skin still porcelain pure but no longer able to maintain a passive disdain. Are those tears, my dear Mademoiselle, you are shedding? Dare I hope they might be for me? Would you join me for a stroll alongside the lake, or accompany me for a swim?

When I step outside my van I will see in the emerging light my girl dancing and singing with her melancholy intensity around a dying fire. Her rhythm responds to a music I do not know, and her songs talk of lands I have not seen, and will never see. She entered my life and left me no wiser, even as you, Mademoiselle, never left me but also did not let me experience your grace—a moment of abandon or surrender, where a conjunction might have been exchanged between us that was not "but." Yet it was not to be. Of course, being of an age where every day enhances more piquantly the possibility of a final night, I did nothing last evening but stare across at the crumbling walls and rich indifference of Nicaea, whose history—unlike any of the other innumerable and forgettable towns on my route—held itself up as a mirror in which I could inspect the fine cut of my failure with all its polished touches and individual tailoring and decide what to do. It seemed then, as it does now, therefore, an absolutely natural extension of that revelation that it should also show me how to die.

I will walk to the side of the lake and, in one movement, enter the water. Feel how cool the water is, dear Belle—can I not, just one last time, call you that without a fear that even this word will be dismissed from your presence with one derisive gesture? Will you not join me? Or do there await others such as myself, of a later generation of failures, who command that you be present yet who will always, like me, disappoint? Of course, it would be inconceivable that I should be a unique failure; that would be too great a success.

And to you, my sylph: Adieu. I will imagine that, after the men have irresolutely searched the surrounding pastures and town, after they have gathered up my belongings and shared them amongst themselves, after they have departed to their villages with the short-lived curiosity of my disappearance flitting through their heads—I will imagine that you will come to the lake and know that my body floats towards the other shore, and that this is how it should be. And you will then also depart; I cannot tell whether you will cry or not. Yet, my love, may you find your village and sing songs of joy once more. May you be blessed with youth—or that youth you lost if that is what you wish—and what all of us in our recklessness imagine happiness to be. I pray you live your life in the way I have not. And Mademoiselle Latriste, in offering you my raddled lips, I bid your cold mouth goodbye: may you find another and more deserving life to serve.

* * *

Synapsis

When the governor told us they were two women—"deaconesses," he said—I had imagined them to be both young and naive or old and stupid. But they were mature

women, perhaps mothers, their bodies firm and well-
formed, and clearly fully aware of where they were and
what they were to expect. The governor had informed
the captain—as if he would know anything about that
sort of thing—that they belonged to a group of
Christians who had proved "particularly intractable."
They were to be "persuaded by any means possible to see
the error of their ways." And neither of them blinked,
though I saw the governor looking around the cell in
mild distaste, trying to avoid their eyes. "But..." And I
saw the governor working to find a word to express that
demurral. He failed, and turned from us.

The captain, in a neutral voice, repeated, "Two
women. Yes, sir," and watched him walk away. When
the governor was out of earshot he turned to us. "Don't
ask," he said contemptuously. "Just do it. Get something
from them. Anything. To please the boss." He glanced
across at the women, who were standing motionless
against the wall.

"Have fun," he smiled to us, and left.

Andronicus was ready to beat them. He started calling them "whores" and "bitches" and after poking his
stick at their breasts and genitalia cracked them on the
knees so that they fell to the ground.

"You must understand," I said, trying to be reasonable and hoping to stop this before it began.
"Andronicus needs to be given license or he will be
uncontrollable. It would be easier for all of us if you
confessed your ideas are blasphemous, and embraced
the gods of Rome." They did not look at me and said
nothing. I turned to Andronicus. "You can do what you

will until I tell you to stop. But you must not touch them with your hands."

I ordered the women to get up, still hoping they might value the restraint I had shown. But they expressed nothing: neither rage nor thanks. They touched their forehead, stomach, and two shoulders with their fingers. Andronicus demanded to know what witchcraft it was they were performing and threatened to kill them unless they withdrew the curse. When they didn't say anything he flung his fist across their jaws. They didn't flinch; seemingly without fear they stared back at him, muttering something under their breath that I couldn't hear. I began to feel my heart palpitating and my armpits dampening. I gritted my teeth and walked up to them, trying to stop my voice from breaking slightly as I spoke.

"I would like to make it very clear that, unless you renounce your false god and swear to honor the gods of Rome, we will have no option but to torture you until you do. We do not want to do this. We..." I looked at Andronicus and then back at them. "We get no pleasure from this. Do you understand what we want?"

Nothing.

"Do you understand?" I asked again.

Nothing. Again nothing. Perhaps a slight smile from the shorter of the two, I couldn't be sure. I felt my heart dry up inside me.

I commanded Andronicus to strip their backs and tie the two women to the beating-posts. I ordered him to give them thirty lashes. First, he beat them on the back of the legs to force them to fall to their knees. Then he began to whip them, carving and slicing into their flesh.

And as the flesh was cut and slit, they began to sing—
their thin voices growing stronger and stronger as the
slashes grew more and more searing. And this is what
they sang.

> *Lord Lord Lord: forgive me for my not giving.
> Establish this point as a place for the engender-
> ing of prayer. Let my soul be infused with your
> seed, and in the darkness make your injunction a
> conjunction, and with two unities form one.
> Allow at this nexus the unity to gather and not
> disperse, to coalesce and not diffuse, so my soul
> may know herself in oneness with you.*

I called out for Andronicus to stop; but when he did,
so did they. It was as if they were begging for martyrdom, for each time I asked them, every opportunity I
gave them, to renounce their worship of the Jew Jesus
and turn to the true gods, just to do it once, even if it
was a lie, they fell silent and dropped their heads. There
were no tears, no whimpers. Even their breath was even
and contained. So I told Andronicus to begin again, this
time letting him lace his whip with salt so that the weals
smarted and wept. And I felt tears come to my eyes as I
saw how their backs were a mess of shredded pulp. Yet,
far from crying out, they began to sing again.

> *Lord Lord Lord: make me a present of your pres-
> ence. At this crossing-point let there be no cross-
> ing over, but an apprehension of all ways and
> nodes of faith. Bring into the ducts of my being*

*the undissolved solution of your spirit, that every
knot may be a yes of you within me, every flex-
ion your inflection, all accidence of my body the
accident of your presence.*

And Andronicus beat, his face contorted by the
effort of his beating—somehow unable to stop. I found
myself backed up against the wall, unable to see because
tears were filling my eyes. They sang and they sang—
and each word they sang was a terrible mixture of
absolute joy and pain, each word timed by the whip that
flailed upon their backs. My knees felt weak and I bent
over and vomited, weakly falling onto all fours.
Andronicus, oblivious to my reaction, kept on beating.
Lord Lord Lord.
"Stop," I shouted. But it wasn't to Andronicus.
Lord Lord Lord.
I meant them. I mean you. Please stop.

*Lord Lord Lord. Gift me the give of my forgive-
ness. Show me the chiasmus of your gift for our
forgiveness and the giving that is our gift to you.
Mold me with the plasma of your love that the
matrix of my soul may conceive in it the synapse
of faith. All I ask is the allness to be upon me, an
answer to the question of my questing. Let me
become a crux for your body, as you were for
mine. Suffer me the suffering of your sufferance,
bond me to your bondage, make a span of my
life for my lifespan.*

Finally they stopped and Andronicus, his arms hanging limply by his side, his face drawn and tired, looked at me. I returned his look and motioned him to untie the women and turn them to face me. Slowly he undid the knots and took them by the shoulders and swung them round. While our faces I imagined were smeared with tears and spittle, grime and sweat, theirs seemed calm, almost indifferent. I pulled myself up and walked over to them, yet it was all I could do to look at them. And then I began to cry again.

"Why?! In the name of the gods, why?"

Nothing. Nothing, of course.

So I commanded Andronicus to take his club and beat them on the back of the head, pulling them up by the hair to beat them down again. This time, however, they began to whisper, each one seeming to answer the words of the other. Hurried, urgent whispers rhythmically echoing their pain and their voices.

Give at the intersection, given in favor and thanksgiving. Give in the touch of body and blood on tongue, palm on palm, cheek on cheek, given for you and you only. Give at the moment of prayer and of union, given when life and spirit are one. Give when the war in our souls rages at its highest, given in surrender and exhaustion as honey on wounds.

Their voices grew steadily louder as the blows fell upon their heads.

Give to ourselves the greatest gift of your self, given to you by that Self which gave you all things. Give us our doubt so it might be forgiven, given to us so we might believe. Give us your will so it might be your future, given to us so we might know the bounty of God. Give us your love so it might be returned, given to us so we might know the belovedness of being loved.

Andronicus took the taller one by the hair and clubbed her until blood filled her eyes and she fell forward. As she died I heard a very quiet "Oh," and then nothing. I watched the other, to see a reaction. Any reaction. There was none.

"If you do not turn to our gods, the same will happen to you," I said, with little energy and no conviction. She looked at me, and, her voice breaking, said:

Give so there may be a given, the compact of word and deed, the covenant of your present. Give so there might be a tale for the travail, the heart has a hearth, the point has a point, the end has an end. Give so it might be over, given as you gave in the grave. Give because I ask, and in my asking hope, and in my hope despair.

She fell silent. Andronicus hit her across the face with one huge blow and killed her outright. He looked at me, and I looked at him; and I saw nothing in his eyes. When the captain came back, he wanted to know what they had said. He seemed to expect something, yet what could I tell him? The nonsense I had heard? No. That was ridiculous. So I told him. "Nothing. They were mad," I said. And left it at that.

* * *

Bizarre PanNicaeas

Sir? Sir? Yes, you, sir. May I stop you for a minute, sir, and take a little of your time to introduce you to my commodities? You perhaps may be forgiven, on an initial inspection, for thinking I am merely another of the innumerable merchants clustered in this bazaar, offering the same poorly crafted watch straps or rings. I beg you, sir, do not rush headlong into such delusion, for this substance is of an especial worth, not crassly measurable in carat or ounce. No, indeed not, sir. This, sir, is nothing less than the quintessence of the elements, cured by dehydration and liquefaction, oxidization and crystallization, electrolysis and hydrolysis, hypostatic purification and mega-accelerated proton-blasting. This substance has been burned by a bunsen and refined in an alembic, isolated in a vacuum and barraged with lasers, exposed on an agar plate and fumigated in the smoke chamber. We have reconfigured its atomic structure and reapportioned its magnetic charge. We have mixed it with sulfur and mercury and filtered it through membranes. It has been analyzed for instability, radioactivity, volatility, acidity, refractability, plasticity, utility, and permeability, and has been found suitable for all occasions, climates, creeds, and tasks. It has been stretched, pulled, weighted, crushed, bent, and dissected, but it has always returned to its original shape, without harm, weakening, or discoloration. The most rigorous methodologists and the most exacting minds have been employed to concoct elaborate hypotheses and experiments whereby this substance might be destroyed, and not one scientist or instrument has been able to bring it about.

Naturally, I would not cheapen this substance, sir, by offering it to you in some trinket, bracelet, necklace, tiara, crown, anklet, bangle, bead, bauble, or curio. This substance deserves more than to be a talisman or token of your visit here, a tatty souvenir of the color and noise of a glorified shopping emporium. No, sir. I offer you nothing less than this, the philosopher's stone. What is it, sir? Why, I'm surprised at you, sir; don't you know that by now? But then, perhaps its sheen dazzled your senses. It is no more nor less than Nicaea.

At last, a customer worth accosting. You don't mind if I say that to you, sir, do you? We get so few people around here who so clearly exhibit the aura, who so obviously are aware of their psychic abilities. You are by any estimation an exception, sir; and, may I say, what an exception! I will show you nothing less, sir, than my finest object. In this box you will find the mightiest force known to man. It has a telluric power greater than any crystal or rock hewn from Mother Earth. It has a brighter gloss than any metal yet refined or created, a greater density than the blackest of black holes in the immensity of space; it is lighter than the tiniest particle of energy. This substance unifies opposites and squares circles. It is monadic and dualistic, inessential and symbiotic, divinatory and pragmatic. It is the lowest common denominator and the highest common multiple; it is paradigmatic and democratic, benign and unqualifiable. It is absolutely hermeneutic and irreducibly multiform, possesses negative capability and infinite tonic harmony. It is a prime number and the sum of all numbers, recursive and finite.

This substance colors the chlorophyll of a plant and shapes the tubers of a vegetable. It powers the microchip and energizes the cathode ray. It compels the combustion engine and splits the atom. It stimulates the solar wind and excites aurorae. It is the motivating force behind all things, sir, and yet impossible to quantify.

What is this substance, sir, so hidden from sight in this box? You do not know, sir?! What if I opened the box? Would that give you a better idea? Recognize it? No? Ah, but then perhaps you might know it in another shape, such as this. Still, no?! But, sir: it is Nicaea!

Feel that, sir. Just feel that. Beautiful, isn't it? That, sir, is the finest fabric in the world. And it's not just any old fabric, sir; it is of a very special fiber, a woof of great fineness, softer than any mixture of silk, satin, linen, polyester, nylon, cotton, muslin, wool or whatever, sir, you are likely to find in any market in this big, wide world. It is garnered from plants grown only for the purpose of producing this fabric, sir; it is then drawn and teased until its threads are invisible to the naked eye; and finally, the most practiced and skilled of weavers and spinners gather on a special day in a secret hide-away, deep in the mountains, and, using the most advanced microscopes, make only a very few individual items from this cloth.

You are very lucky, sir, since I have a wide array of these very few individual items made from this special weft. I have here towels (body or hand, sanitary or bathroom), sheets, pillowcases, napkins, cloths for table and dish, curtains, comforters, shirts and sweaters (short-sleeved or full-length), cardigans, blouses, leotards, pullovers, scarves, cravats, mittens, camisoles, briefs, socks, garters, slips, tights, suspenders, chemises, negligees, petticoats, stockings, basques, T-shirts, shorts, bikinis, underpants, long johns, vests, corsets, trusses, halternecks, thongs, bodices, pantyhose, pantaloons, nightgowns, pajamas, knickerbockers, brassieres, and, of course, handkerchiefs.

You will be aware, sir, as I discern you are a man of some polish, that dyes so frequently destroy the fabric. We have, therefore, made it our policy not to dye our garments, which is why they still appear invisible to the naked eye. Be assured, sir, that not only is the fabric delicate to the touch, as you have already experienced, but it is also, as you perhaps have noticed from the shimmering light illuminating this shop, exquisitely patterned with chinoiserie and curlicue, interlaced with gold filigree and inlaid with mother-of-pearl. It can be monogrammed on request.

Naturally, you might be feeling alarmed at using such a cloth for a mundane task such as drying yourself after a wash. But fear not, sir. This material requires no

washing, will dry the wettest of bodies or most extensive
of spills; it will retain water or allow osmosis; it will neither tear nor wear; it will neither lose its pattern nor fray
at the edges. It can be cleverly wired for uplift or support, tightened to shape or compress, or cut away for the
sheer, plunging look.

Are you still unconvinced, sir, even after so detailed
and—dare I say?—passionate a description? Perhaps
you are more used to this substance under another
name. Am I right? Do you not know it as Nicaea?

Forgive me for saying so, sir, but you do not look like a
man who is content with what you see around you.
Within you, if you will pardon the liberty, I discern a
questing soul, with an almost feverish interest in knowledge qua knowledge, a man always on the verge of
adventure, or discovery, or revelation.

If I am right, and I will admit that experience has
rarely proved me wrong, may I draw your attention to
the range of goods I have displayed here? You have
probably been around many of the shops and stalls in
the bazaar—I would not expect an open-minded man
such as yourself to be anything less than thorough in his
quest for perfection—and you may have heard the stall-
holders attempting to sell you substances that are the
most miraculous yet discovered or created. I would ask
you, please, to do nothing less than dismiss the hawkers
and charlatans and their sham wares from your mind. It
is unfortunately the case that, in these days of affluence,
sharks and wise guys of all kinds are flourishing with
their bargains and giveaways that seem to offer so much

yet actually give very little. It is, I am afraid, the spirit of the age.

I will not lie to you, sir. I do not stop every child of Abraham who walks this way. I do not attempt, if I may be frank, to throw pearls before swine. I have found it at once useless and dispiriting. What I do instead is to concentrate on those who have a discriminating eye for quality, and an ear sympathetic to intelligent argument. I ask for nothing less than a noble stature and the visible gleam of intelligence from a customer before I will even offer him or her the time of day. This may be presumption of the highest kind on my part, sir, but you must forgive me; I merely believe in quality. Quality above all.

I offer you the highest quality when I offer you this Nicaea. It has a particular scent and juice distilled from a bouquet of the most aromatic herbs and spices from around the world. It comes in the form of powder, perfume, roll-on, spray, cologne, concentrate, potpourri, cream, pill (soluble or otherwise), liquid, or oil and can be administered to everybody, children or adults, with unlimited dosage at any time of day, as often as is desired. It can heal all diseases, balance the humors, remove stress and unhappiness, and alleviate back pain. It is nontoxic, easy to swallow, good for the teeth, and soothing for even the most severe of psoriatic or seborrheic conditions. It reverses premature balding, eliminates premenstrual tension, increases fertility in male and female, and provides additional nutrients for the amniotic sac. It soothes indigestion and rids one of flatulence, halts dysentery and eases constipation. It is high in fiber and low in cholesterol; it garnishes a dish most succulently, and fills the house with a delightfully uplifting smell. It ensures sound sleep, ecstatic highs, and longevity without side effects, ethical dilemmas, or expense. It can revitalize dying houseplants and recycle non-organic waste without releasing harmful chemicals. It can clean dirty heads on cassettes, and provides a much-needed alternative to fossil fuels. It can rid many Third World countries of their national debt, and reduces unemployment. It is guaranteed to last forever and requires neither replenishment nor readministering. It is precise in its healing and all-encompassing in its offering of well-being. It is available to everybody from anywhere in the world, and requires but one readily available quality in the patient if it is to succeed.

This quality—and by mentioning this quality, sir, I hope you will discern that this is where I differ from the other imposters in this bazaar—this quality, which we so often disempower in our ridiculous shortsightedness, is the catalyst for this Nicaea, sir. It is something you clearly possess in abundance, and which we all, poorest and wealthiest alike, share in some quantity, no matter how disreputable or unthinking our existence. This substance is vital, sir, for without it, everything I have offered to you is useless. Without it, sir, Nicaea is a mere placebo, a cure-all, a lotion any witch doctor could compose from the dung of the earth. Without this ingredient active within you, Nicaea will provide you with no benefits and merely leave you with a bitter aftertaste in the mouth. This ingredient is critical; it is the wellspring from which all of the goodness bursts. The man or woman who understands he or she is possessed of it, and knows how to stimulate it, requires but Nicaea to fulfill his or her life and live to eternity.

What is it, sir? Am I possibly correct in believing that you do not know the name of this material? I find that extraordinary, sir, absolutely extraordinary. I took you for a man of more acumen; I would have thought it was obvious.

This element is Faith.

* * *

The Iteration of the "I"

I, John of Lincoln, being sometime physician in the army of the victorious Emperor Alexius I Comnenus, sent by God to do battle against the barbarians for God's glory, do hereby record that on Friday night last, in the year of our Lord 1106, were heard the last words of a nun of St. Mary at Trier in Germany, notorious for the events here at Nicaea but ten years ago, when Kilij Arslan I was forced to surrender the town to Godfrey de Bouillon of the true faith.

For it is said that, being abducted by the Seljuk savages to whom we were laying siege and being most foully abused by one of their number, this servant of God was released in an exchange of prisoners and allowed entry into the city, where she did most desperately berate and decry this man who had ruined her in the eyes of God.

It is further told that prayers were offered up for the salvation of her soul, by noblemen and men of God alike, that her defilement might be forgiven in the Lord's eyes; and, behold, he in his goodness stretched out his hand and forgave the fallen woman. Yet shortly afterwards, the ungrateful woman vanished with that same barbarian whom she had said brought about her very destruction; and she was not heard of again until I chanced upon the lady begging on the street, sitting in her own squalor, and heavy with child, shouting words that seemed but the cries of a madwoman. I took pity on the wretch and brought her into my home and gave her succor.

After I had nursed her for some weeks, for she was most gravely unwell, I asked of her history, and what evil force had taken her away from the Lord a second time; or whether the Devil himself had goaded her into pursuing the pleasure of the flesh, by which all are lost. But she was unwilling to relate her history or her reasons for turning herself from the true faith in such a manner.

A few weeks after I had found her, the child was born. But it was dead and the woman pined. Although I applied all the knowledge I learned from my teachers and offered prayers to God to give yet again intercession for the soul of his handmaiden, I found I could do nothing to save this poor woman, for she did but prepare her body for the grave since the death of her child. Her soul was in torment, and each night her cries troubled the air.

She would scream forth sinful thoughts no amount of purging could stop; being accusations against herself and this man, blasphemies and condemnations such as were never heard by Christian ears. Finally, when it seemed as though she would depart at any moment and her ghost was ready to leave her tortured body, I gave her my blessing and said a brief prayer, resolving meanwhile to set down her last words; for I hoped truly I might more easily understand the suffering of such a soul in the full and timely examination of a tongue in the written word than by listening to the torrent of words that poured forth from her mouth.

I therefore do set down here these her last words. I have for many hours studied them and do not understand them still; for I believe they are words not of our world. I am not sure of what form the spirit that possessed her was made, nor its origin; for it is as if Good and Evil were at war in her soul, and she spoke in a tongue I fear and do not fully comprehend. I do not know whether the lord to whom she called was this barbarian who had so terribly mastered her, or the Lord whose mercy had forgiven her once. I have, therefore, sought to distinguish as best I can them one from the other through my writing—in order that I might represent this woman in the truth of her innocence and not in the folly of her guilt. I can only pray God forgives her a second time and that wherever her soul rests now, it is at peace. This is what I wrote:

"Yes to say yes I will, and yes to say I want to, and yes to say no if I wish, and yes to all things as long as I allow it. Yes to say yes I trust you, and yes to say trust is my gift, and yes to allow you, but yes to say no if you wrong me.

"But no, Lord, no to always, no to accept you, no to deny me, no to know me and no to discard me. But no to not accept me, no to no one except you, no to be not me but you, no to not me.

"Yes to you always, yes to you when not now, no not now, and no to the pain, and no to the force, and yes to my no.

"I am rock. I am solid. My hands are with me. My legs are with me. My breasts are with me. My mouth is with me. My eyes are with me. O my eyes are aflame with love for you, my Lord. Let me see you, my Lord. Let you enter into my eyes, let me know you through my eyes, let me win you with my eyes, and let me never lose you with my eyes. I am aflame with myself. I am risen with myself. I am risen with my body, Lord. See, how my body lifts itself above myself. See, I am everything. My eyes see the world. They see me, for I have in my belly the world. See I grow. See I grow."

At this, she reached out and touched her skin where the child had but lately been. God is my witness that no one would not have been moved by the sorrow on her face when she found there was emptiness in her womb. She was silent a long time thereafter, and did stroke endlessly her belly where the child once grew. Then quietly and yet in a stronger voice she began again.

"I am bone, Lord. I am flesh, and my hands are filled with blood, Lord. The blood fills my cheeks; it is a river in my heart. I am your servant, Lord. If you so desire me, enter me in your love, Lord. But give me. Do not take me. Give and enter and do not leave. Do not leave me here. Take me with you. You have taken me, Lord, but you have not taken me. You have left me. Let me reach you. Do you not see my hands? Do you not see my hands filled with blood? See, these my hands are your hands. See how they touch you. See them touch your face, Lord."

Until that moment, I had not thought she had noticed my presence by her bed, for it had seemed to me her eyes were turned inward toward her innermost torments. But she lifted her hands and touched my face. I verily believe she took me for her abductor or the true lover of her soul; I can only guess at what she was thinking in her sadness and her affliction. Again, as with her feeling with her hands her belly, sorrow once more settled on her face as she saw how withered and sere were her once youthful hands. A cry shook her body, and I was fearful for her life. I was barely able to make out her words in the screams that followed. But this is what I heard.

"O my love, these hands are pale. Where is the blood I shed for you? When I reached below into my self I found blood on my hands. Where is the blood now? Did you not fill me with your blood? Did you not fill me with your spirit? I am filled with your spirit and your blood. I have given you your blood and spirit back in my womb. Where are you now, my Lord? Where is your love now? Why are you not here? Why are you not with me now? Ach, the ashes, spit out blood, ashes. He is here, fire and ashes, spit, spit out the ashes. He burns me with his eyes, burns my body, my hands, my eyes. Burns me, no, no, not now. He burns me. Please, Lord, save me, save me from this. Save me from him and his kind. Save me, Lord, please, take me, Lord. Take me from these ashes. Take away my body. Blood. Blood and ashes. Save me. Lord. He, now, O, he now. No, he. No. Lord. Please."

As she spoke, her hands ran over her whole body, tearing at her clothes. As much as I tried to cover her body, so much would her hands pull all clothes away. Because she seemed a thing possessed, I let her have her will, and soon she was entirely naked. Her screams had removed all the strength from her voice. It now became a moan and at times she almost choked, so great was her misery.

"These hands, they are sweet hands. But O, how pale are these hands. These are my hands. See, I offer them in salutation. They touch and I offer them in prayer. Lord, these are my breasts. I offer them to you. Lord, these are my legs. I offer them to you. I offer all of me to you. Make me whole. Fill me with your spirit once more. Be here with me now, Lord. Be here."

Suddenly, she arched her back and a frenzy surged through her whole body. Again she shouted into the air, every word she said racking her body yet more. I saw her eyes, and they were ablaze with a fury I have not seen in a hundred of those possessed by the Devil.

"But no. No. No. No. No. No. No. No to leaving me, no to not knowing me, no to not fighting. I am bone. I am flesh. I am spirit, whole and aflame. I am one. I am one with myself. I am I. These my hands are myself. These my legs are myself. This my mouth is myself. These my eyes are myself. I am myself. I am spirit. I am blood. I am filled with my eyes and my flesh. I am lifted up. Yes to touch. Touch my hands. Touch my mouth, my breasts, my arms, my legs, my soul. Let me welcome you as a brother. Let me feel you as a friend. Let me reach for you and love you. Let me love. Let me open my heart to you. Let me sing. Let me give and take your body, your love. Let me enfold you in me. Yes to all. Yes, in me and from me. Yes to say yes to say yes to say yes."

She repeated these words many times, so many times and so fast I was not able to record them. And each time she said these words, her sobs grew, until a sweet balm of tears filled her eyes and she became calm, and she was silent a while. Then, as if in a trance, her body became rigid and cold—for I felt it myself. She began to speak, her voice quiet at first but then rising to a shout at the end. It was not a shout as one in the last torments of despair, but the shout of one in bliss, as though she had seen a vision of God. This is what I heard, and so such will I record.

"Lord, I am with you and I am with myself. I am yours and mine. I am reaching out to you."

Her hands reached out into the air, clutching and hugging to herself that which was only apparent to her inner eye.

"Let me reach out to you, Lord. Let me feel you. He is gone, Lord. He has vanished, Lord. The ashes are gone. The blood has gone. You are with me, Lord, and he is not here. I am with you alone now, Lord. O reach your hands to me. Let me touch you. Let me reach out to you. I can feel you. I can see me. I know you. I know you are coming to me. I can touch you. I am with you. Lord, I am with you and in you. You are in my body. I am in me. You are in my soul. I am aflame with you and with myself. I am one with you, Lord. I am all you and all of you is in me. I am bone, Lord, and I am spirit. I am whole with you and I am whole. I am one and I am peace. I am all things. I am here. I am with you. I am above the world. I am with you in all places. I am one with the heavens. Lord, I am with you forever. Lord, I am body and self. I am touch. I am sight. I am here, Lord. I am here. See me, Lord. See me here. You see me, Lord, and you know me. Lord, I am here. I am with you. I am of you. I am the world. I know you, Lord. I am here. I am here. I am with you. I am in your soul. Your soul is in my eyes. I am in your eyes. I am with you forever. I am with you in heaven. Here. I am here, Lord. Yes, I am. Yes, I am here. Yes, Lord. Yes. Yes. I am. Yes I am. Yes, Lord. Yes I am. Yes. I am. I."

So saying, she gave a great cry and sank down in death. Thus passed away a tortured soul. May she rest in peace.

* * *

It's So Nice Here

So I said I was going to stay.

"Here?" he spluttered.

"Why not?" I replied.

"No. You mean Iznik?"

"Yes."

"But there's nothing here. You said so yourself."

"Adam." And I felt very clear-headed and assured. "There's nothing anywhere. I am only going to stay here for a few days."

"What do you mean 'there's nothing anywhere?'

What about Antalya or even Bodrum? There's plenty of 'there' there! They're much more interesting places. Anyway, what do you mean by 'a few days'? We're going back in a few days." He paused, and smiled a slight, ironic, irritating smile. "Where we're going back to, I'm not entirely sure. But going back we are, nonetheless." I could see behind the face that he was genuinely surprised and bemused—perhaps also a little anxious. I have to say I was pleased about that.

"I'll meet you at the airport," I replied, ignoring his questions and surprising myself at how calm my voice sounded. "At the check-in desk. I know the time and I have my ticket." I paused and felt the silence between us. Twenty years of silence between us, and now a few months more of it—even though this time it is a different kind of silence, somehow lighter, of less consequence. "I need time to think." I heard my voice softening, making itself gentle for him, coaxing him, acting like the female conciliator I had been too often, far too often. I tried to drag it back before I lost it again—just as I have always tried and failed to do.

"But what will I do?" he said.

He looked at me, with misery hanging from his face like a dying leaf. Suddenly I felt the power of my anger pulling my voice back to me. "Adam. I don't give a damn what you do! Do whatever you want to do. But for once in my life I want to do what I want—and what I want is to stay here. Okay? Now that's all I ask. I'll be fine. I'll be careful...if that's what's worrying you."

He says nothing, merely looks unhappy, trying to perform triage on what he probably feels is his wounded pride. It has the desired effect. I add, repeat, reassure—all of those things: "I'll be at the airport. I know what to do. You remember: I've been here before."

He looks out at the water.

"It's difficult for a woman traveling alone." His voice is quiet and severe.

"I know."

"You'll get a lot of unwelcome attention."

I look at him. He seems unaware of the irony. "I'm used to it."

"It won't be the same without you," he adds quietly. So *that* is what is really on his mind!

"I expect it will be," I reply. "I'll be with myself most of the time."

"I meant it won't be the same for *me*." He is irritated, but worried about angering me and thus completely ruling out the possibility I might relent.

"I know what you meant, Adam."

"Please come with me."

"I seem to remember once you talking about how much better it is to travel alone."

He is silent. Something has been broken.

"Please come with me," he says again. He turns away from me and I follow his gaze, watch his quiet voice float over the surface of the lake toward the town. I feel tenderly toward him. The whole thing is ultimately folly, when you think about it. The two of us should know better—him with a young family, me with, as he says, a perfectly adequate husband.

I think again of Helen and the inamorata of courtly love. All those men, throwing themselves against the walls of Troy for an illusion, the knight of faith rubbing the unhealable scar. What drove them to do these things? And what were they at once so attracted to and so scared of that they had to vilify the loved one or render her an abstraction?

"I can't," I say.

"Why not?"

I go over to the rock where he is sitting.

"Because I can't. I just need some time."

"I see." He gets up and gives me some more money and says he'll help find me a hotel. Then he gets the bus back to Bursa and I watch him roll away through the dust. I turn back and walk through the town to where the fountain is and the shadow puppet theater was. They have tidied it all away except for a few chairs scattered around.

I sit down on a chair and take out my journal and write to you. And I've been here so long now that it's almost completely dark and it's only a dim streetlight and an amazing moon that's giving me enough light to follow my words on the page.

Across the square is the road to the lake, smooth and silver in the moonlight. Adam tells me that this was where they made a statement of faith once, and I can understand why. Whatever it chooses to call itself, whether Iznik or Nicaea, this place encourages creeds, and my decision to stay is part of that encouragement: a statement that focuses on an "I," a declaration of permanence, an alignment with something greater than what we can imagine.

I lift my head and see, moving through the shadows,

a man and a woman walking. They are casually dressed, both in jeans, she wearing a headscarf that, even from this distance, I can see is patterned with flowers and leaves. They are holding hands. They walk towards me, and I can see how young they are, perhaps no more than teenagers, a diffident, frail mustache on his upper lip, her frame as slender as a boy's. By the way they move comfortably in and out of each other's space I presume they are in love.

The moon spreads its light around them like a benediction.

When he sees me, the young man is startled, and he guides the girl away from me. She, however, turns her head and looks at me. She is wearing make-up that exaggerates the largeness of her eyes and the smoothness of her skin and makes her seem older than she is. It is, I imagine, the effect she wants. On her lips there is the hint of a smile that I do not understand although I throw meanings at it like confetti—that she has a man and I do not, that she is young and I am not, that she believes in love, and I...

She turns away again and walks into the shadows with her young man. Through the space between the houses where they walked I can see the lake, relaxed and expansive beneath the moon. I open my journal again and lift my hand to write. I think of you—the sharer of my blood, the mother of my abandonment. Like you, I am washed by lunar cycles and reddened by love. I think of a shower of red rain and a woman on a shore or a parapet, looking out, scanning horizons, her eye upon a departing other, and yet herself unseen. My hand, shaking slightly, stops over the blank page. The nib touches the paper and my hand begins to move. I see the black line curve and slide across the whiteness before it rests at the end of the sentence.

It's so nice here.

* * *

Altarations

The act of choosing what to describe is everything, for in choosing I create. If I had chosen the stars, and the silence, and the warm spring air, and the wind breathing on these old city walls, then the mind would have turned to intimations of a responsive God, or night thoughts and meditations, or the delicate thread of the sensuous and exotic orient. Or if I had told how even now I look at the lights and hunched buildings, how the noise of cars and buses stalks the streets, and how the eye follows the arcade of orange on the road to Istanbul, there would perhaps have grown in the consciousness images of the dust and sweat of mortal endeavor and the great urban existence of the cityscape of humankind. Or if, finally, turning to either side of me, I had chronicled each and every movement of the diffident lovers silently passing my eyes, or the hushed togetherness of the family, or the brief shuffle of a lone walker, then what would have appeared would doubtless have been seen as the expression of a sentimental humanism, of brotherhood and sisterhood couched in the impassive warmth of a spring night.

But I chose to begin with you, and, perhaps as a result, for the whole day I have tried to quantify your life by trying to clasp your death, manhandle the spirits of your displacing, grapple with the unreformable truth of your going from me. I have tried naming you in diversity and playing you symbolically in my desperate imagination. I have offered apologies and apologias, thematic structures and the afflatus of my creativity. And none of it has worked.

You appeared to me in the morning—an unreformed Banquo of accusation from my consciousness. I loathed it, your self-righteous contempt for my hopes to chart a new way to conceive of you and God. Yet, even though you are not here, talking to me, are you not here in the air this night, my friend? Indeed, are you not everywhere, forming my language, or the words the lovers whisper to each other, or what I write now? Is not what we speak a revivification of the dead before us as we use their words, their images, the palimpsests of lies and evasions that are our memories of them?

Perhaps, indeed, everything we do when we talk of the dead is not a denial of death, but instead a celebration of it. All our language becomes a vibrant epitaph to their being and their departure. In all we say, in all we write—and perhaps this is as true for all that remains unspoken and unwritten—we are confronting our mortality through our dialect, establishing our right to existence and nonexistence, demanding eternity to listen to the voice of mortality.

Yes, there is talk to fill empty spaces. Yes, as you pointed out, I still want my existence to be well-spoken, and allow the rhetorical trope to adopt a persona instead of the unvarnished honesty of conversation face-to-face. Perhaps this is because I still believe in an ordered hierarchy that will in some way reveal to me a direct and polite line to God. Yet today has shown me, in some way, that in every act of discussion there is a literal shaking asunder of language and our contact with people. We die and are memorialized a little each time we speak. That is the bequest made to us.

It is measurable in the sound of the entropic universe speeding away from a center, the sound of a distant unity that once formed itself and spoke. It surrounds us in every single particle created and destroyed in and out of time, never observed except when no longer truly observable, never perceived but always present, never actual but always potential.

It is evident in the traces of the continuous repetition of human existence offset against the particularity of every single life, our tiny selves within our universal imaginings. It is ascertainable, more than anything it is ascertainable, through the simple truth of having once known and been with you. Beyond everything and within everything, there is the absolute truth of your life and death, something beautiful, as hard as granite and as soft as the night, as bound in its atomic configuration as it is as expansive as the universe.

It exists when I imagine it and exists when I do not—enveloping me from without and pouring out from within me. It is selfless and yet full of the self, monomaniacal and all-effacing, free-spirited and strong.

It is an act of dedication and sacrifice, perpetual and unique, that allows us to alter and to altar all that we have been, are, and will be.

It is everything.

It is Nicaea.

* * *

Heimweh

It means "homesickness," but the sound of the word in the head summons up much more than nostalgia for your country. Into the mind march the images of the wanderer far from the mead-hall, the love-maddened poet lost in a reverberating forest of songs and sounds, or the prophet in exile meditating in the desert. It speaks of homelessness, of the lack of a roof and the lack of a homeland; it has within it the sigh of the need to feel centered without worry in the absolute confidence of rightness. It yearns for an end.

Within its echo is contained its unorthodox answer: heimweg. The word this time does not stretch into infinity as does heimweh, where the "h" leaves all hope and despair open in its breathless expectation. The soft "g" has a stronger—although only barely stronger—sense of finality. Heimweg is about the movement homeward and the road that must be taken to reach home: in its unity it contains both promise and actuality, another of those many words that have resonances beyond what can be written, and hold within themselves the truth of existence.

As with all the similar endings, there exists the dislocation of translation, made more poignant in this case by the actual fact of these words used for a specific place and themselves being the acts and expressions of movement and desire.

I end with heimweh because it was my last sensation of Iznik and its shriven icon Nicaea, just as heimweg was my last act as I took the night bus from Bursa to Istanbul around the Marmara Sea. At the bus station in Bursa, people departed from and arrived at this new, beginning city, as old as the mountain that spawned it. In the sky, stars were dying and beginning. People whose lives were being changed that night, or even those whose lives seemed the same, were all beginning or ending. Beginning and ending were everywhere, states of being and yet continual movements, the image of a road beginning or ending here or somewhere else, swinging in an arc to the north towards and then away from the distant, sinister hills.

And heimweg and heimweh held equal prominence in my mind, indistinguishable one from the other, except for that momentary lingering on the second syllable that turned action and direction into longing and dispersal. It was the same with this place, this green place, and the city walls and the road to Iznik; thinking on them and forging them in the hard fact of decision, I delayed too long on their weak, fragile final syllable and converted all of them into the desire and yearning for the impossible. So I oscillated between heimweh and heimweg and settled on neither.

I left in darkness, as I had arrived, with the lights

stretching up the mountainside to where Ülüdag rose blackly above the city. The bus station shone absurdly bright at night, claiming its rightful role as the true center of the town, involved as it was with the ebb and flow of those arriving and those departing. I left its brightness and we set off on the road to Istanbul, heading north and then east past the brooding hills and the silent lake where Iznik lay in wait. For hours we moved through the darkness, with no knowledge of where we were, the bus a wayward and unruly ship rescuing stranded travelers from the pitchy sea of night. There were sensations of waves and troughs, and beacons marked our progress as we trawled through unnamed towns and unnameable villages. Eventually, after a stop for tea and fitful moments of sleep, we reached the outskirts of Istanbul, until at dawn as a welcome and a farewell we crossed the Bosphorus and saw in the gray light the great mosques of the golden city.

And I thought then, as I half do now, that I had arrived at Nicaea; for Istanbul would solve at once the urgency of the correspondence between heimweh and heimweg, by its being a gateway to the West and an airport to home. Istanbul would not trouble me, because I did not wish to know it as I wished to know Nicaea. Istanbul did not command my presence in order to be able to exist in the glory of its past. Nicaea did. Nicaea was always mine to create and remained indifferent to my creation. That was its terror and its beauty.

We arrived at the bus station and soon I was at the airport and in the anonymity of another territory, at once the country's and no one's home. And I could already feel within me the growing sense of comfort, of things understood and settling, of things coalescing in the mind without struggle or contempt. Even as we lifted into the air and I saw the ground sink beneath me and thoughts of Iznik and the lake and you haunted my mind, that feeling washed over those thoughts, bathing them into submission and letting them rest at the bottom of my mind.

This was my journey. This was my ending. This was where I had arrived. I had understood that to understand will never be possible. I had seen something only to know it was not what I was looking for, merely a remnant of something I had thought necessary to have. It was the facsimile of countless errors of judgment, the map of every single journey taken towards that unreachable city. I had traced in the imagination the known chances of multiple and multiplying dislocation and difference. I had stopped the wrong bus and taken it just the same, in the hope—and always in the hope—that this bus might roll past signs to other places on the periphery of a destination. For to search for Nicaea, either directly or indirectly, is to destroy the opportunity of finding it. And it will never be found.

As the plane lifted from the ground, what I knew was that, at least for a moment, heimweh was becoming heimweg, and that made me content. Now it merely makes me sad, for Nicaea still complicates and ramifies and has almost wrestled from my grasp and splintered on the ground of my unbelief. Nicaea in history became the sad and unimpressive town that is now Iznik. Nicaea in my mind became something else; what I am not sure, but bound up with sorrow and love of you, my friend and friend no more. And I fear the ultimate question of Nicaea's validity will never be answered in life, although Nicaea's ultimate question is the only question worth answering in life. And all of my feelings indicate that Nicaea must be answered. It must be answered, in triumph or in sorrow, in penitence or in strength, in faith or in despair. But it must be answered. In the end.

In The End.